Three
Short
Novels

(First paperback edition May 2023)

IBSN

978-0-6450447-2-0 (Paperback)

978-0-6450447-7-5 (eBook)

Also By Rory Haymont

The Dreamer

Zen

Bruja

Kirby

Three Novellas

Proximity

The Hand of Tæranon

The Survivor

Nance

The Blue Groper

Names

The Baker's Dozen

Short Novels

The Girlfriend Experience

Reaper

The Blue Groper

Proximity

The Reputation

Short Stories

Clean

Holes

The Hostel

Death Row

Sheds

Crayons

The Dog's Dream

Revenge of the Geriatrics

The Art Piece

The Last Embrace

The Donation

Bottom Feeders

Run

Reaper

Prelude

The car in which her Uncle had brought her home in was disappearing into the crowded streets. The rebellious part of her wanted to go back to the markets for a while, but it was time to be getting home anyway. She needed to help her father start the evening meal.

She had to cross the remains of a bombed out building which was being cleared away for redevelopment. Looking down to step over some of the remaining rubble, she saw something remarkable. It was a smartphone. Superseded by a few models, but in good condition. There was a small crack in one corner of the glass. Probably from when it had been dropped.

She walked along looking the gadget over. She'd never held a phone and didn't expect to own one, unless she was married to someone who might be able to afford it and choose to let her have it. Still some distance from the small block of flats where she lived, she remembered what she'd seen in magazines and on television. She tried to unlock to phone but it only brought up the password screen.

Even still she started to pretend to take selfies. She held the phone out at a distance and struck various poses turning her head to the side and making pouting or kissing lips.

She held the phone up and pretended to take photos looking up at it..

As she did this, she heard a strange noise and bent her head back further to look straight up to see what it was.

Sore Hands

His hand ached. Especially the tip of his index finger. He'd never done so much writing in his life. He'd advised the team that every night he'd retire to the hotel room and write from nine. People were surprised that he wasn't circulating more after the various dinners or other celebratory gatherings. He'd said from the beginning he wasn't going to glad hand the Washington elite or give audiences to the endless stream of people who wanted to informally seek positions or favours.

He started work at six in the morning and was probably far more available than his predecessor had been during the transition. He had an efficient, well-functioning team that he trusted. He'd decided during the Primaries that if he was successful, he would acknowledge people with more than a few bulk e-mailed platitudes. He'd make the effort to let people know that their support had really mattered.

There were three levels of response. One was the emails and letters, but for everyone who received one, his staff tried to do some basic research on where they came from and who they were, via social media or elsewhere. Everyone got a Friend Request from the President Elect. Six people were working nine hours a day to get these messages of appreciation through to small donors, volunteers and Party workers. They noticed that a lot of people who had contributed comparatively large amounts as small donors, were very hard to track down.

The second tier were major donors, senior Party officials and union leaders. They had an individual letter written by his personal assistant Kimmie, supported by those providing good research for reference purposes.

Each of these he signed in ink and where possible, delivered by hand.

The third tier were the Congressmen and Senators, his adversaries in the Primaries, the biggest donors, close colleagues, team members, friends and family and the mentors he'd counted as pivotal in his career. These all received a handwritten letter. His team provided him with a list of dot points about any recently arrived grandchildren, Olympic Medals or mountains climbed in the past, changes in career

or major illnesses so that he could carefully personalise each one, in addition to what he already knew. Most of them were one page, and he had taken to writing in fairly large letters. Some, like the one to his Highschool English teacher, the man who told him he had significant talents and that he shouldn't waste them, received a four-page letter, recounting his career and giving him a heartfelt thanks.

And so; his finger hurt like hell. When he couldn't stand it anymore, he'd call it a night, calculating whether he had enough time to complete the list before Inauguration Day. He would deliver these letters by hand if it was at all possible. If not, he would see if the Governor of the State they lived in could do so.

It was after eleven when he would usually give the writing a break. He'd revisit the daily briefing the current Administration provided to him, rather reluctantly. He'd generally fall asleep doing this and would be back up at five and working at six, the Transition Team arriving by seven.

Tonight, there was a quiet tap on the door. He went to narrow space that confined the entranceway into most hotel rooms and opened it. The two men gave each other the kind of brief off-set embrace men share to signal affection but not intimacy.

'The traveller returns. What news from the east?'

'And west. And everywhere in between. It was an ambitious itinerary.' The visitor smiled. Revealing a little weariness which could not be concealed.

'Yes, it was. The guy who wrote it must have been some kind of sadist.'

They sat at a small table. 'Scotch?'

'Why not. I've been trying to fend off Business Class booze for a couple of weeks but the last two flights I've just given up and said; 'hit me.'

'I'm sure there's a ten-page report nearly complete for each port of call, but I thought that since this hotel is on your way home from the airport ...' It was not. '... we could catch up for the highlights.'

The man's reports ran significantly more than ten pages for each location, but he knew Gene would have Kimmie condense them to one page each and the rest would be consigned to the dustbin of history.

'And I know what you're thinking. But it's going to be a two-page summary she'll be asked to prepare. But I'll expect the top three positions in State to learn the full reports by rote.' Gene smiled. Everyone loved it when he smiled. Many people often wanted to please him because his smile made them feel good.

'One of the highlights, if you can call it that, was that there weren't any earthshattering surprises.

Which is probably a good thing. The major outcome was that everyone I met was very ready to welcome an informal envoy prior to you taking Office. An envoy that listened without much in the way of a prepared position.

They said what they thought of the US and made observations about how the relationship might improve.'

'The devious plan worked.' Gene was enthusiastic and he knew his colleague will have set the perfect tone.

'Yes, ask people what they think and then listen.'

Gene wanted to get the message right around the globe that there could be a reset of the relationship. Some would be wary of upheaval while others might assume the open restoration of ties was a green light for them to return to the human rights abuses of the past. There would be a hundred different responses from a hundred countries, some with multiple dynamics important to the US in only one nation. Gene would be putting together a team who could manage this without him ever hearing about most of it. Just the key nations of strategic interest.

Gene Carlson, President Elect to the United States, looked satisfied. 'The main message was that we were ready to listen and the doors that may have been slammed by the previous administration, don't have to stay that way. Sounds like they go that.'

His unofficial envoy, Greg Watson agreed. 'Pretty much. The individual countries, after welcoming the new kid in town, rolled out fairly predictable story lines. The Chinese subtly asked if we wouldn't mind standing aside while they quietly took over the world. The Russians, hell Gene, the Russians lied for two hours straight. And the funny thing was, they knew that I knew they were lying, and they were fine with that.

The Europeans were worried about the Russians and didn't want us to further dilute our role in NATO. The British wanted us to help plug the hole left from the complete hash they made out of their relationship with Europe.'

'The Israeli's were happy as long as we never said a single positive word about Palestine. Preferably no words. The Saudi's want us to sell them as many advanced weapons as their oil money can buy and never mention the human's rights issues, we'd be condemning anybody else for. I got the sense it was implicit that we didn't mention that the arms we're supplying them are sometimes deployed on their own population and impoverished neighbours.'

Gene sighed. 'That's international affairs for you. Once you've had a good rest, I have another circumnavigation of the globe planned. This time visiting our neighbours in the north. The Nordic set, Canada, Greenland, Norway. Even little old Iceland. The same story. Pretty much. But with more of a 'we love what you have done with the place' flavour, given we might even learn a thing or two. I'd like to develop more alliances where the US doesn't usually go.'

'Like Canada?'

'Where's that?' They both laughed.

Gene continued. 'As you know, I have Jimmy Jay working his way through the great continent of South America on a similar mission. Below the Tropic of Capricorn has been pretty plain sailing. Further north from there... it's harder for those countries to take any change in position from the new Administration seriously. He's in central America now and the skeletons are making a God damn racket in the closet.'

'I prefer my gig. The rifles are stored a bit further away from the meeting rooms.'

'Yes. He's doing Africa next. Selected locations.' Greg sat quiet. Making sure there was no suggestion he would like to reshuffle the existing accountabilities.

'Anyway, I'm sure all of this stuff will pale in significance next to domestic affairs, but I want to be well off the starting blocks on foreign affairs so nothing can bite me on the ass on day one.' Gene slid a manila folder across the desk. 'There was another reason I asked you to stop by. I've been mulling over the list of those I'd like to appoint to Cabinet. I've asked a select group of colleagues to look over the potential appointees, and the portfolio's they've been recommended for.'

'Because I didn't want to do this over the phone or e-mail, you're input is going to be the last to come in. I'd like to finalise the process of consulting with nominees and make the announcements in the next few days. Here's the list. In some cases, there's only one nominee in others there's several. You can provide notes on each person if you want to or mark the colours green for good, blue for 'I don't know them' and red for 'keep away'. I've completed this process with five very different people and ended up with similar feedback. I'll be interested to see what you come back with.'

After scrutinising the single page from the folder for a moment he observed. 'I see you've found some fellow with exactly the same name as me to take over the State Department.'

'Yes. A good man. Has a tendency to make the same lame jokes again and again which can be tedious, but otherwise perfect for the position.'

'Well thank you very much. For the feedback on the jokes I mean. But Gene, however much I'd like to take the job, I can't see how this could be good for your Administration. Certainly not at the beginning.'

Gene picked up on the hint that his friend wanted the opportunity but thought the second term more fitting.

'There are a dozen more deserving of this role Gene and a couple of dozen more who aren't but are expecting to be tapped on the shoulder for it. Rightly or wrongly, I'm seen as a senior staffer who's ridden your coat tails since you were deputy governor in Missouri.'

Gene could be prickly. 'Greg do you think I don't weigh things up before making a decision. And if I thought I could get a better outcome, do you think I'd pick you. You know me. I wouldn't pick you. Now you look me in the eye and tell me two things. Tell me you don't want this job and tell me you can't do it as well as anybody else.'

'You're right Gene. I want the job and I believe I could do it. I'd love to do it and show people what could be done. But how will my appointment be received. Confirmed by the Senate even.'

Gene was somewhat annoyed now. 'Greg, never confuse my job with your job. What you're talking about is my job. If you're concerned on my behalf, on the administration's behalf, these are problems that I was elected to manage. Do you think it was easy to get Candice as my running mate? Most people said it was impossible. But there she is.'

There was a brief silence before Gene said. 'Give me your response in twenty-four hours and mark up of the rest of the list.

As you see, there's only one person listed for State, so you'd need to suggest an alternate if you know of a better candidate.'

'Will do Gene, and I'm sorry if it came across like I didn't appreciate the opportunity you're presenting to me.'

As he was saying this, there was a soft bell from Gene's phone, which was sitting next to the writing pad. He picked it up and looked at a text. Greg was surprised to see him throw it down so hard it slid along the desk and hit the wall.

His voice was now terse. 'We'll need to wrap this up Greg.' The whole issue of the appointment to Secretary of State forgotten. He pulled out another sheaf of papers. 'Here is a list of positions held by Republicans which would typically be changed out with Democrats when a new Administration comes in. The ones marked in green, I've asked to hold fire before looking for another job because they may have an opportunity to continue. Those marked in red we don't want.' There are quite a few unmarked. I want you to scan those names and look for anyone you know who is a good operator and we should keep. And mark up the ideologues or those being run by ideologues.'

Greg was a bit tentative. 'Sure, but I imagine there's a great many Democrats expecting some of those jobs. That's what usually happens.'

Gene's irritation went up a notch. 'Well I'm not going to be a 'that's what usually happens' President am I. And I was careful to make no promises to anybody on this front. I don't want or need a bunch of 'also ran' sycophants. If there are good people already doing a good job and know the ropes that's who I want. And it's a good start to the bipartisanship I intend to lead with.'

Greg had never seen his boss quite this worked up. He was known for having a smile like Eisenhower. He was engaging and almost always even tempered. The 'Genial Gene' nickname was inevitable and was almost always found to be apt.

Greg wasn't going to accept what he felt was an exaggeration and potentially even a slur on the people who put them where they were. 'Sorry Gene I don't agree with that. There aren't many sycophants seeking appointments, but I take your point about keeping the best talent in place and I'll get both lists marked up and with Kimmie by morning.'

The wind went out of Gene's sails suddenly. 'Thanks Greg. And thanks again for the envoy stuff. I'll appreciate it if you give that job serious consideration.'

'Will do.'

A simple nod between them marked an end to the meeting.

The Unwelcome Visitor

Greg opened the door to find a man with his hand raised in the process of making his first knock. He was confronted with a tall thin man, possibly mid-seventies with grey hair, swept back from his forehead. Some grey curls, almost ringlets, fell on the thick velvet collar of his heavy back coat. He had a long face, thin lips that now shed the tiniest hint of a smile of greeting. His almost black eyes looked out from somewhere terrible.

He let Greg pass.

As he rode the lift to the lobby, now having to face the hour and a half taxi ride; going right past the airport to get home, he thought about Gene's visitor. Since he was a boy, as his father had taught him, when he met someone new, he automatically stretched out his hand and said, 'Pleased to meet you, I'm Gregory Watson.' And in all his life adult life he'd did that. But to do this with the grey haired man had never entered his mind.

Gene and his visitor had met only once before and that had been a bitter, angry meeting. The bitterness and anger were still barely below the surface for Gene. The man had sat quietly then, as he did now. Sitting without being invited to do so in a seat still warm from the last visitor. Gene poured himself a scotch, one more than his usual quota and sat down opposite the man at the small round table.

The man looked to the bench and said. 'Glenfiddich.' Without much hope.

With a display of incredible reluctance, Gene got up and fixed his visitor a drink. But rather than hand it to him across the short space he slid it across the table. He did this with more force than he'd intended. Had the grey haired man had not been very quick to catch the drink, it would have landed on his lap.

He gave no sign of noticing the slight and was pleased to have a drink without speaking for a few moments.

'You know Gene; you're about to embark on the opportunity of a lifetime. An opportunity that few men in history have been fortunate enough to have had. I understand enough of your policies to know a great deal of good could come from your Presidency. Will you squander all that in churlishness? The interests I represent have orchestrated a situation whereby some of your policy must be subjugated to their influence. Unpleasant as that it, these will only form a proportion of your legacy. That is unless you cut off your nose to spite you face.'

'How the fuck can you sermonise to me?'

'Merely an observation. You can take it or leave it of course. Shall we move on.'

'Let's talk about why the hell you turn up with five minutes notice.'

'If you think it through you would understand. Also, could you pass me you're phone please.'

'My what?' Gene didn't.

'Gene, do you want this to be a long visit or a short visit. It's up to you.'

Having been called churlish, Gene now had to make an effort to not be. The man didn't need Gene's password. He navigated as it lay on the table. Several innocuous looking apps functioned as voice and video recorders. They had been remotely activated for the past hour and recorded Gene's previous meeting. 'Gene, eventually they may not be able to hack your phone. But I'm sure it would be a little inconvenient to have the entire contents of the phones of anyone you know remotely being managed, hacked or wiped clean. So why not accept things the way they are. This is a tiny fraction of the risks you face as you know.'

He wiped the surface of the phone and handed it back. As the President Elect had done only a few moments before for Greg, the man produced a piece of paper. In this case pulling it out with tweezers and sliding it across the table. 'You're Cabinet along with some other key appointments.'

Gene looked at the list. 'You must be kidding. Tell your masters to get fucked.'

'Are we going to go through every time Gene?' The man was earnest, not offended.

'Yes. We're going to go through every time.' Gene wanted to ensure he conveyed the impression there were limits.

Gene could hear the man was now working through a script.

He started to have his suspicions he wasn't alone in his predicament. 'Do you know how hard it was to make it look like sixty million dollars came from small to medium donors. Your people are having trouble finding them to write thankyou letters to I believe.' Gene got a feeling from the man's his heart wasn't in this. However for his own reason's he wanted Gene's compliance as much as they did.

'I didn't ask for it.'

'You wouldn't have been elected without it combining that and the effort my 'masters' expended to support your campaign. Half that again was spent to sabotage the campaign of you rivals both in the Primaries and in the Presidential race. And your fingerprints are all over that process. It need only be revealed.'

'Your people want a thankyou card from me?' Gene's voice flat. He knew what was coming.

'They want what they paid for.'

'Well if they've paid all of that money then I presume they'd rather get an eight-year term, than a four-year term, which is all they'll get with the clowns on this list.'

The man sighed, heavily. 'You were never given the opportunity to see all of the video Gene.' The man had no enthusiasm for this task. He laid a large tablet on the table and played a video. Gene had seen some early scenes and he knew it was him. He knew where and when it was recorded. He only barely remembered the details of being in the room because he'd been floating in such a cocktail of booze and whatever they'd spiked it with.

The man's voice was flat. 'The actor took over from you when the sex started getting rough here.' He stopped it for a moment.

Gene imagined the man probably shouldn't have shown him a detail like that. 'You won't remember much of this because you were so heavily drugged, and you were taken out of the room as soon as he arrived. But the actor was an almost perfect look alike, though the video is still carefully edited. The footage was not supposed to be of high quality. It was produced to be what it is. Blackmail footage taken by a cheap video camera concealed in a good position to capture what occurred.'

'The girl is now being beaten to death on the video Gene.' He said, embarrassed. Gene could sense self-loathing, not deeply concealed 'You ended up with her blood all over your clothes. Her clothes have your semen on them. And more stored away in her body in the shallow grave not far from the place you were staying for the conference.'

The man's face was sad. Disgusted. Not so different to Gene's. 'The actor they'd found was drugged and was deep in the sea diving later that night.'

'How do you live with yourself.'

The man held his phone in a certain complex way and lay two fingers on Gene's phone. 'We're all bound by chains Gene. The links are those we love.'

Gene was quiet for a long time and took out a pen. He circles five names and pushed the list back.

'I'll tolerate these.'

The man looked at them for some time, breathing heavily. 'They'll insist on Defence, the EPA and Labour.'

'I'll accept Defence. You can tell them that whether they like it or not this *is* a negotiation. They can publish their video and I'll make my excuses and burn my career and try and take as many of the fuckers down with me.'

'Okay Gene. I'll try to get this across the line for you.' He made the same maneuverer with the phones. 'Unfortunately Gene the investors look for their return. You are ultimately only on character in a cast to fulfil a greater strategy. And power hungers for more of the same. The man's eyes seemed black. He realised the phones. 'Before you get all gung-ho about coming out in the open, remember there are other people at risk here. You must pay a little. Or they might pay a lot. Depending on how you conform to what my masters want. You might see the consequences for what you've decided. Or you might not. They have plans stretching ahead for years for those that try to expose them.'

As he said this there was a quiet bell tone on Gene's phone, which still sat between them. He looked at it with the same irritation that characterised the meeting. But the text read. 'Still up babe?'

He stared at the message. He'd brought the people he loved most in the world to within one degree of separation of these evil bastards. He heard a different sound, as a message tone came to the phone in the coat of the man sitting opposite. Pulling out his phone he said. 'I'll leave you.' Putting it away. 'You should call her. It's not looking too good for your mother-in-law in Barbados…according to her.' The man smiled thinly. 'Although it's well known you dislike her, you might want to visit. It would make good copy, and you may not be aware, Claudia has decided to fly in from London to surprise her mother and offer support. It would make a nice reunion.'

The man stood and took the two steps towards Gene to hold out his hand. Gene's stomach had been sliding to think that his most intimate relationships were being monitored. That these people knew more about his family than he did. Gene looked at the man.

'You might get me to do a lot things. But never that.' The man shrugged. He picked up the paper from the table with tweezers and slid it into the manila envelope, turned, and left, wiping the door handle on the way out.

Gene looked again at the text from Amancia. He didn't call her.

The NASA Project that Wasn't

'The Armies Chief Egg Head has had his people scanning the publications from the B list universities, and they've come up with a name who's written some papers that suggest he can give them what he wants.' The Colonel's voice was navigating through unfamiliar territory.

'Which is?' The female voice didn't like the sound of this assignment already.

'He wants to thin out the 'also ran' egg heads from his group. This university guy is going to be given some work from their team to do, problems to solve, that kind of thing. But the team are going to be told this is coming straight from a world-renowned AI genius.' The Colonel tried to sound enthusiastic, be he knew what her answer would be.

'I'd be guessing the team members that say it's amazing work are toast. Nice. '*And thanks for spending your career here guys.*' She didn't like the sound of this assignment.

'It's a rough and mean world the AI game; apparently. And if this guy shows any promise the Head Egg might throw him something to work on that he needs done pronto. To see if he has potential.'

'And I'm his handler.'

'You could frame it that way.' The Colonel responded to a very forthright First Lieutenant. 'Yes. We need to take him out of his current environment, get him settled, and focused on delivering outcomes for NASA as soon as possible.'

'NASA?' Lieutenant Odette Symmon's eyebrows were rising with a 'here we go again look.'

'Did I fail to mention that this project is being run by the US Army with the generous participation of NASA. A third-party arrangement sort of thing.'

'The kind of arrangement that NASA haven't been invited to the party.'

'Why trouble them Lieutenant? Why have the wearisome meetings? The negotiations? All we need are some letterheads and signature blocks on e-mails. Even a few emails sent accidently with a few organisations and more NASA people in the e-mail chain. Lots of phone numbers to call. All of which lead to one phone line in this building.'

'That one' She pointed to the phone on his desk, and he continued.

'But you won't be answering that phone Lieutenant because you'll be enjoying Florida.'

'Florida?'

'Yes. The Florida where NASA is.'

'The NASA that has nothing actually to do with this project.'

'That's right, but for our University man, it would be logical to have him near where NASA is.'

'But he can't meet anyone, because the no one's there working on this.'

'No, but we can organise a hell of a backstage pass to NASA and the airbase. The Head Egg may drop in, so you need to be close by.'

'I'm moving to Florida for a month.' There was a tone in her voice that suggested it might have been nice to have been asked.

'For six months Lieutenant. People advised me you don't have much of a life anyway. Bit of a workaholic I was advised.'

'How kind of them.'

'If this goes well Lieutenant, a recommendation for Captain will be signed and submitted the day you return. I'm well aware it's overdue and you've earned it already, but I'm going to shamelessly hang it out there. A nice incentive in addition to the more straightforward being an Order from your commanding officer combined in an elegant combination.'

She smiled. 'No one else wanted to do this.'

'We must play the hand we're given Lieutenant.'

'And all of this in aid of? Building a better bomb?'

'The bombs we have are great. It's getting the damn things to drop when we want, where we want, and goddamn it on *who* we want them to be dropped.' He waxed lyrical. 'And ideally we want those bombs to do all this while we're sleeping or walking the dog, because these bombs should know what they're doing and stop bothering us with details and get on with it.'

'I thought we've been doing surgical strikes for years.' She observed dryly.

'Such cynicism is beneath you Lieutenant.' He continued. 'Algorithms Lieutenant. We get every scrap of information that we're ever going to get via our esteemed colleagues in the countless intelligence agencies this country can be proud to have, and let AI do the rest. It's a bit like the driverless car. People are less comfortable with us bombing somebody when there's no 'pilot' involved. But there might be a ten second window that only AI, our trusted partner, could foresee and capitalise on, to make the target an ex target. They're already way better than the human pilots, but this project is about lifting automated target acquisition and reducing false positive so that it's infallible; Almost.' He smiled winningly. 'Let's let those Reaper drones loose. Let them loose. Machine Learning. Let them learn.'

Lieutenant Watson knew that no one else in the Colonels staff was allowed to enjoy his inherent levity. And she appreciated that. She now knew he shared it with her because he was certain she had no one to talk to about it. She knew she was very fortunate to report to him, even if he still favoured men for promotions, based on apparently primordial instincts.

'So, no more wedding parties evaporated? Ever.'

The Colonel chose not to respond to that. 'I'll expect a daily update.' Odette picked up the package of information about the mission, saluted her Colonel and wondered as she walked away, yet again, why she'd elected to go into this branch of the service. Then she thought 'What the hell'. She turned around. 'Sir, you could submit it now.'

'Submit what now?'

'My promotion to Captain Sir. You could submit it now rather than when I get back.'

This caught him unprepared. 'And why do that.'

She had a pleasant smile. 'Because I deserve it.'

He thought for a moment, shrugged and said. 'Sounds like a good enough reason to me.'

An Interview with Archie

There was modest applause as the Tory politician arrived in the chair next to Peter and acknowledged the audience, while crossing his legs.

Before Peter Lacey, host of the long running late evening interview program could make the initial remarks, Archie was on the front foot speaking with great confidence. 'Why the dickens have you invited me onto your remarkably successful program. What, five years running is it? I'm one step above a nobody. And a fairly small step. Is this some awful harbinger of decline Peter. Aren't you able to get the quality guests that you once did. I was surprised to get the call. Flattered of course. But then I thought, O dear, Peter's program must really be on the slide. And then I didn't feel so good.'

This threw the audience off kilter. Indeed, the person in charge of lighting up the APPLAUSE sign was confused and left it off.

Fortunately, this was the kind of situation Peter enjoyed, and one of the reasons he'd invited Archie was that he was known to be unpredictable, but had an interesting story.

'How did you get to see my notes Archie. I was going to use this episode as a plea to potential interviewees.

People might say. 'If Archie can get on then why don't I give it a shot. Indeed, we have hit the absolute bottom of the barrel next week when the PM takes a seat on the program. Hopefully it's all going to be up from there.'

There was relieved applause and laughter.

'Warm greeting aside Archie. Why did you come on? And you agreed to have nothing out of bounds in the interview.'

'As you know I'm not contesting the next election. There is a fabulous candidate I've been, well, trying to mentor. She doesn't seem to need it though. More women in politics. That's always been my mantra. Although I accept the *always* may be in more recent years.' Most forgave him as a late learner, because he'd demonstrated a vehemence for the objective late in his career.

'And I suppose I've been someone with a certain reputation, and I thought it might be good to clarify a thing or two. People think I've had a particular task and that's the way the Party does things, but there's more to it.'

'Well people call you the Reaper Archie, it's a sobriquet you find distasteful.'

'And yet you use it.'

'I had to get you back for the introduction, close to the bone as it was. But whatever the nickname, tell us how you got it.'

'One day at the beginning of my time as an MP, I was an assistant on something or other to a Minister for something or other and we were meeting with the PM. The discussion turned to moving one of the team sideways as a prelude to moving them out.'

'Sounded damn inefficient to me, but also, not what most people would really want to go through.

How they'd like to be treated. Certainly I wouldn't. I'd want someone to respectfully give it to me between the eyes.' He paused reflectively. 'I thought that was what the senior people were supposed to do, but they played politics even when they didn't have to. I offered to go and talk to the person. I described where they were headed and suggested we see if there was an alternative within the Party or Government that was of interest or how a respectful departure would look from their perspective. The person involved didn't like the news, but they were glad to get it before things went sour, or opportunities vanished. They came up with a list of opportunities and a way was found. The person retired from government last year.'

'So how did it work Archie. The PM gave you a list to work through each Wednesday.'

'No. Slightly more subtle. Hints and suggestions often. But hints no one could misunderstand. And then I'd make a time to go around to see the person involved. What was interesting was more than half the time they were relieved. Wanted to change, step down, move across but didn't know how to ask, or didn't want to let the Party down. I'd listen to what they really wanted and, sure, lots of times it was never going to happen, but sometimes the stars aligned, and the slot was sitting there waiting for them. Others needed time to stew.'

'But one way or another their office was always cleaned out within a week after a meeting with you.' Said Peter.

'Without fail.' Said Archie. Unapologetic. 'Hence the reputation. But as I say, some moved to another office they wanted more, other moved across to a part time role while they and others made an assessment. Others moved out. Not everyone left the building because their office got cleaned out within a week. But it sent a message.'

Nodding Peter said. 'You know Archie, we called several people who had been the focus of your ministrations and nearly all of them said you had worked with them tirelessly to find a good fit for them anywhere in government or in some cases the private sector. Many of those people say now, they're in fulfilling careers because you took them out of their instable political careers and helped them realise, in more than a few cases, their true calling.'

'Do you have any idea how much I had to spend to ensure you got that feedback.' Archie smiled. 'But Peter, there was a class of people you may not have canvased. If you didn't work hard, do a good job, if you weren't trustworthy and if you didn't act in the interests of the Party, you were out on your ear. I dealt with a few cases with this malaise. And for me, it was a good day at work to be permitted kick those people out and see someone productive move into their place.'

'You're a company man Archie.'

'Absolutely proud of my Party. Always. Almost. Which is as good as you'll ever get in politics in any day or age.'

'But all of this took its toll.'

'Yes.' He paused for quite a while. 'Every door one passed had an occupant hoping I'd keep walk by. The people who were disaffected and angry were of course more vocal than the those that had a satisfactory result. Some people would take things through a formal grievance process.' He laughed. 'Always ended up much worse off because ultimately the PM took accountability and never once left me hanging. But yes. It took its toll.'

'All those looks from the open doors had an effect.'

'Yes Peter. You want me to talk about that do you.'

'Well it's something I'm well versed in also Archie. I can tell my story after if you like. But it's less interesting.'

'I'm sure that's true.' He smiled. 'I'd spent most of my working life where alcohol accompanied lunch meetings as part of the job. A drink after work and a drink at home were the norm. As time went by in my role as a...relocations specialist...continued I found the drinks count increasing at lunch and I'd have drinks after work whether the occasion called for it or not. I'd never drink heavily at home, so I simply began to drink in the car, or have neat scotch with no ice in the office. I must have been a functional alcoholic to some degree, as they didn't immediately engage a new removalist to shift me out. But a few colleagues for whom I have a great deal of respect, were courageous enough to tell me that I was on the road to ruin and doing damage to the Party.'

'And yet the concern from my fellow Parliamentarians wasn't enough to break its grip. It was the change in how my family viewed me. I opened the door one evening and my wife of thirty-five years and my twenty-five-year-old daughter both looked up and for an instant I could see the same thing before the smiles of greeting covered it. They were disappointed in me. I was in the thrall of this thing. Yet they saw I wasn't reaching out for help and so I obviously didn't want anything to change. I kissed them both hello and I went to the liquor cabinet and took an armload of booze out onto the back patio and set it on a table. One after the other lifted the bottles up and I began shouting, enraged, that this blasted liquid was destroying the most treasured things in my life. I smashed every bottle and went back until the cabinet was cleaned out. Then I went to the three stashes I had hidden and brought them out smashing them and shouting. I can't say on television the words I was actually shouting of course, but I cursed that this flavoured liquid had turned me into its slave.'

Peter knew how to help someone segue to break the tension. 'And what happened then?'

'Well I had a hell of a mess to clean up. And some of the bottles I'd broken weren't mine. They were some of Cheryl's favourite liqueurs, brought from overseas. She applauded the symbolism of it all, but she was a little conflicted about the methodology I'd chosen.'

'And was that the end of it? Was that what it took to break the chains?'

'No, no, no...' his voice faded away. 'I would weaken again, but the instant I could gain enough resolve to decide I was the one in control, I'd smash that bottle, no matter how much or little was left in it. Soon I seemed to be cleaning up broken glass all over the place. But it got less and less frequent. Haven't smashed a bottle in a few years now. But no one who's truly been an alcoholic is ever so haughty to say they have it beaten forever. We're dealing with such a demon.'

Peter was about to start the slow wind up with his final guest on a bit of new material. He had some observations from Senior Ministers that he wanted to weave through, and perhaps get a response here of there before closing out the show. But Archie got in first.

'Well to you viewers at home and with us here in the studio audience, that's the end of the show and sadly, the end of the 'Lounge Room' as a program.' Some applause commenced but Archie talked though it. 'People in the BBC thought it would be ironic, and a little fitting if I was the last guest, and the one to *do it*, unscripted, in the vein of what Peter and I have been talking about just now. Next week there's going to be a highlights program of the 'Lounge Room', mostly of me I'm told. Before that the BBC will be announcing a new talk show. Thanks for viewing.'

There was scattered, confused applause.

After a pause, cameras dropped down and the floor lighting lifted so the sombre audience could walk up the stairs, mumbling and muttering, to the back doors. Peter looked across at his Producer who was as surprised as he was and shook his head and shrugged at the same time, he was then engaged a conversation with an intense woman in a jacket and long skirt.

'Didn't really go off as funny as we thought it would when we dreamed it up. You know. Trying to convey the…irony.' It wasn't hard to see Archie was feeling bad. 'Still, you know Peter, once you look back on it, with the benefit of time, there's never been a talk show that's finished with a twist. The 'Lounge Room' is going to be remembered as a great show with a memorable finale.'

Peter smiled across and said. 'Aren't you supposed to find me a job.'

Archie laughed. 'Let's have a talk about that later. The boss got a bit of a farewell gift for you. Even though you never did get to interview him, he wanted to pass on that he was a regular viewer. It's behind the curtain I'll go and get it.'

Peter sat there alone. The studio lights were now dimming, the cameramen had left. The program had had a five-year run. That was about the broadcast life of a show like his. As with anyone else, he'd hoped for a few more years. But if he was going out, he was glad Archie did it.

Archie returned with a small hamper with a card. Getting a gift hamper from a Prime Minister was strange. Getting a mean little one was hurtful. He read the card which said the kinds of things you'd expect. Archie smiled. 'Pull on that string would you please Peter.'

Peter pulled on a little string coming out of the hamper. In doing so a huge crackling display of light and sound went off above their heads. CONGRATULATIONS PETER. 200 EPISODES.'

As this was happening the audience was being directed to their seating coming around the studio floor. They were all clapping in time and laughing. As they'd come out of the studio, they were immediately corralled in a waiting area for the cue, the situation having been explained to them. The floor cameramen returned, although there had been handhelds filming discretely the whole time.

Peter had taken the bait and he wasn't going to try to pretend otherwise. His Producer and some notables from the BBC came to congratulate him. He gave a warm embrace to Archie. He loved making good television, and this was memorable. But back in his dressing room, he knew it was a much more dramatic setting for the inevitable.

Inauguration

There was not a cloud in the sky. But breathing was to draw in tiny blades of ice and blowing them out as smoke. People were dressed accordingly. Probably because such warm clothes were generally on hand for winter funerals, those on the podium and in the crowd were almost all in black.

'Our nation is a nation divided.'

This got everyone's attention and was not the first line the speech writers had written.

'When you travel overseas and ask people where they think America is headed many will say. 'Civil War.'

'We are a nation divided along lines of race, wealth, education, political ideologies, and media bias.

We're divided on how we interpret what our freedoms represent and our responsibilities under the Constitution. We are divided in our conception of the role and scale of government.'

'Yet we are the first and oldest democracy of modern times. The Founding Fathers could not have predicted what the world would be like more than two hundred and thirty years after they ratified the Constitution. The prescient checks and balances they put in place have gradually been eroded by unrelenting partisan politics and the skewing of the composition of our judiciary. Preferential treatment for faith-based schools and other institutions has, along with the politicised judiciary has weakened the Separation of Powers and fourth estate is compromised by media manipulation inconceivable even twenty years ago. And the heavily resourced and relentless attacks on the independence of the Legislative Branch of government by small groups that dominate wealth and power lobbying for legislative outcomes that serve their interests.'

Some listening thought that was a speech a President might give at the end of his tenure, not the inauguration. Such as Dwight Eisenhower gave and warned against the 'Military Industrial Complex'.

'We've had divisions before when we confronted Civil Rights as a nation. We had division before the US joined the war in Europe, with many of our citizens against the idea. The divisions between rich and poor, scandalous as they are, were worse in the nineteen twenties. The intense and sometimes nasty rivalry between political parties in our country, though not so entrenched, is over two hundred years old and the partisan nature of media is nothing new, though the media landscape has changed dramatically and is more susceptible to money and power.'

'However in the past it was almost unavoidable that people would be exposed to a diversity of views while they came to a position or eventually staunchly developed an ideology. But that process is fading.'

'Citizens can be encouraged to go where only one point of view is represented. This can be utilised by internal and external powers in a way very different to what those consuming the media realise. These entities may simply be seeking to drive wedges between us and will guide people to stronger and stronger views in any direction, it doesn't matter to them as long as it's not moderate. All our divisions are being further widened by these unseen forces.'

'Why? Because to some entities, including foreign powers, a divided America is a weakened America. And for them a weakened America, is a good America.'

'Yet as a nation, we've reached our hands across divisions in the past. Now we need do it again. Or we should contemplate what our country will look like if our divisions continue to widen. My first priority will be to work and collaborate with anyone, to narrow these divisions. To support processes that bring us together and not drive us apart. And one way to do this is to fix things. Because when things are broken, it's a good place to drive wedges between us.'

'In an Inauguration Speech a President might provide glimpses as to what she or he sees as major areas of public policy. Aspirations. Audacious change. I give you the reverse of that.'

'We have good rules. Good regulations. Good laws. But the system is broken in many places. We keep putting new rules on top of old rules or new laws on top of dated laws and take nothing away. We have processes or procedures that are good. But aren't being funded, operated appropriately or enforced. We have legislators gridlocked because they sometimes agree however alignment will work against them personally as a Party member or their overall Party at the poll. Or it will leave insufficient distinction between adversaries.'

'I'd like to challenge everyone, from Congress to State legislatures, to City Councils to School Boards to agree what can be dealt with, with little debate to clean house of defunct laws and statutes, regulations, and by-laws. Be open to compromise and ratify quickly what is a self-apparent good. This might get people in a bipartisan frame of mind. Then look at your legislative calendar and see what might be possible to come to agreement on in the near term. Give a little, compromise, for one year. The Opposition Party will want to distinguish themselves for the next election, and rightly so. Let's have a year of bipartisanship and then return to the usual contest of ideas which sustains any democracy. And I intend practice what I preach. And some in my Party may not always like it, but I'm going to compromise, and I'll be looking for compromise.'

'And for everyone else who's not a legal or regulatory decision maker, we're starting a 'Let's Fix What's Broken' campaign at the individual level. The First Lady will be leading the movement. We can't promise you we'll fix everything. But anyone can report laws not working or regulations not being observed by authorities, promised funding not being distributed or with unreasonable delays, people being enriched by specific laws or regulations and many other examples which will be listed on the web page. Those managing the Project, which will be bipartisan and include legal and public policy experts, will be identifying clear examples of something broken and will be developing proposals for specific or systemic changes. Amancia would like to hear about all of it because she will be looking for trends and themes emerging. As I say, we may not resolve every issue locally, the Project will try to fix the systematic failures initially, but people may wish to set up individual chapters to focus in more on local issues. But don't get angry. Systems don't respond to anger. Get conciliatory. And accept it won't work every time. But at least give it a try.'

'In addition to this. We'll be planning and designing a resourced program for the three years after we have the 'Fix it' year. We'll be working then to close a lot of gaps in race and gender equality, in education, health, and in basic wages. We'll ask for; plead for, moderates from both sides to try to close these gaps. So that it won't be so easy for faceless organisations or other countries to drive wedges between us. If we can take even a few steps closer to being a unified America, it will mean a lot. We're going to roll up our sleeves and fix stuff. Not exciting. But once we get things fixed, we'll have a solid base to work from on strategic issues.'

'Together.'

The Lecture Hall

Mansour looked up at the steep gallery of the lecture hall. He had spent his time as a student looking down at the professor lecturing them on calculus or advanced algebra in Tehran. Dense mathematics. His first professor would challenge the people in the lecture theatre to figure out answers to complex questions. To resolve the puzzles nature had crafted and hidden for them to solve. And algorithms, these were destined to be his personal passion. It's certain that none of the other students back then were quite as devoted to the subject as he was. However everyone still paid attention.

Now things were different. He paused and looked up to a sea of faces and every single one was looking at a laptop or tablet screen, or flicking though pages on their phone. He could see a few listening to music, and one even turned to the side with white earbuds in trying to have a quite conversation, undoubtedly about something other than mathematics.

Usually when he looked up, he would see at least a few people looking down at him. Maybe not with the rapt attention he used to pay to his lecturers, but at least paying attention. But at that moment there was not one single person in the hall looking at him.

He knew he shouldn't pause too long while looking up at the metaphorically empty hall, as this would look strange on the video. All his lectures were video recorded and put up on the course webpage along with his notes and diagrams to be downloaded any time it suited one of the students. He was advised his notes needed to fairly closely reflect the contents of examinations.

The students could get everything they needed without needing to turn up and could miss a substantial amount of the lectures provided there were reasons given, which were never followed up on in any event. The theatre was only half full, which was a good turnout compared to what sometimes occurred. Especially if there was a major sporting event on, or it was the day after a large communal celebration which precipitated widespread hangovers.

He imagined how odd he would be in this group, positioning himself in the hall so he was eye level with the lecturer. Taking note, almost frantically, hoping to be asked questions. In Tehran this being a rare occurrence because he was always right.

His extracurricular studies generally put him several lectures in front in the series, so he would pester the professor with questions the rest of his cohort were yet to learn or in some cases, would never be confronted with.

Unfortunately, the last lecturer in Mansour's student career had lost his passion for the subject. He was focused on retirement. He did however give Mansour advice about how to pursue a career in academia. 'Don't.' He had said dourly. 'Help them build rockets.' This advice came along with the message. 'Don't ask any more questions. They take too long to find the answers to.'

It wasn't difficult for Mansour to finish top of his class, though, religious studies took more effort for him to excel at. Once he began his PhD it was simple. He completed this on an obscure corner in the field of algorithms which, although not attention getting, had been little explored by other academics. He won a place as a mathematics lecturer in a University in a small Iranian city and enjoyed being able to create a curriculum, considering both those interested in the subject, and those not. Although he knew his style could hardly be characterised as entertaining, he made efforts to make his lectures as interesting as the subject allowed. Unfortunately, his lifestyle became more and more characterised by political pressure and ultimately surveillance. Not because of his boring lifestyle. But the decisions of family members.

Now in the lecture hall in the mid-west USA, he came to himself all of a sudden. He had no idea how long he'd been lost in a reverie, but every single person in the lecture hall was staring at him. Phones ignored, earbuds out, looking over laptops.

He smiled. 'This is how to do it.' There was some laughter, and most of the 'attendees' drifted back to their usual occupations, although he noticed a small smattering, chastened by the incident, providing at least some degree of attention.

The lecture came to its conclusion, always on time and not before or after. The students shuffled out. Many scrolling on their phones as they walked down the narrow path between seats.

He gathered his papers and the memory stick with his lecture presentations. He had a lecture preparation period next, which he found amusing. The lectures he needed to prepare to keep the university satisfied had taken him a few days for the entire course. Three years ago. He read journals. He got negative feedback if his lectures became too complex, and the same applied to the difficulty of exams.

They needed people to pass. There were financial considerations and only those spectacularly bad could be justifiably failed. If they were good at sports or the child of a wealthy donor, one on one tutoring was to be arranged and, in some cases, specially crafted make up exams.

But this is where fate had delivered him. He'd moved to the United States when he was visiting his parents and was advised they were leaving Iran that night. They 'emigrated' to work for the US Government. He had to begin again with only three years credit towards a degree. The final year of the course work, PhD, and the lecturing he'd done in Iran all counted for nothing. He was bitter for some time that at his age and background he was now returning as a student. Also knowing he would never return to his homeland. But his parents had made stipulated to the US he join them. They all knew his life would be made untenable in Iran.

He often thought about where he would be if his life could have continued as it was.

Now lost in his second reverie for the morning he looked to see a woman standing quietly waiting for him to emerge from wherever he was.

'Ah. I'm so sorry. I hope you don't think I was being rude. I didn't notice you there. How can help. I don't seem to have seen you in the class before.' Perhaps she primarily undertook the course via the recorded lectures but had some specific question to ask he thought.

'I'll take that as a compliment, but I'm not a student. A little old I imagine.'

He sallied forth with what he hoped was understated Persian charm. 'I would hardly have known. But how may I help you miss?' She smiled again. 'It's Odette. And shall I refer to you as Professor Adraki or…?'

He relaxed. 'It's Mansour, of course. You come to me no doubt with a question on algorithms, a question which has been plaguing every waking moment and maybe even your dreams.' He said this with a trace of hope as well as humour.

'Um…not exactly, but it's not so far from the truth. I represent an organisation that uses algorithms and AI in a range of applications, and they follow the journals, especially the smaller publications, because the mainstream journals want to play it safe until the supporting evidence is overwhelming.'

'Exactly Odette. This is what I believe happens. And I do not accept their philosophy. That's why I never publish in the bigger journals.' He smiled.

She was uncomfortable from the outset to be deceiving this man. 'It seems that some people, people who know rather a lot about the subject, think some of the things you write are … what's the word… prescient.'

'A very generous description of what I've been trying to contribute.'

Odette dragged her black hair tightly against her head between her fingers, as if she was accustomed to have it tied back. 'Yes. The people I work for, those who read your papers, also scrutinised your thesis, I think they said it came together as, 'a coherent projection from a little examined vantage.'

Mansour could only smile. He'd run out of the capacity to respond to so many compliments because he'd never needed to respond to more than one on any specific occasion. He was impressed that they'd unearthed his Iranian Doctoral Thesis.

'You may be disappointed to find out, that I know as much about algorithms as I do about the quantum physics.'

'Both noble and difficult subjects.'

'But I'm the nearest available contractor who works for the organisation that's interested in your work, so they've asked me to come and discuss some possibilities and terms.'

'Possibilities.'

'Yes. My employer has a large team working on a range of algorithmic based problems for various applications. They would like you to critique their work as an entirely independent party, separate from any preconceptions, team dynamics or hierarchical expectations.

They'd expect you to point out areas of strength and weakness, and ideally suggest improvements, corrections, or alternatives.'

Mansour felt two things at once. There was the surprise and excitement about such an opportunity, and the disappointment at being, essentially, a reviewer. From what he could gather there would be no opportunity to collaborate with other scientists, nor produce papers from this arrangement. Like it or not, it was being published that built careers.

He smiled somewhat sheepishly. 'My weekends are very full of extreme sports and parties so I'm not sure I'll have enough time.' It was abundantly clear to Odette that Mansour's weekends would be free for algorithms, if they were not already taken up with recreational algorithming.

'My employers said to tell you this will be a fulltime commitment. It may last six months, possibly more.'

'Well, Miss... Odette, I cannot afford to lose my place here, humble as it is. So, although I would be more than delighted to take on the role you've described, I must consider the long term.' Mansour said this with a heavy heart.

'My employers anticipated your concerns and have taken the opportunity to speak with the University Vice Chancellor and have gained approval, if you chose to accept the offer, for you to return to you existing position with no loss of advancement towards tenure or any progressive entitlements due to you. And you would have an assurance of this via a formal contract with the University. You would receive double the salary you currently earn while you work on the Project. As an incentive.'

This took some time to digest. He'd been watching a movie recently.

He tried to watch movies that improved his capacity to understand the idiom and culture of the country he'd moved to. He remembered a gangster saying. 'I'll make you and offer you can't refuse.' This was certainly that kind of offer.

He looked at the dark haired woman. She was fine featured with fair skin. A mask of good nature seemed to overlay a native earnestness.

'And who's your employer Odette?' He knew the answer. 'The United States Government.' She replied. 'NASA.'

Big Bear and Honey Bear

One of the few compensations of the roster was the sunrise. Duane didn't like night shift. It felt unnatural. He missed sleeping next to Honey Bear. He hated feeling awful when he transitioned back to dayshift. That had led him to consider asking for permanent nights. He and Honey Bear had talked about it. She said she would work night shift at home, right along with him. Work the horses morning and evening, pretty much like she did anyhow, and work on her online business through the night.

He tested the water with a few people of his rank who knew a thing or two and was told it could never happen. They said it would foul up the roster. It was two weeks dayshift and two weeks night shift. Like it or lump it.

He didn't want to transfer away, and the performance reviews and even the looks he got from officers told him he was at the bottom of the list in terms of any advancement in rank. He didn't help himself.

His huge size accompanied by a distinct lack of zeal about his job left him watching the few promotions that became available being taken by younger, slimmer men. There were far more transfers out of the base than promotions. People came in, staying only long enough to develop a thorough dislike for the place and its function. Along with a quite contempt for what they saw as the hick town that serviced the Base. They'd transfer out as soon as it earned them a few lines on their CV.

Duane had sat through this since they'd come home seven years before. Honey Bear hadn't renewed her contract with the military and returned to the family farm twenty miles east of the Base. Earlier in their careers they'd enjoyed a rotation to bases in Germany and the Philippines, but they'd never be leaving their home now.

She'd given up any outside work so that she could care for her father while he died. It hadn't been an easy death nor a quick one, and Honey Bear refused to put the old man into palliative care. He wanted to die on his farm.

By the time the old man died five years later, Duane was the longest serving soldier on the base by over a year, and yet had no seniority. It would be another five years before he could get the full retirement benefits they counted on to be comfortable in their old age.

Honey Bear's internet venture made a bit of money but the small farm and the horses in particular cost a lot to keep. Duane had been in the Service since he was a kid, but he didn't have a lot to show for it. If it hadn't been for his father in law's farm, they'd be living in a cinderblock place in town; with a mortgage.

The sun had breached over the hills east of their farm. A small creek formed the boundary of their place and a reserve. To the north the neighbour's houses were all on the far side of their acreage, nearly a mile away.

The sun was well above the hills when he pulled into the driveway and stopped in front of the pleasant farmhouse. It was all they would ever need. Honey Bear couldn't have children, so she adopted horses instead. She was always through the door as soon as he pulled up, and once he'd stepped out of the pick-up, he was smothered in one big long hug.

'Welcome home Big Bear.' Their nicknames were quite accurate descriptions as well as terms of endearment. They were big people, but they'd decided not to be ashamed of it, or feel like there was something wrong with them. It's how they were. Honey Bear did make efforts to stop them getting any bigger, though the end of nightshift breakfast suggested otherwise.

Duane arrived home to a full spread of bacon, eggs, toast, hash browns, hotcakes with syrup and sausages. This was accompanied by coffee and, because this was Duane's 'evening meal', beer. He couldn't drink before leaving for the base late in the afternoon, so he got in the habit of having a few beers in the mornings on night shift. Once Honey Bear found out he couldn't do permanent nights she started to keep him company and do the same shifts he did.

'How was the Inauguration Speech.' Big Bear asked, having missed it.

'Oh, I don't know, mostly about how people in the US all hate each other and how he's going to fix all that up. Said he was going to try to get Democrats and Republicans working together among other things. Pipe dream stuff.'

He gave a shrug of agreement. They'd never seen a politician they trusted.

'I'm pretty sure what he's really planning is to take our guns away.'

'Yeah. That's the Democrats for you.'

'So how was your shift?'

'Pretty good. Organising short notice despatch for people in Iraq.' He smiled. 'You've got to know who to speak to on both sides of the fence to get things there on time.'

But she could tell he was uncomfortable about something. 'What else?'

'They want to train me up to be one of those Drone pilots. Actually, not a pilot, not one of the guys that fly them. One of the guys that monitors what goes on and lets them know if there's a problem or something.'

'And is that a good thing?'

Honey Bear was looking for some guidance as to how to react but the breakfast she'd prepared was getting cold so they could talk more later.

The Unwelcome Visitor Returns

His security detail said he had a visitor from Uzbekistan in the briefing room, who had requested a moment of The Presidents time and had some useful information to share with respect to the politics of the Caspian.

Gene was tired and was about to ask them to get Greg to deal with it, when he thought it was interesting part of the world to get a first- hand briefing about.

Once he entered the meeting room and saw who was there, he was tempted to turn around and walk out. But he knew the man would simply use his remarkable contacts to be sitting in another room, the next night or the next and have the President called to him. He asked his security to remain inside but at the door. The security man held up a phone. Gene looked slightly confused. Then realised what the unwelcome guest wanted and handed his over.

The man arose and offered his hand. On this occasion, he was in front of his staff, who were thinking the President was meeting with a foreign emissary. They would have thought it most unusual for him to refuse a handshake. Gene's eyes were steely as he shook the man's hand, who's eyes gave the appearance of regret that it was only in these circumstances that Gene would do so.

'I appreciate my views are of no interest to you Mr President, but I believe your inaugural speech was of a very honest and ambitious nature and had the kind of sincerity absent from politics for years.'

Gene sighed, and with only partial sarcasm said. 'I'll take a compliment wherever I can get one at the moment. But I doubt you've come here to discuss anything associated with sincerity.'

'I'm afraid not Mr President. My masters have sent me to convey a list of; requirements which they would like to become a program of policies to the extent you can directly implement them through Cabinet, or where budget allocations or legislative approvals require it, urge these outcomes through the House.'

The man handed Gene a list and the President looked over it. He shook his head. 'How can these people expect me to maintain any credibility if I prosecute an agenda completely at odds to my election campaign and policy track record.'

The man slid out a page from under an envelope with the writing facing the President. 'I can only assume there is some urgent objective to create such a dissonance. Mister President.'

'I know what the answer is going to be if I say I won't do them all. I'll attempt what's on this list but it's during a term, not a year. I'll give them some results soon and give myself some pain, by getting a number of things through Cabinet. The Legislative agenda I can only do my best. It'll be my Party I'll need to convince. This is Bipartisanship on steroids.' Gene looked down the list again and felt defeated. He tried to imagine how he was going to get these objectives next to what he'd already committed to and commenced.

'I'll provide your feedback that this is a full-term list of things to do.' The man said this with reluctance. Anxiety seemed just below his otherwise calm veneer. 'I have no doubt there will be more. But we shall see what we shall see. Mr President, I appreciate you're busy, or tired or both so I'll leave you to get back to your evening.' The man was about to stand when Gene said.

'One moment.' Gene was curious. 'Because I'm reasonably easy going, many people call me Gene, when protocol would require they call me Mr President and I've never given them permission to do otherwise. You could call me Gene or anything else without consequence. So why call me by my title.'

The man was sombre. 'My masters hold everything that is dear to me lightly in the palm of their hand. But you're still my President.'

They stood together and Gene reached out his hand. 'It's been lousy to see you.'

The man nodded and left.

Florida

They pulled up at the low block of apartments in Florida within sight of Cape Canaveral. Mansour had expected to get a taxi, but Odette called and said she'd arrived back in town and would come and get him from the airport.

His temporary leave had been arranged easily, the Head of his Faculty said they were viewing it as a sabbatical. He got a sense that the US government had provided some incentives to the university. Mansour had paid his rent in advance for six months and given the few plants he had to a neighbour to look after.

Odette's cheerfulness felt a little forced. When he asked what it was like working for NASA, she reminded him that she was only a Contractor and did logistics projects, generally associated with short term external specialists. She did contract work for the Airforce Base also.

'Projects like me.'

'Yes. Though yours is a situation I haven't been asked to manage before Mansour. I get a sense you're a little disappointed that you won't be working directly as part of the team, and it's a little unusual for me to be involved in a Project of this duration.

I imagine it's so important that in addition to bringing in several recognised specialists, they have set up this 'Devil's Advocate' arrangement for you.'

He laughed quietly. 'They bring in an unknown junior lecturer from a University with small prestige to defeat the claims of some of the greatest minds the US can pay for.' He didn't sound like someone enthusiastic about rising to that challenge.

'I think you're selling yourself short Mansour. NASA understands much of what you achieved in Iran wasn't recognised, but they haven't discounted it as the Universities have. As I understand it, you're considered to be somewhat of a maverick. Albeit the quiet kind. And someone who can see things from a different perspective.'

He smiled 'Like the Devil.'

'How much fun is there being an angel.' She was trying to stay positive.

'And how much sorrow in being a devil.'

The apartment building was on the shore side of the road. It was the kind of place with one small elevator for each block and covered stairs at the front running to each level at intervals. The car was parked right in front, and he took the two modest size bags up to the third floor. The apartment was luxurious to Mansour's eyes. There was a sweeping vista over the bay and down along the beaches. Plush carpets, tasteful furnishings and genuine art pieces. He would later find a refrigerator full of all kinds of food and alcohol.

'I did up the second room as a kind of workroom where you can spread things out and write things down. Calculate stuff or whatever.'

It was at times like this that Mansour got the impression Odette was pretending to be more naïve than she was. She led him into the room and he laughed. The ensemble bed and mattress had been laid against the wall. There was a raised map table with stools in the centre of the room, and a mobile tilting chalkboard filled one corner. One wall had a fixed whiteboard and facing it was both a modern projector and an old fashioned Overhead Projector.

He walked up to this and slid his fingers down the neck. 'You do know no one uses these anymore.'

She laughed. 'I thought you might like to see one again. My father was a lecturer and I imagine he's about the same age as your father. I thought he might have told you about these. I got it on eBay for twenty bucks.'

He looked up and smiled back. 'It's a trip down memory lane. My father told me that sometimes the students who did best were those who were good at deciphering the scribbles on the plastic sheets that went with these things.' He was amused to see one. They were being phased out as he began his studies. 'And the chalk board, with wood framing is good quality. The board is barely used. eBay?'

'Yep. It cost a little more, but it's all on NASA's dime.'

'And I imagine you expect that I'm going to fill this up with long complicated formulas, with rubbing marks here and there to make corrections and refinements? Like in the movies? I'm sure it's the kind of thing a devil would do.' Mansour realised that although he spent a great deal of time alone, he would find working in this situation, all day, every day, lonely.

Even the students that didn't listen were company.

Odette was watching these calculations being made behind those brown thoughtful eyes. 'Oh, and NASA have said this project is high priority and they've assigned me to help you in any way I can. Hence while I'm not dazzling you with my skills as an algorithm grand master, I'll be helping out with some chores around here but also showing you around the area. I assume you've never been here, and you can't think mathematics every day I don't imagine.'

'No. Your assistance with...ah...chores, would not be suitable.' On this Mansour would be unmoved. Or so he thought. 'You're obviously a person of significant talents and capabilities. I could not permit you to be doing menial duties for me. I will do them. Thank you for your offer and I appreciate that it was well meaning.'

'Mansour there is a self-interest angle in this for me. I'll take you to Cape Canaveral and we get a backstage pass, our own personal tour guide. Who knows we might get to wear space suits. The same with the Air Base. I'll do the shopping, vacuuming, keep the windows clean and you do the showers and toilets. I only live a couple of miles from here which is why we picked this place. I'm a contractor. If I only do half a day's work, I only get half a day's pay.'

Mansour still didn't like the idea. Apart from growing up with his sister and mother he had never spent much time in close proximity with women even though he might have liked to. Even in his early forties, ultimately he was shy among western women. As he chose to pursue opportunities in his field, he wasn't near an Iranian enclave with Iranian women. He'd hoped his time at this University would allow him to eventually move to such a place.

Odette took his silence as a yes and said 'Great, I'll let you get settled in and start the process of setting up a VIP visit to Canaveral.'

Soon after she was giving a progress report to the Colonel.

'Is he settled in?'

'Yes Colonel.'

'No expense spared?'

'He's a frugal man, if we went over the top he'd know something's wrong.'

'Whatever's the right balance is, find it.'

'When will he have something to work on. He's not the type to sit around watching TV or walk along the beach.'

'Tomorrow. It's coming tomorrow. We've made a change because there's been a push from above to get this working. Rather than get this guy to send in some diversionary crap to trim the dead wood, we're sending out chunks of the main product to see if he can find flaws and add any value.'

'That's good to hear sir. That's pretty much what he thought he'd be doing. Oh, and if you could remember to organise the VIP tours of NASA and the Airbase. Spread out by a few weeks perhaps.'

'Will do.'

Garbage

They had dinner on the balcony. The aromas brought back many memories for Mansour. Even though he had dined at restaurants that served the food from his homeland, he had missed sharing a meal at home. And he was an abysmal cook. His Sheppardess was not.

That's what he'd begun to call her in his mind. He was a goat who knew a few secrets and she kept him close. Perhaps waiting for his turn at the altar.

'You disappear a lot.'

'Disappear?'

'Yes. Off into your own head.'

She wore the blouse and jeans which was her custom, but tonight they were a better cut and there was a slight trace of perfume. He felt inadequate wearing the clothes he wore every day. He made an undertaking to himself to go and buy some casual clothes. But then he would probably need the Sheapardess's help.

'There you go again.' She smiled across at him. The sun was dipping down over the bay.

'I want to thank you for this beautiful food. You are a magnificent cook. It was about this my mind was wandering.'

She took a sip of wine. 'I'll admit I did have to do a bit of research, and to be completely honest, I did a trial run at home.'

'I'm the beneficiary of that. Khoresh and Lavash bring back fond memories.'

'What's it like in your country.'

'Well, not to be pedantic, but this is my country now.' He smiled. 'I

was being pedantic though wasn't I.'

'I'll get over it.

'My homeland, in terms of the ordinary people, is the same as here. People work, they're concerned for the future of their children, they love their country and its heritage. They are ruled by ideologues who are bad.' He laughed. 'Just like here. And badness or goodness are relative things. Iran lived many years under the Shah. Was he better than the Ayatollahs? Maybe, difficult to say.'

He was reflective. 'I like to think of myself as a Persian. Persia is a country with centuries of remarkable history and heritage. It's a country that values poetry and all knowledge very highly. Most of the Muslims are devout but not xenophobic nor see themselves as superior. Some on my mother's side of my family were Sufis.'

'What's a Sufi?'

'They are a mystical sect of Islam. Many are ascetics. Some of them beg and then give most of what they get to the poor. They love poetry and prayer and dance.'

'Are they like those Devershers I've heard about?'

He smiled. 'Not the Whirling Dervishes, they're Sufi's yes, but from Turkey. My mother's people do dances but a bit different. But I'm sure I'd still become dizzy.'

'You didn't keep up the traditions.'

'No, like my mother, I believed that Sufism and algorithms were incompatible. Now I'm not so sure.'

'Speaking of algorithms, it's been a few weeks, how's the assessment going.'

Mansour was pushing the napkin gently against his mouth. 'Oh, it's Garbage.'

'Garbage?'

'Yes. The whole construction is misguided. Because those assembling it wish to achieve multiple complex tasks, they have used a number of algorithms which served one purpose each. They have tried to adjust them and connect them together to work as a whole. Very complex and challenging. But it's garbage. I didn't want to raise it until we'd finished the meal which I'm so grateful for. My bags are mostly packed. Of course, with you I've used a word people might find offensive. It would be best if you'd characterise my feedback using the word *flawed*.' Mansour was annoyed by the task he'd been given once he'd understood it. That's why he'd used the word.

This progress report surprised the Colonel.

'Garbage?'

'That's what he said.'

'We have some of the most brilliant algorithm heads on the planet and this guy from, shit I don't even know where he's from, says what they've produced is garbage.'

'That's about the size of it.'

'Has he illuminated you at all as to the aspects of the work that are garbage?'

'He has, reluctantly. But I had no idea what he was talking about. He had his bags packed and wanted me to arrange a ticket home. Didn't want to upset the big dogs because he thought he wouldn't get a paper published for the rest of his life. I told him they don't know who he is so he should write a critique and we'd send it through.'

'Can't he help us tweak the damn thing.'

'He says the fundamentals are wrong for what it's being asked to do. Needs a rebuild.'

'Shit. How long.'

'We didn't speak about it because he's not expecting to be asked, but I suspect it will be weeks not days.'

'We have people wandering the middle east we would really like to depeoplise with this thing soon. Send the critique.'

'Okay Colonel.'

'No problem Captain'

'Captain?'

'Congratulations.'

The Interview

Peter felt the manna from Heaven raining down upon him. He knew that his daughter Racheal went to the College in London with the US President's daughter, and they'd struck up a friendship. He'd restrained his desire to ask questions about her. And then Racheal invited Claudia to dinner. Peter had decided not to even mention the US Presidency, he would however enquire after her mother Amancia, and how her grandmother, who was in care facility in Barbados, were faring.

His scheme worked brilliantly. Claudia didn't mention her father at all during the meal. A few days later, Rachel said that her friend had so much respect for the way he'd approached the evening. Especially as a former journalist now talk show host. She was sick of being quizzed about things that were nothing to do with her.

And then the call came. His Producer told him that the Whitehouse had been in touch and the US President wanted to make an appearance on the show. It would be after the visit to the G7 summit in Berlin and while he was in Britain for follow up talks with the Prime Minister. After a moment or two of disbelief, there was joy, then a bit of fear, then a return to joy. It was no doubt to do with Claudia, but there were half a dozen other shows that were more prestigious.

The night arrived, and looking out at the audience, he said something he never thought he'd say. 'Ladies and gentlemen, if you could give a warm welcome to the President of the United States.' There was applause greater than might usually have been for a President, as during the visit he'd made it clear he was the staunch ally the British were looking for. Yet there was a small pocket making calls which were unflattering in one corner of the sea of faces.

Once they were settled, Peter led off with 'Mr President' but Gene interrupted him and said that since Peter wasn't an American citizen it would be fine if he called him Gene.

Peter said he would do his best, but the title was a somewhat embedded. The first thing that Peter had to ask was why he'd come on his little program when there were so many options.

'My daughter Claudia is friends with your daughter Rachel. Claudia was telling me about this show that Rachel's father does, that virtually no one ever watches. She said I could go on and say pretty much whatever I wanted, and no one would notice, which I thought would be nice for a change.'

The audience appreciated this and Peter took it in good humour.

Gene smiled. 'The real reason is that the media in the US is partisan. The networks that think they aren't, are left leaning, but they don't want to admit it. The right leaning networks are unapologetic about their biases. I've decided to do long form interviews only outside the US. I believe interviewers might have some different perspectives on our politics, and the situation in the United States overall.'

'Well.' Said Peter. 'I'm right across all of that stuff you talked about.' Peter was impressed with the rationale for the interview. 'I suppose the observation many people make, is that you're Presidency is schizophrenic. Through the Cabinet, or as a driving force though the Legislative Houses, you're prosecuting foreign policy, internal affairs, military expenditure, labour, and environment policies that many seen as regressive. Areas of race and wealth inequity, strengthening of emergency preparedness, better resourcing and expanding national parks, affordable housing programs, shifting the focus on the so-called drug war to treatment and rehabilitation are more progressive. You're improving health and education in a superficial way, but not touching the expensive fundamentals.'

Peter didn't like having to put this line of questioning to this Gene, but it's what he would ask anyone other in the circumstances. 'In fact, you're being referred to as the best Republican President America has ever had.' There was a loud murmur in the lower left corner of the audience.

'I'll take that as a compliment and a very significant compliment. Abraham Lincoln was a Republican. As was Ulysses S. Grant whom I admire as I do much of the policy and many of the achievements of Dwight Eisenhower. Even Richard Nixon, whom I'd never like to be compared with, started the EPA and George H W Bush signed in the Clean Air Act. The gap between parties is harder to bridge now then in days gone by.

Bridging it in any way can be viewed by the constituency which voted you in, as a betrayal of trust.'

There were loud murmurs of assent and a few audible calls of. 'Because that's what you're doing.'

Gene could see some of his people moving closer in to be prepared if the group became threatening but gave a small shake of his head.

'You mentioned schizophrenia Peter. I don't know enough about that condition to say if it's a good analogy, but I think what people are saying is my Presidency looks like it's all over the place without one single driving agenda. And, at the moment, I admit it looks that way.'

'And that's because I'm a President for all the people. Those who voted me in, those who didn't, and those that didn't vote. They don't have a simple, clear driving agenda. Is the United States a simple place? Americans have a mosaic of needs and wants and concerns and fears. Some of these things are long held policy ambitions on the Republican side of the House. Others the Democrats. And my view is, I represent all Americans and I should make my judgements on a case by case basis, and not a partisan basis.'

A young woman in her early twenties stood up and started to speak from a piece of paper. Her hands trembling. 'Who can I trust to vote for Mr President, when just about everything you said you'd do, everything you promised you'd do, you haven't done. To us it looks like you're doing the exact opposite.'

Again, his people moved closer in and again Gene shook his head.

'We voted for real reductions in arms spending and real increases in spending to get our country from around the bottom in modern democracies in education and health performance and remove us from the top of the list of the number of incarcerated people per capita in the world. An increase in wages for the working poor Mr President. A class of people many countries don't even have. Where's the President we thought we could trust during the elections?'

She sat down and because it was a British audience and the President was being interviewed there was only a smattering of applause.

Peter tried to lighten the mood a little by saying. 'Thank you for the question without notice from the floor.'

Gene smiled and looked across at him. Ready to answer. 'It's true. I haven't delivered on my promises, two years into my term. I live in a world of meeting with powerbrokers on both sides of the Party system to try to strike a deal across a table. I live in a world where the interconnectedness between health and insurance is so complete, so bound up, there seems to be no line anymore. Prison guard unions, the left, have teamed up with the prison management companies they work for, to lobby for laws to maximise incarcerations through criminalisation of as many things as possible. I live in a world where I have one House held against me and everything's a negotiation.'

There was broader applause from the audience though not resounding. Gene looked at the young lady who had crumpled sideways into the arms of a friend.

He paused and sighed. He simply could not do this. A kernel of an idea began to form. And the price he was going to have to pay.

'I'd like to revise my answer a little. First to recognise the audience member who identified and took the opportunity to pose a penetrating question to the 'Most Powerful Man In The World.' She put herself up against someone who has spent much of the last twenty-five years speaking, in one place or other, in one way or other, about politics and I gave her that kind of answer.'

'Here's the answer I'd like to give you. Yes. I have betrayed your trust. I haven't achieved the things I promised to or haven't progressed them as well as I could have during the two years I've been in Office. Yes. These things are difficult tasks but I was elected to deliver outcomes on difficult tasks. That's what a President has to do, make difficult decisions and encourage others to do the same. I know I've failed in meeting the expectations of many of those that worked tirelessly on my behalf and voted for me and encouraged others to get out and do the same. I'll give what you've said very careful thought as I plan for what will be my final two years in Office. If you and a friend would like to join myself, the First Lady and Peter and his wife and our respective daughters for dinner I'd be delighted, and I'll be very happy to continue to listen to what you have to say.'

This time there was warm applause and Peter wrapped up the segment with no comments.

Later that evening, Gene thought it was funny that when they were all around the table, Merci, the girl who asked the questions, was much more interested in talking with Rachel and Claudia and they all disappeared somewhere as soon as the mains were finished.

She'd done what she set out to do and got what she wanted. She didn't need to repeat herself. He respected that.

The Girl in the Market

He had seen her in the markets. She was not supposed to be there unaccompanied, but her mother was dead and her father, wheelchair bound, was indulgent. She loved to walk among the stalls and take in the scents of the spices and the dried fish and meats. And look at all the things her father couldn't afford. She would be wearing the Hajib as soon as the change in her body came, which would not be far. And while she was looking forward to womanhood, she was enjoying the last months as a girl.

But her Uncle had seen her from his car. She had only visited her father's brother on a few occasions. Each time her father had made some apology and left after only a short time.

She was put immediately on edge when a man with a foreign accent got out of the car that had been weaving its way through the crowded streets. He asked her to come and speak with a passenger.

The window came down. She'd never spoken to her Uncle. She'd always been in another room, with her aunt and cousins. He berated her for being alone in the markets and said that she was bringing shame on her father.

Her eyes downcast, she was bidden to get in the car to be taken home. They came through the narrow streets to an open space that should not have been there. A bomb blast from the still smouldering civil war had destroyed it. It had been a ten-story building. She had lived there with her mother and father and her baby brother. The rubble had almost all been cleared away now. She assumed they had found the remains of her mother and brother.

Her father's legs would not have been there. They were amputated in the hospital.

She and her father now lived only a few hundred meters from the space. One of the windows of their small flat looked out over where their old home had been. It had been left as rubble for two years.

The car slowed. There was a road cleared right cross the ruined building site to the front of their block of flats. Rather than drive into the open to take her to her door, they pulled up at the far side of the bombed area and her Uncle pointed to the cleared pathway and told her to walk straight home.

As she opened the door he provided a parting rebuke.

The car was disappearing back into the crowded streets. The rebellious part of her wanted to go back to the markets for a while but it was time to be getting home anyway. She needed to start dinner preparations.

Halfway across she looked down to see something remarkable in the middle of the path. It was an iPhone. A few models back but in good condition. Where it had been dropped on the ground there was a small crack in one corner.

She stopped, looking the gadget over, never having held a phone and unsure she'd ever own one. She was immediately fascinated. She thought about what she saw in magazines and television. She'd tried to open the phone, but it only brought up the password screen.

Then she started to pretend to take selfies. She held the phone out at a distance and struck various poses turning her head to the side and making pouting or kissing lips.

A man in a second story room saw a person in the empty space, which he glanced at frequently. On this occasion to look for her return. He pushed his wheelchair to move back the curtains. He shook his head smiling. She was the last of his precious family. But she was more. She had a strength and generosity of character that made him proud. And probably too indulgent.

She held the phone up high and pretended to take photos, the pretend camera pointing down. As she did this, she heard a strange noise and bent her head back to look up.

Honey Bear

The hug was not quite as long, and not as tight. He picked over the usual beautiful breakfast buffet she'd prepared for him. He said he was exhausted and might go straight to bed, without even sharing a beer on the porch.

'What's going on.' Honey Bear's voice was as hard. Even though people in the service had used the same nickname for her as her husband did now, they also knew not to get her hackles up. It could get ugly.

Big Bear said 'Nothing.' As convincingly as an eight-year-old.

'Well.' She shook her head. 'I'm real disappointed, Big Bear. You're keeping something from me after all these years.' Her voice carried real disappointment and hurt.

She was about to get up and leave him to stew on that for a while when he said. 'I shouldn't have done it. I took a video of it on my phone. I'm not supposed to even have my phone in there. I sneak it in to play games on it when nothing's happening. Which is most of the time.'

It took Honey Bear a moment to process this. 'What did you take a video of?' She asked.

'A girl. She was standing in this square. I didn't know who it was until we got in closer. The Drone had deployed the ordinance before I got an alert. As the bomb got closer, I got clearer footage, which doesn't usually happen. Something new they were trialling. Cameras on the ordinance. It was just a girl. Taking selfies. That's what it looked like. And then she was gone.'

'And she was standing with some terrorist the drone was targeting.'

'No. She was all alone.'

'Can I see it.' Said Honey Bear. She watched it several times.

'Just a child.' She said quietly. 'This doesn't make you proud. Was there some kind of debrief with you and the pilot and the higher ups?'

'There was no pilot. These ones use all kinds of information to acquire a target automatically. I'm supposed to monitor. Press a kill button.' Big Bears voice tapered off.

'Could you have killed that missile Big Bear?'

'I don't know. The bomb had dropped but there'd been no warning signal. That high up I couldn't tell if it was a woman or a man or a child.'

'So, you had no chance to kill the shot until it was too late?'

'No. I didn't. What are we going to do?' He said this quietly. He'd accept her decision and he was glad to have handed it over to her. Honey Bear had made many of the important decisions in their lives since before they'd been married. He sometimes believed he was a weak man and knew that some others viewed him that way.

He would always come around to the view he was with lucky to be with a good person he trusted.

She sighed. 'If you agree; I'd like to get this up on the internet. I don't want to live in a country that does this to a kid, wherever she's from. We seem to be drifting more and more further away from what we used to value. To me, if we don't do something here, this sort of thing's going to get worse, and as you know, the Brass'll sweep it under that big carpet covering up so many things like this.' Honey Bear was reflective for a while. 'When we first joined the service, it was this kind of thing we were there to stop. Innocent people getting killed by bombs. That's what I thought anyhow. I'll talk to a guy on the net I work with, and I think he'll be able to get it up there without anyone knowing where it came from.' She said this, but not with complete confidence.

All the News

It wasn't hard to foresee that the President's interview on the 'Show that no one Watched' was soon leading the twenty-four-hour news cycle. Newshounds looked for precedents of a President that said he had sold out his constituency. The young woman's complaints were a good summary of the President's apparent duplicity and yet many in his Party were reluctant to come out against genial Gene. It triggered foment in the Democrats which boiled over into the daylight led by people with the same frustrations, who believed that the bipartisan deal making was being tipped far too heavily on the side of the Republicans. However many Republicans came out against this analysis.

Some of the things occurring that might look like the brainchild of conservatives were not the will of a large number of people in that party who made analysis of situations as carefully as democrats, but from a different vantage. Both parties hosted ideologues for whom analysis was narrow, shallow and cursory.

The President had achieved a great deal and had several long hoped for and much needed changes pass through a minority Senate. But the dollar value of these initiatives were a fraction of the military spending and tax concessions to already bloated corporations.

He was sitting reflecting on the Presidency that might have been. He knew he could run rings around Democrats and Republicans alike and fame them or shame them or badger them into delivering something good, not just hollow compromises. He could have taken on big business and redistributed a tiny slice which would make a huge difference to lower class Americans. He could see a nexus in every place he went, and he could see how to break it. But he wasn't allowed to. He was being forced to strengthen them, to make them unbreakable. And those close to him, and those who worked for him, could see this mood of conflict and entrapment, and found it confusing.

He had a ringtone for family. He'd often forget that every word was being monitored and he'd treat his calls as private.

'Hi Cloud.'

'Dad, was it one of ours?'

'Was what one of ours?'

'It's all over the internet. There's this middle eastern type girl taking selfies and a bomb gets dropped on her. Are you in a meeting or something?'

'No...I'm moping to be perfectly honest. You want to send a link. I'll get it investigated.'

'I'll send it now.'

'I'll call you as soon as I know something.' 'We don't drop bombs on kids do we daddy?'

Gene was tempted to talk about the realities of almost any war and that on many occasions more civilians die than combat troops. And the US could hardly claim to have clean hands in terms of children killed in either traditional wars or the more prevalent recent wars with 'Non State Actors.' He gave a balanced answer. 'Not like this we don't, unless there's been a major mistake. Which I'll get fully investigated.'

'Thanks Dad. Sorry to bother you.'

'It would be completely impossible for you to bother me. Call me soon. I need you and your mother. You know that.'

Secretary of Defence

'Mr Secretary. Good to see you. Please take a seat over there.' Gene gestured to the two seater couches facing each other with a coffee table between. Once they were seated the Secretary of Defence looked at the President inviting him to lead off since he'd called the meeting. Gene pulled out his phone and held up the blurry footage of what looked like a girl taking a selfie prior to the image disappearing into a flash and clouds of dust.

'Was this one of ours Mr Secretary?' Gene's voice gave nothing away beyond simple curiosity.

'Gene, you may not know, I just gave the press a statement on this. These days footage can be faked very easily, and no one has come forward to claim responsibility. There's no intelligence to suggest the event in question even happened let alone it was one of ours. There are numerous terrorist drones out there now that do this kind of thing and worse. The usual objective. Make us the villain.'

'A couple of things Mr Secretary. First, I never gave you permission to call me Gene. Second, I didn't ask you if it could be faked or if it could be a terrorist drone. I asked you, was it one of ours?'

The man opposite him shifted position. 'There is the possibility, Mr President, that it was one of our assets which was responsible.'

'A possibility.'

'That's right sir.'

'You're telling me right here, right now, that you don't know if it was or it wasn't.'

'Mr President, if I tell you something, you can't later un-know it.'

'What was that? I won't be able to un-know something.'

'Mr President there are things which it's better you aren't directly informed of, so that at some future time you can deny any knowledge of them and do so with integrity.'

'I see. And how are these decisions made. Decisions to protect potential damage to my integrity.'

The Defence Secretary was uncomfortable at having to spell such a thing out. He considered it implicit in the relationship. 'These decisions occur very infrequently and after careful deliberations of the Secretary involved.'

'I get it now. The people who I appointed to positions, and whom I ensure are paid in those positions, have formed some kind of secret protocol to not tell me things in specific circumstances. Anyway, we'll get back to that in due course. You told me there was a possibility that it was our strike.'

'It is possible yes.'

'I'm now going to ask the question a different way, and I don't want to hear about any of this un-know bullshit. Have you seen evidence that it was our asset that did this?'

There was a long pause.

'Are you going to answer Secretary Dobson.'

'Mr President I believe any kind of release of this information would not be in the national interest Sir. Quite the contrary, it would damage our interests and that which we're continually striving for.'

'Secretary Dobson, I want the original video sitting in my inbox in five minutes. If it's not there, I'll be asking the next person down in the chain of command all the way to the people who peel potatoes for the prisoners in Leavenworth.'

Dobson pushed himself up in a crotchety old man sort of a way and was about to walk out of the office to make a call when Gene said. 'You'll make the call here, right here.'

'Mr President...'

'Unless you have something confidential to discuss, to which the Commander in Chief is not a party; you'll make the call here. Sit back down.'

Dobson was looking at 'Genial Gene' with surprise. He had never seen this persona in any of the public life nor the Cabinet meetings he'd attended. He placed the call on the mobile and once it was answered he didn't introduce himself but merely said, 'I need to speak to Myers.'

Dobson looked up at an urgent tap on his shoulder, Gene was motioning for him to hand over the phone. The request was so commanding and unexpected the Secretary handed the phone across automatically.

'Hello, who am I speaking with? General Myers, good. Yes, it's me. I've been meeting with Secretary Dobson and I need a copy of the video in which a girl is killed in a drone strike. That's right, the one on the internet.' Gene listened for a moment. 'Secretary Dobson assures me it was one of our assets. Are you contradicting him General?'

The President listened for some time. 'I'd like the unedited version with a minute of footage taken by the drone before and after the attack. It needs to be in the original resolution, I'll be sending people from my office over to check on that once the what you have has been provided.'

Dobson sat quietly fuming, wanting to burst into the conversation and unaccustomed to lacking the ability to assert control. When the President was speaking into the phone it was with a voice of someone who was tired of bullshit.

'I'm finding it a little hard to understand that getting a video file to me is going to take several hours of authorisations. What part of 'Commander in Chief' don't you understand. If I have to get into the Presidential Helicopter, myself, and fly to the Pentagon and sit in your waiting room until you're able to get this thing released, you're going to find out how much carnage a Commander in Chief can wreak on a career.'

After a moment more the President hung up with nothing further being said. He placed the phone on his desk and walked back to lounge area. The President looked directly at Dobson and waited until the Secretary of Defences eyes come up to meet his own. 'I imagine you have someone under arrest for the leak.' The man said nothing. 'Listen, if this is another thing you've chosen not to tell me for my own good, or the country's own good, let's cut right through that shall we. Is there a Manning squirrelled away in some facility somewhere? Took the video out on a memory stick maybe.'

'Manning. That perverted fuck. No, we fixed all of those potential threats. People aren't supposed to have phones in there but this guy somehow used to bring his in to play some fucking video game instead of doing what he was supposed to. Which was watch the monitor.'

Dobson was filled with disgust. 'Then he filmed the monitor. That's how we caught him. He reran that specific segment twice. What did the halfwit think was going to happen? Then the traitorous prick loads it up on YouTube.'

'But you can't reveal that you have him because that'd confirm that it's our drone. So where is he now?'

'At one of our holding locations in Virginia being questioned.'

Gene laughed. 'Short list of questions and answers I'd imagine. What's the way forward for him.'

'He'll sign a non-disclosure and get a dishonourable discharge on another charge and we'll let him know we'll grind his traitorous ass to dust if the piece of shit ever talks about it.'

Gene seemed to be losing interest in what was being said and with a 'wait here please' he went out and spoke to his assistant Kimmie.

He'd picked up and put Dobson's phone in his pocket. Gene went back to his desk and when the Secretary of Defence asked if he could return to his duties, some of which were pressing, he was merely told; 'No.'

A moment later the Secretary's phone rang. Gene answered as if it was his won. 'General Myers I have a question for you. Yes, the video has arrived thank you for that. I would like the person who leaked the video brought to my office.' The President sighed during the pause. 'Is there someone else I need to speak to General. I'm losing patience here. We're the largest economy with the most advanced military in the world and I can't have a man brought two hundred miles. Is there someone else who can expedite this?'

After another pause Gene said 'Yes.' And again put the phone on his desk. Gene could see the man on the lounge was building up a head of steam.

'The President of the United States... spending time on this, this kind of garbage. This ...'

'Bullshit.' Proposed Gene helpfully. 'I've only learned that I had no ability to choose what to spend my time on because I'm only a 'need to know guy.' The President sighed 'Now Mr Dobson you've had a distinguished corporate career and I hope you manage the next half an hour with the professionalism you've demonstrated during your service to me.' Gene went to his desk and pressed a button. Two Whitehouse security men came into the office, wearing the blank faces of security men and runway models everywhere.

Dobson stood up and pretended to find the situation amusing. 'You're kidding. What am I going to be handcuffed now? Is that it?' His voice turned nasty. 'This day is the day you'll regret the most of all Carlson.'

'Had to do it the hard way Mr Dobson.' The President Chief of Security, Spicer, arrived for instructions. 'Please take Mr Dobson to a secure room and place him under temporary house arrest. He's not to have any outside communications until I instruct otherwise.' They were leaving when the President said.

'Mr Spicer, a moment.' Contrary to stereotypes, the good natured and affable man returned. 'Did you do as I asked?'

'It's happening as we speak sir. Computer unplugged and Wi-Fi disabled. Hard drives all in a pile. Online storages quarantined. Work and personal.'

'Get tech on it as quickly as possible. If we find anything we'll move straight on to his house.'

'And we're looking for?'

'Influence peddling, sharing secrets with corporates, secret commissions, porn. Anything you can find.'

'His house would be out of our jurisdiction Boss.'

'We'll go only if there's a good reason from what we find here. Work with the local law enforcement and turn the place over. Leave it very tidy though. Make sure his wife is taken away somewhere with a friend if she'd there. Kimmie can arrange that.'

Once Spicer had gone, he opened up the hidden screen in the wall and played the file attached to the email he'd been sent. It was surprisingly clear.

Different to other Drone footage he's seen. There was satellite infrared and a camera mounted on the missile in a split image. A young person, probably a girl, doing the defining act of her generation. Taking a selfie. She moved to a couple of poses and then for a fraction a second she looked up. You could see her face clearly. Then there was a flash and a pall of thick dust. The satellite hung in the, taking footage, dispassionately. The drone waiting for more targets.

Some people came into view running into the area, the video ended and then restarted. Again she looked up. At him.

He got on he the phone and said to his Chief of Intelligence. 'I don't care what their acronyms are I want them all to stop what they're doing and start working directly for me. I'll be sending out a list of questions and based on the answers another list. Anyone doesn't like it I'll arrange the severance package for them.'

A Complicated Puzzle

They were having lunch on the balcony. Mansour had cooked on this occasion. Resorting to the internet to prepare what he thought might be a curry which had some of the flavours and spices of Persia within.

'I'd like to be honest with you Mansour. I'm going to miss working with you when this contract winds up.' Odette was a confident person and so she said it that way.

Mansour was less confident but said. 'I feel like that.' She reached across the table and briefly squeezed his hand.

They sat together for a while until Mansour said. 'I finished it a few days ago however...it's been pleasant.'

She smiled. 'You figured it out? Got it all as one piece to do they want it to do.'

He smiled a strange smile and said. 'No, nothing can ever do what they want it to do. As in so many things in life, you simply can't remove the human dimension. No. I've submitted an algorithmic puzzle. It may be the most complex ever made because who would be given the time for such a thing and who would take the time to do it.'

'And what happens if you work out the puzzle.' Odette could see her mission collapsing around her.

'Oh. The simplest of codes. To make a word the letter A equals one, and B equals two etcetera.' He smiled apologetically 'It spells out the word 'Drone.''

A Simple Plan

To Sebastian's masters it was a simple plan. One this President could align with easily. A girl is killed in a drone strike. However an Iranian agent had piloted it to make it appear to be an autonomous drone for the United States. Poor quality footage would be released and within half an hour the Iranian and his US army accomplice commit suicided before being captured capture. With compelling evidence uncovered. A script was prepared to demonstrate an autonomous drone could never mistarget in such a situation.

The narrative he would give provided evidence no civilian was ever killed by such a drone and there was very sound mathematics to prove it.

The narrative prepared by defence, true or not, was that civilian deaths were dramatically reduced because of autonomous, machine learning AI drones. Some of the worst terrorist leaders being successfully removed from circulation, were the cause of tens or hundreds of deaths each year. Even when the girl held the phone of a high value target, which was placed by a Syrian insider, they could prove an AI drone would not deploy. The dead Iranian agent and his collaborator, a US Army Captain, would make it obvious that the Iranians wanted to undermine AI drone projects. This confirmed they were one of the weapons most feared by the enemies of the US. One outcome of the plan would be that it was obvious the intelligence agencies had failed to identify the pair, operation on US soil, and their plan. Their leadership would claim they were underfunded. A good outcome all around.

Instead, the footage was released far too early by an army monitor who was not supposed to be monitoring *that* drone and not have access to the ordinance footage which was the subject of trials. This meant the incident came out before the Iranian and the US Army handler were ready for capture and the target was humanised so much it made the whole affair a global media frenzy. Then the Iranian and his collaborator disappeared right he was to be captured enroute to the airport. The Secretary of State went with the script that it wasn't a US drone because within half an hour of his announcement he'd be supported that it piloted by an Iranian.

With no Iranian narrative ready the Secretary of State mismanaged his meeting with the President which should have been a simple plea for patience, he would acknowledge it appeared to be a mistargeting by an autonomous drone but needed only a few hours to complete the investigation.

Then their go between Sebastian failed to force the President to meet with him prior to the announcement. All the President was to say was that he had been made aware of the incident, was very concerned about it and an investigation was under way with more information was pending. It was not too late to get the initiative back on track. Better in fact because the preliminaries by the President would lend credence to the eventual finding about the Iranian.

Instead, the President made uncharacteristically dramatic decisions, completely contrary to the objectives of the plan. The outcomes of the plan were supposed to be laid in front the American people and later the Senate Committee on Machine Learning. A justification and a favourable sentiment created about the use of the technology on many weapon systems. Instead, it was in disarray.

A Message from the President

He'd been preparing notes for his brief speech to the nation and was told there was a visitor to see him. As usual there was a compelling reason causing his staff to urge him to attend a meeting with this silver haired man.

Not today Gene thought. I'm not doing it.

He spoke from the podium with a simple 'Good Evening. Many of you will be aware of a story concerning a young girl in Syria, who was killed by a missile which appeared to be deployed from a Drone. The United States Government, by way of the Secretary of Defence, has previously indicated that there was no American drone operating anywhere near the area in which the girl was killed.'

'I'd like to advise you, that based on an investigation I've initiated, the young person in question was in fact the victim of a mistargeted US drone. I say mistargeted to give assurance that the young person in the video was not intentionally killed.'

'It sounds inadequate for me to say only that this is entirely unacceptable. However, I intend to put measures in place to demonstrate, I hope, how serious we take the matter and how much I wish to assure you, Americans and all nations, it will not happen again.'

'The mistargeting was carried out by an algorithm driven drone. Many of you will not be aware that some drones are deployed, search for and identify targets based on the rapid acquisition of self-assimilated data which draws upon existing intelligence, and continually updates during a mission. It's a form of what's known as 'Machine Learning.' The missile is deployed without reference back to a human pilot. Monitors may or may not be in a position to cancel the deployment. The advantage to the military, I'm advised, is there may be only a very small window to complete a mission.' Gene said. 'In this case the Drone was targeting an ISIL terrorist, who was known to be preparing an attack on US Troops in Iraq. This particular terrorist had been active in the area of the Sinjar Mountains and had also been one of the leaders in the attack on the Yazidi's, a group of ethic Kurds. Five thousand Yazidi civilians were killed, and thousands of Yazidi women were forced into sexual slavery. Several of our allies supported the mission to target this individual terrorist.'

The intelligence services had pleaded with the President not to reveal any specifics about individual terrorists as it would immediately alert him to the fact that he was a target and drive him underground.

The President wouldn't be swayed and said it was central to the explanation of what had occurred.

'The drone was following the man I described for some time. He walked out into a space open enough such that, there would be no casualties which is a safety metric for the US Army must meet.' But it was more of a 'sliding scale of collateral damage' depending on the value of a target calculation. This particular target would justify two dead and twenty injured. A detail the President didn't need to know about.

'While in that space he discarded his phone. A moment later, the young person picked it up.'

Very few people had seen the higher resolution pictures of her. Behind the President emerged still picture of her in various poses of taking selfies.

'The young person reactivated the phone although she could not get through the passcode.'

The vision stopped on one last haunting image. The girl had been holding the phone high up pretending to get a selfie from above. Hearing the noise her arm was lowered, no longer obscuring her face. The face looking up was one the face of aspiration, and the small joys of a little mischief.

'I've instructed our military that until this matter is fully investigated, there is to be no utilisation of machine learning targeting systems, most especially the Second-Generation algorithm responsible for this mistargeting. Deployment of any armaments from Drones must be initiated by a pilot, working with a monitor. I will be mandating that the Monitor will be of more senior in rank than the Pilot.'

'I've also placed the requirement on the US Army, overseen by an independent panel, to investigate the value provided by the extent of drone deployments. I've set forth interim guidelines which limit the utilisation of armed drones for attacks to within areas where US troops or our allies are currently in active combat or have bases on the ground to protect. If there is a clear and present danger creating the need to deploy a drone outside of our active combat areas, I'll be consulted and make any decisions personally.'

'I'll be requiring independent analysis of mission data from all machine learning deployments from the past two years to identify any other cases of mistargeting where civilian have been killed or injured.'

'I urge the Senate Committee currently hearing evidence on Machine Learning in Armaments to examine this case and any others like it before completing your findings.'

'We still have every reason to be proud of our armed forces and the men and women who serve. Part of the reason for that pride is we fix things if they break, and we're not afraid to admit it when we get things wrong. I would like to express my heartfelt regret to those relatives and friends of the young person who died due to an avoidable error. Should any relative of the girl wish to contact our Embassy I would appreciate the opportunity to speak with you personally and again express our regret at what occurred. Thank you.' His media people had advised the press he wouldn't be taking questions.

Amancia was in the wings of the press briefing room and gave her husband a long embrace. 'Lots of people in the Administration and big business are not going to like it, but you stood up and did the right thing. That girl didn't die for nothing, and there's a lot of people who feel that way.'

Everglades

They had parted awkwardly the evening before. It was the intention that they would drive to the airport together and probably have an awkward farewell. When Mansour awoke, he could smell chicken bacon and eggs. He came out to see Odette cooking up breakfast as if ready to go out for the day. 'I thought a cooked breakfast might make up for a lifetime of lies.'

He thought about that. 'Hardly a lifetime. I knew it was all a falsehood when they sent me the first algorithms. There was only one purpose it could be put to, machine learning. They weren't garbage, much room for improvement in my opinion but not garbage, I said that because I felt angry, and betrayed.'

'And I was lying up close in person.'

'Yes. Don't take it so hard because I should have left then. But I stayed on. I enjoyed the special treatment trips to NASA and the Air Base. And, you know...'

'Yeah, well. I had an idea. That we put off the airport and have one last day doing something. You may not be in Florida again and I've always wanted to go, so I've arranged a ride on an airboat in the Everglades.'

'The Everglades.'

'Yes. The ones that are three and a half hours drive away. We'll stay down there overnight. Then one night back here and...' she shrugged. '...we go our separate ways, I guess. What do you think? Unless you have someone waiting for you to get home.' She laughed. 'Like I don't.' It was the first time she'd laughed. It was the real Odette now.

'Well...it's an interesting idea but I don't want the Army to...'

'Nothing to do with the Army. Going to switch cars at the hire a place, fuel, foods, hotel room, all on me. The actual me. The not the lying, scheming me.'

'I don't believe that, but I do believe you will already know I must pay half of everything.'

'Never saw that one coming.'

After breakfast, and with a hint of friendly sarcasm she said. 'Throw on your causal clothes and let's roll.' As if he had some jeans and a T shirt in his bag, rather than the six pressed plants and business shirts.

Driving down to the air boat tour, they could finally relax and share a bit more about one another. Mansour was impressed she was a Captain and asked how long she thought it would take before she made General. She went through a long of list of made up things she would never do to make it to that rank.

He asked if she thought it was too late for him to join the military. She asked if he spoke fluent Arabic. When he said no, she said his prospects were not good, especially once they figure out the puzzle, or worst still, try to program a drone with it.

They'd stopped for fuel and Mansour insisted on taking the first turn to pay. When he returned, Odette was looking at her phone which she avoided around him as she knew he thought the practice rude, partly because he had to cope with it on such a vast scale every day.

She told him one thing that she'd been taking an interest in was the Senate Committee hearings on Machine Learning in Armaments. It was ironic that the findings to date had been unexceptional.

And she showed him a news article with a grainy black and white film embedded which was drone targeting imagery but one that strangely gained resolution as it approached. There was a person in an open area. As the image grew clearer it was a girl or young woman taking selfies. She looked up prior the scene disappearing into an explosion and then a swirl of dust.

Asked for comment the Secretary of Defence advised that 'No US Drones had been operating within hundreds of miles of the location the footage was taken in.' He suggested that terrorist drones easily had the capability to carry out attacks such as this, designed to undermine American efforts in the region.

Odette shut down her phone. 'I hate my job.'

Mansour said Machine Learning could work very effectively on the targets with exact measurement and understand typical performance metrics. Tanks, boats, planes, specific personnel vehicles. With human targets, as they had seen, there would always be a percentage of innocent people killed, and it would be up to those utilising mathematics driven devices to decide what is an acceptable rate of the killing of innocents was.

She looked jaded and said. 'It's difficult to measure and so I suspect they don't. This was an instance where the target was a non- combatant, and someone was both courageous and foolish enough to leak it.'

Retirement

'A visitor for you Mr President.' He'd been kept waiting quite a while but was put in a lounge which allowed him to see the broadcast. Big Bear walked into the room exactly the way someone would who was never expecting to. Facing the President but also stealing glances around at all the famous parts to the oval office he'd seen on television or the movies.

Gene, in his usual way, come around his desk and extended his hand. Now the President had Big Bear's full attention. 'Master Sargent Duane Combs Sir, an honour to meet you.'

Gene loved making a pompous ass like Dobson call him President. But to Master Sargent Combs it was. 'Gene Carlson good to meet you Duane.'

'How about the five-cent tour of the office and then we'll get down to it.' Said the President.

Duane was fascinated by the history of the items which each President could draw on individually to fill out the display areas of the spaces if they wanted to. Duane could see the sitting President thought highly of Truman.

He was soon seated opposite Gene at his desk, and they had a TV screen against the wall so both could see it. 'Duane did a pilot sight and deploy this bomb?'

'No sir. There would have been a voice of the pilot in my earpiece, generally with questions and so the sighting isn't as smooth as you see here.'

'I'm going to run through this frame by frame Duane and I want you to tell me at what point you can say this is not an adult male. Possibly holding a gun.'

They ran though the frames and came to one which Duane said he thought it was not a man with gun a few frames later it was a girl taking a selfie.

'Now I'm going to run it at normal speed.'

There was only a fraction of a second that the nature of the drone target became obvious. They did the same with the satellite image which never gave a clear picture of who the person was.

'Could you have reacted quickly enough to abort the mission.'

'I don't believe in that short time the bomb could be disarmed. The ordinance was deployed before anything but a figure of a person was clear anyway. By the look of the photography, even if it was disarmed it would probably still have hit the girl.'

'And you're quite sure of that.'

'Yes and...' He was wondering if he'd get in trouble for telling the President something that was common knowledge in certain circles.

'And?'

'I don't really think the Army likes to have unexploded ordinance in non-combat areas, or anywhere I guess. It can be examined and put on the news and such.'

'Monitors are mainly utilised to avoid non-combatants prior to deployment. And in this case you'd be having a conversation with...'

'A machine I guess. I just advise to abort the mission with a button.'

'And is the mission always aborted?'

'I'll be very honest Sir. I'd only been in the job a month. It's not a situation I'd been confronted with. There's hearsay that a monitor's abort is sometimes ignored, but that's only hearsay Sir.'

Gene changed tack. 'I imagine you're a very popular guy on base.'

'You might call it popularity Sir.'

'And the Army, after providing you with some accommodation for a few nights recently, offered you a discharge.'

'That's correct Sir.'

'Do you believe you did the right thing, bringing this to the public's attention, knowing that the military would otherwise have buried it, as we saw in the announcement from the Secretary of Defence.'

'Well yes and no sir. I'm still not comfortable with loading up sensitive stuff on the internet, because I'm Army, and have been all my life. That part will never feel right.'

'So why do it.'

'I don't want to live in a country that kills kids and doesn't do anything about it.'

'Good answers Duane. I'm not going to lie to you. I could have done without this right now. But it's my job to make sure we find out about these things and stop it rather than stand by and let it happen. And you didn't stand by and let it happen. I've got someone from Army HR coming over. You're going to be given an honourable discharge and a full pension, unless you'd like a promotion.'

Duane smiled. 'No Sir, the pension and discharge are very good of you Sir. I wish...'

Gene wondered if he was going to ask for more which would be disappointing.

'I wish I'd voted for you Mister President.'

Gene laughed. 'I'll let you in on a little secret. I didn't vote for me either. It was supposed to be a media whistle stop to have me vote at a swing state. There was some organisation issues and in the SNAFU I didn't vote.'

Gene walked him to the threshold and after they'd make their goodbyes Gene put a hand on his shoulder and said. 'You're a good man Master Sargent.'

Duane remembered that. Eventually.

The Intangible Asset

They had a pleasant afternoon on the everglades. Odette said she'd had to choose between high-speed jet boat or a sedate airboat journey out into the glades spotting panthers, alligators, and bottlenose dolphins. She knew which to pick.

That night they had a nice meal on platform that stretched right into the glades. Odette asked a passer-by if they wouldn't mind taking a photo. They heard someone talking about the President giving a briefing regarding the drone strike on the 'Syrian Girl.' It was on high rotation on the news. Mansour, was, on this occasion an avid consumer of mobile device content, they found get a site which played the entire speech on Odette's phone.

Mansour looked confused. 'Why is your leader telling the truth.' He said in a parody of a middle eastern accent.

'I think it's a once in a term aberration, although he was testing the waters of honesty last week in Britain.'

On the drive back the next morning Odette became preoccupied. The Second-Generation reference. 'It didn't sound like the Machine Learning project you were working on was ready to test. You must have been working on Gen 3. And they wanted it in a hurry.'

'Pedantic I know, but I didn't actually work on it. In terms of providing any useable input. I don' think their current algorithms were for a new generation. But for use to demonstrate the algorithms themselves were infallible in terms of mistargeting. If the Army says an extremely complicated algorithm is infallible, most people will accept that and those that do suggest otherwise as friends or enemies may have a bad time of it.'

Her phone gave the WhatsApp chime. They needed gas and it was Mansour's turn to fill it up, so she looked at the text. 'Call Quacker on 3215 777 627. Purchase a phone to make the call.' She was in the process of dismissing it as a crank call when she thought of Colonel Fowler. Quacker.

After having to drive to the next small town for a phone she made a voice call. 'The everglades wasn't in the plan.' Came the familiar voice.

She was about to explain why when he cut her off. 'Listen. I'm on a pay as you go cell phone. Drop Mr Adraki at the stairs to his apartment. Leave immediately for the airport. Do not return to your apartment. Check into the next flight to anywhere and stay in the air while you organise connections to Washington. When changing planes stay airside in a crowd at all times. Get a random taxi part way along the rank to the Pentagon. Have your driver come with you and wait at reception. Text me on this WhatsApp number and I'll come for you.'

'Colonel...'

'It's an Order Captain. Do it.' The line went dead.

Mansour had returned from where he waited on a park bench when he saw she finished her call. She gave him what she assumed was the universal finger to the lips; the 'be quiet' signal.

She asked for his phone, and she put both of hers next to it and wrapped them in a towel and then in a basket covered by another towel and clothes.

'Mansour. We're about to find out what 'A bad time of it' is when you don't like their algorithms. This is extremely serious. Listen to the whole thing first. There's a team of men coming to both of our apartments waiting to abduct us, then kill us. They are probably going to let us go into the apartment because they think we don't know they're coming, and they'd rather not do it in the open.'

'I don't think it's your mathematics they wanted, although they may have been surprised at how good it was. I think what they wanted was your nationality. They wanted you sitting here, doing what they would say was short contract work for NASA, and you managed to hack the system. You got a Reaper Drone to target an innocent civilian to undermine confidence in the whole program. They'll say Iran is trying to undermine US drone capability, particularly Machine Learning Drones. And if Iran is afraid of them, the US should have more of them.'

'I came to a ...Democracy?'

Odette considered this. 'I think it's more of an Authoritarian Democracy. Don't waste your time on it Mansour. If you want to be alive a few hours from now we're going to need a plan and ...'

Mansour held up his hand. 'I'm sorry. I need a moment or two to absorb things.' He said this in a self-depreciating way. After a few minutes he said. 'Please continue Odette.'

'If we try to take off, running us down is what they're good at. Small infrared drones and all.' She smiled. 'We have to surround ourselves in people we can trust. Which means outsmarting or outliving the ones we can't. Although I'm not a specialist in this kind of combat, I enjoyed these subjects at Westpoint and I'm handy with sidearms and rifles. Shooting on the range fills in what my Colonel characterises as having no life. If only we had a few rifles.'

'You're not going to like this at all Mansour, but your only role in this will be to hide until I call you out. If you're anywhere they can see you, I'll have two things to focus on and your chances of defending yourself against these people is...' she was going to say non-existent. But she said. 'Very low.'

He took another moment. 'I'm sure you can appreciate the humiliation. But I cannot defeat the logic.'

She told him where she needed him to hide, and explained her basic plan.

They pulled in front of the stairs and carried the few light bags they had taken south. Odette had praised Mansour for being someone who still took photographs with a camera rather than his phone. On the stairs she asked how much space for a video remained on the SD card and he said there was enough for half an hour. She didn't erase the photos of them in the everglades.

In front of his door, she opened it and pretending to have a conversation with him on the threshold and slid a bag inside. There was no reaction.

They went in and Odette quickly turned the video on and placed it discretely on a shelf in the kitchen facing the front door.

Mansour crawled backwards into the triangle the mattress and bed base made against the wall. He lay flat with pillows she pushed in all along his body on the side facing out.

She stripped the sheets and bed covers from the other bed and towels from the bathrooms and put them against the wall right next to the opening side of door. She always carried her service side arm but would need to get hold of another weapon for them to have any hope against what she imaged would be a three or four man team.

She got rubbish liner bags ready and put them under the coffee percolator. Plastic bags were filled with Mansours Computer and drives. Mansour was such a careful person he carried a backup computer as well as a backup drive. She put the backups in a daypack and went to the veranda where there was a dense patch of garden below and threw the bag into the thickest patch. Fortunately, it didn't hang up on any trees and disappeared deep into the tropical growth.

A vehicle was pulling up and she ran to the window. It was swinging around to back up. A large white van with a small laundry service logo. Odette checked Mansour was in place. She told him 'Don't worry.' Which he thought was ridiculous.

She went and covered herself in the bedding and towels next to the door. The magnetic key unlocked the mechanism and the door began to open. The visitor walked carefully in. As expected, scanning all around the room. But not expecting to be shot from the pile of bedsheets behind him.

The next entrant ran in quickly while shooting. Assuming the shots had come from in front and she shot him up through the chest. She heard the radio of each man receiving the message. 'Hold back!'

She knew anyone coming in now would be careful and heavily armed.

But they had a set time to complete the mission. She wanted them to overrun it. She quickly grabbed the weapons and radios from the soldiers on the floor and ran behind the kitchen bench which faced the door. She shot the man who'd come through the door first as he tried to get up.

Her gun was levelled at the door waiting for someone to come through. Hearing a sound just in time she dropped to the floor. One of them had climbed down from the apartment above onto their veranda, the door into which she had carelessly left open. She was now trapped in the far inside corner of the kitchen with automatic weapon fire turning the rest to splinters.

She knew he wanted her to be distracted with her head down. But from her little corner of shelter, she kept her eye on the front door and when a figure came through, fast and diving, she was hitting him all around his body armour before he could aim his gun. He slid dead on the tiles.

The man who came from the veranda had access to the Master bedroom without passing the kitchen.

Fortunately, he didn't look down inside triangle of the leaning bed, assuming Mansour had a gun. He started shooting carefully along the base to ensure he would hit someone lying on the floor. Odette came around the corner to start firing when she realised she'd wasted the entire magazine at the man in the door.

All she could manage was the unbelievably stupid. 'I'll need to get another gun.' To the man's back. That did cause him to stop the barrage at Mansour. He was convinced the target was dead, but equally convinced he couldn't afford to check on him given that this slight, dark-haired woman had killed the rest of his team and would have him trapped in the room if he didn't move.

Once she'd picked up her gun, she heard the shooting stop. She didn't go back. She spent a moment to pick the location with both the best cover and the best view of the two doors. Eventually her adversary had to come out, choosing the running and firing tactic. It didn't matter, she had time to take shots with a dead man's side arm. This took her mind back to being near the top of the class for sidearm marksmanship at Westpoint. She felt a bit guilty about it, but she was enjoying her job again.

Mansour emerged without being called. He was filled with concern when he saw the many cuts and bruises which were mainly from the disintegration of the kitchen. But one bullet wound to the shoulder 'Small stuff. You?'

'I have this hole in my...um... thigh which is sort of leaking blood but not streaming blood which I assume is good.'

'I'll put a bandage...' 'Guys. Status?'

Odette picked up the radio. 'All dead soldier. How about you come and join the good guys.'

'Ma'am I'm the driver for this mission. The team coming over from your apartment are a few minutes away. If you move out now theirs will be a clean-up operation pure and simple.'

'Soldier, I think you have about as long to live as we have. Good luck.'

'Mansour, get every gun and everything that you can see that has come into contact with blood and throw it into the pillowcase.' She then had an intense call on the phone she had only just bought. She was giving her credit card details which to Mansour, seemed surreal.

He then witnessed the strangest and most disturbing thing he'd ever seen. Odette took a very large, sharp kitchen knife and went to each of the bodies and took a section of hair and scalp the diameter of an apricot. She appeared to be trying to include some bone in the sample.

She recovered the camera and said Mansour may need to be a cameraman soon. 'Do you think you can climb up to the veranda of the apartment above?' He nodded. 'You go and climb up. I'll bring the bags. I want my shots to come from this door, and then we move.' Mansour did what he was told. In a perverse way, he was enjoying his job that day also.

After thirty seconds she saw a second van driving in. She wanted to hit it before it backed in, to make it harder to drive out and block the other van in. Just as it was about to swing around to reverse beside the other van, she fired into the windscreen and windows. She took the time to try to shoot out ever tyre that she could see on both vans and then climbed up to the veranda above. Mansour smiled, proud that he'd been able to bring everything with him. In two loads.

They slipped out of the door and ran around the landing, shielded by a brick wall, which was a long, wide arc on the fourth floor to the next brick stairwell.

Odette took the risk to move one more stairwell away to get themselves a long way from the vans, but also have an unobstructed vantage point to shoot from.

She opened the radio channel. 'Stay in your Van till we go. Otherwise, I'm going to shoot in every door I go past saying you're terrorists.'

'Ma'am, we're cleaning up. We're going to get out. No weapons. If you want to kill unarmed men that's your choice.'

'You asshole. That's what you were planning to do to us five minutes ago. Anyone gets out of the Van, armed or not, I will kill them. Clear on that.'

'Clear.'

'Clear what.'

'Clear Ma'am.' Odette though it was amazing these people would so easily demonstrate they were ex-military.

'Where are they.' She said to herself. The call she'd made a few minutes before, on a clean phone, was to a genuine business, she was sure of it.

She got herself in position with a rifle to focus on the van to let them know she would follow through. The man getting out of the van calculated the time required cross from the van to the shelter of the stairwell. So had Odette. It was a long shot, especially with this kind of rifle, but the figure fell to the ground and didn't move again. Odette hoped Mansour got good footage on that one.

'What happened to being clear on something soldier. Where's the trust.' She said this with a mix of irritation and adrenaline fuelled playfulness.

'We're losing our sense of humour over here Ma'am.'

'That's strange, the morning's been one big laugh after another for us. Ten against two. You with semi autos and me sidearm.' Mansour could see Odette would have loved a combat role.

As she was thinking this very thing herself. He saw her look at the entrance to the carpark and say. 'Thank Christ.'

A cab entered the complex. Then another. Then another. They kept coming. She nodded and they ran around the complex and down the stairwell in front of a cab. She'd paid for thirty more and asked, that once were going, and to the degree possible, the cabs travel as a group. The destination was the city hospital. It was a twenty dollar fare. For thirty cabs that would be six hundred dollars. Odette had paid two thousand. She knew there was a limit to the number of witnesses these people's masters would tolerate.

Slow Erosion

It was early evening. Gene had a dinner appointment in half an hour with someone he'd forgotten the name and affiliation of already. He'd have to call Greg to remind him.

He got the call. That curious message that there was someone he needed to meet in such and such a room. It was important. He knew who he was. He knew he'd passed on the meeting the last time and that would have caused problems. He went along.

The grey haired man was there. But reduced. He stood and shook hands. 'Mister President.'

Gene was weary. 'And how should I greet you?' The man hesitated. 'Sebastian, Mr President.'

'Please call me Gene, Sebastian. It seems we're in this awful predicament together.'

The man said nothing. He had a message but had either forgotten or was too fearful to deliver it.

'Care for a drink Sebastian. Beer, wine, spirits. You're choice.'

The man looked up a little surprised and said. 'A glass of dry white wine would be nice.'

Gene sighed. 'Let's share a bottle.' He stood up and went to the door.

They sat in silence until the wine arrived and a glass each was in their hands.

'My master's anticipated you would like to make an address with respect to the mistargeting issue. They prepared some…talking points. I was to deliver them to you earlier in the day but could only gain access to the Whitehouse shortly before the address. It's a curiosity that their designs in this area have been reduced to ruins anyway.' Sebastian provided this esoteric comment with satisfaction.

'I didn't come to see you that time. Though urged to by some of my staff.'

'I don't know if it would have mattered. Your address was written. They want any charges against the former Secretary of Defence, to the extent they involve the Whitehouse, dropped.'

'You know what a sick person he is. Some of this is in the hands of the police.'

'Yes. They'll take care of that. It's the White house investigations into collusion that needs to be terminated.'

The man was beaten. Grief stricken.

'You have grandchildren Sebastian? Hope I'm not offending you about guessing your age.'

'It's fine. Five. Three to my son and one each to my daughters.'

Gene felt sick because he knew the answer. 'How many do you have now Sebastian.

'I have four left. Last night my daughter and her husband. Their house burned down. No one got out alive.' The man seemed to sit there, but in another dimension at the same time.

There was a long silence.

'I'm so sorry.' After another pause all Gene could say was. 'Show me what they want.'

Before doing so he said. 'I'm to tell you, a man you thought very highly of; a mentor. There was a break and enter last night and…I too am sorry.'

Gene sat quietly for a time. Sickened. What had they done to an eighty year old man?

Sebastian ignored the process of the tweezers and Gene looked down the list. It was virtually a complete reversal of what he'd said the evening before. He gave a little bark of disgust. 'How can they possible expect to get what they want if I have no credibility.'

'The factions. Most are pleading to go more slowly. They have a plan for the next Administration, and it doesn't include you. But there are interests the reversals you've announced. It's not as ham fisted as it might appear. Your administration was always to be shorn of integrity and legitimacy, but not yet.' Sebastian was looking down.

One or more of his remaining grandchildren were probably riding on what Gene might do or not do.

He started annotating the list, mainly with dates, in some cases a short note. Beneath this he wrote. *'You'll get what you want. It will take time, but only a short time. My position is worthless without credibility. Give me Time. Gene Carlson. President of the United States of America.'* He signed it.

'If I could put a wax seal on the damn thing I would. My fingerprints are all over it.'

Gene looked at the man after he'd read it. 'Do you think it will be enough?'

Sebastian shrugged. Conveying in the small raising and falling of his shoulders that expressed thanks but that it was probably only a matter of time for him and his family. He smiled. 'In any event, there will probably be a new messenger from now on. If they exhaust my motivations, then they need another who can be…. made pliable.'

They had finished the bottle before they realised it.

'I hope that's enough. I imagine if I showed in any way, I was trying to help you it would have the reverse effect.'

'Yes.' Sebastian said simply. 'Goodbye Gene.'

Gene's dinner meeting seemed unbelievably droll compared to the previous encounter, irrespective of its unpleasantness. Appearing pleasant and interested were simple autopilot functions he was born with and had honed over the years. He also had a useful knack of seeming unhurried but also winding things up at the same time. Greg was more than happy with this outcome. He asked to catch up with Gene in the Oval Office.

Gene knew to stick to only one kind of booze a day, so he asked for some wine to be delivered. He'd had another half a bottle at the gathering.

He and Greg sat on the couches opposite each other. Greg was a little uncomfortable. Gene got in before he said anything. 'You don't have to say it. The entire Executive Branch of government seems to be turning to shit, while I seem to either wander aimlessly or reverse my previous position shamelessly. Is that what you were going to spend fifteen minutes trying to say diplomatically.'

Greg smiled. 'Yeah. Getting it in one sentence is pretty good.' He looked across at the monitor in Gene's desk and saw the still frame of the girls face from the drone footage. Aspiration and mischief he'd called it.

Greg noticed Gene, whom he'd travelled with constantly for years, was drinking more alcohol faster than he'd ever seen him do before. He knew he'd been drinking before he arrived at dinner. He also knew that if he tried to get anything out of Gene in this mood, it would be clever deflections, which The president was also an expert at.

He didn't offer up an excuse, only a statement. 'The Address last night was tough for one reason or another. Today hasn't been easy. I plan to hit the ground running tomorrow.'

In the end it didn't matter. During the meeting, a message came onto Greg's phone. Very few people could send him a message, so he always looked.

'Shit.' He said. 'The King of England's dead.'

Gene thought of all the disasters he had to manage. 'What an inconsiderate prick.' He said. And they both laughed.

Medical Treatment

Mansour was dead. She had been stupid enough to allow themselves to be examined and treated separately, though separated by only a curtain. She'd organised, at considerable expense, a shared room and she was in the process or organising personal security.

Mansour had an 'in and out' bullet wound in the soft tissue of his thigh. Apart from helping her gather evidence, he had been pressing a towel either side, so that by the time they were in the cab there was very little blood on a new towel.

Odette had a shoulder wound that was more serious than she realised to the extent that it would permanently affect the full extent she would be able to move her arm.

What looked like a male nurse came into her partition. He had a needle. 'Who are you?' Then she yelled at the doctor and nurse treating her. 'Who the fuck is he?'

'He's...I don't know. It's a big hospital.' The Doctor said.

She tore away from the bandages they were placing and started yelling for security to catch him as he ran. Going around the partition she said. 'Did a man come in here with a needle. Did a man inject you Mansour?'

Mansour nodded. Immediately realising what this meant.

'You fucking idiots!' The staff thought the dark-haired woman was going to start throttling them. Which was what she intended until she recovered some self-control.

They were moved into the shared room and had only settled into their beds when Mansour began to convulse. It was over quickly. Odette had started to inveterately film everything. But she didn't film Mansour's final moments.

She asked the doctors to describe what happened and state the cause of death on film. She wasn't feeling anything anymore, but she was going to run down everyone involved in this. No matter how long it took.

And then the FBI came. I'm Special Agent Lewis. We'd like to get a statement regarding the incident earlier today at the Beachside Motor Lodge. We also understand you may have evidence relevant to an investigation the Bureau's been conducting for some time.' That's why she was alive and not knocked out and taken from the hospital. They knew she had the evidence because of the pieces of scalp missing from four men's heads and a lot of missing guns and computer equipment. They needed it to come with her. The security Odette had organised hadn't arrived yet.

Some evidence was in Motor Lodge. She hoped. Some was in a daypack on the floor pushed into the corner under her bed under a pillow kept cold with ice she planned to ask for every few hours.

They were pleasant. A man and a woman. 'I'd like to examine you're badges pleases. And photograph them. Slide them on the floor.' She was filming the interaction and was holding a scalpel as she filmed. As soon as they'd arrived, she'd pressed the button for assistance.

Special Agent Lewis said. 'I assure you we will apprehend the people accountable for what happened to Mr Adraki.'

'Slide over your badges or fuck off.' They started to approach so she dropped the camera on the bed and held out the scalpel. She knew both had the kind of training that meant they could easily take it from her.

'I'm afraid you'll have to come with us Captain Watson.' Said the female agent. Odette knew a needle was carried out of sight.

A nurse arrived. 'Please stay where you are.' Said Odette with all the authority she could muster. 'These people are trying to kill me. You can say I'm crazy. That's fine. Please stand right there.'

The nurse held her hands up. 'Okay. But I can't let you leave the room with that. I'm sorry.'

Odette threw it on the bed and immediately slipped behind the nurse and began running down the hall yelling 'These people are trying to abduct me.' She had insisted on keeping the jeans a blouse on irrespective of the blood stains.

She started to get attention but no intervention. They had a needle. She had two things they hadn't accounted on. An almost incandescent rage and another scalpel. Surprise was the only thing she could use to stop them dragging her out of the hospital, which they could do on any one of several pretexts with their badges. Odette was faster, both in bare feet and overall. She allowed the female 'agent', presumably with the syringe, to come closer behind. She turned quickly and side stepped the woman, grabbing her hair and began to slash her across the face as rapidly and deeply as possible making her pursuer forget the needle. As the woman fell, man behind had slowed down but had enough momentum for Odette to drop down and trip him. While he was down, she slashed across the back of his neck. As she pushed up to attack she'd held a swath of his hair and slashed across his face in a blizzard of cuts. She thought of Mansour and drove the scalpel into an eye. They were soon writhing like blind bloody worms on the corridor floor. She heard people coming. Her mind was sharp with adrenaline. She got some towels to soak up some blood from each of them. Grabbed the needle and ran back to her room.

She knew others would arrive soon. From her room she saw them arrived and take the 'agents' away after an argument with hospital administration.

No one was taking this scalpel away.

Barbados

'Come on Greg. Every Head of State worthy of the name is going to be there. Those that don't will be singled out as assholes. I'm not going to be the exception because you and everyone else think I need a week off and simultaneously get back to my real job.'

'Also, I want to get a stopover in Barbados, I'll only be getting off the plane for a few hours or in order to see as little of my hideous mother-in-law as politeness allows. I'll be expecting an urgent call on the bat phone from you twenty minutes into my visit with her. Make that ten. No five.'

One of the things that had brought Gene to where he was, was that he could, with a clear head, which was normally the case, assimilate, weigh, balance, prioritise, package, and sell an array of issues, often complex, in rapid succession.

In the two and a half days prior to the Regents funeral, this is what he did. He drew down on some of the things on Sebastian's list by having his now hand-picked Secretary of Defence rapidly complete and prepare findings on some aspects of the Machine Learning issue. He met with senior Republicans and told them it was time for some Quid Pro Quo. He gave them his own list and he wanted it progressively announced. If they thought he was weakened and they had him on the ropes, things were going to get very nasty. He'd be picking up the phone and he told them who he'd be calling and about what.

This was the Gene he missed in himself. He never blackmailed anybody. He was good at connecting the dots about what was in the public domain. But mainly he appealed to people's sense of right and wrong. They'd been dragging their feet and he knew why and if he turned the glare of the media onto them it would not be a good look.

He got a few 'absolutely will announce today' and a whole bunch of 'we'll think about it Gene'.

As he shook each hand on the way out, he said. 'I might be the monkey on the chain today gentleman. Next month it might be you.' Most had no idea what he was talking about.

As Airforce One landed in Barbados, there was a small crowd. A delegation of Caribbean Island Nation leaders had been invited to an informal opportunity to mingle with the President on this short notice visit. His research and speech writers had done a stellar job and he relied on them much more than usual. But at the end, he dispensed with any pretension as to the purpose of his visit.

'As you know, I'm visiting on my way past to farewell a truly great monarch, and my mother in law is from in Barbados, as is my lovely wife. Although this wasn't a trip planned months in advance, I think it's better. We've got a few hours to mingle. Talk and listen and I think it offers a good opportunity without the expectations of some kind of Summit. I have to be visiting my mother in law by nine or else...' His voice went quiet and he looked from side to side. '... is Voodoo real?' There was a good deal of laughter and no small amount of surprise.

Soon he was standing beside the bed of the ageing woman in the most prestigious aged care facility on the island. He had been listening to the conversation between Amancia and her mother with the same irritation he always felt. Nit picking the luxury she enjoyed, forgetting the squalor that would otherwise have been her destiny.

There was a phone call from Claudia. But Amancia worried about leaving her mother and husband alone. Thinking about it, she'd never let that happen before.

Once alone the old woman pinned him with a glare. 'You can fool the whole world you know. All your friendly ways. I can see that mean streak big and wide that you cover up so well.' The woman's eyes were black and had narrowed. 'And you stole my only child away with lies. You're an unfaithful man. I can see it.'

Gene didn't care any more about consequences. 'You're a bitter, ugly old hag, and the only thing you ever did to improve yourself or move forward in life was let your daughter marry me. Now you live somewhere nice which you aren't grateful for, and you pretend to be so incapacitated that everyone will fawn all over you and do whatever you ask. You can move around fine you're simply lazy. If I had to encapsulate everything about you in one word it would be nasty. You're a nasty old bitch.'

Amancia came in after this last word had died in the aether. 'Your mother was telling me how awful the slums she grew up in were, and how grateful she is to have ended up here. I got a call from Greg. Schedule change. We have to get going asap.'

Amancia wasn't bothered by this. Short visits to her mother were fine it seemed, as long as they occurred. Gene positioned himself such that Amancia left the room first so he could look back and give the old woman and smile and a wink.

But Amancia had other news.

Claudia and Rachel

Amancia had something she wanted to discuss, but in the privacy of Air Force One. Once in their suite she turned and held him. 'They've eloped. Got married a week ago. They weren't expecting the Queen to die or us to be in Britain. They were going to plan a big reception at some time that suited you.' She shrugged irritably. 'Us.'

Gene held her quietly. Happy for the two girls, avoiding international attention for what was allegedly 'their day' yet it didn't always turn out that way for brides, and especially in their case. He thought a big reception bash was a great idea.

'I always dreamed our only child, a girl, of having a beautiful wedding. You know.'

Gene always knew how to handle Amancia. She was a smart, good person. He would never offer a solution. He would wait a few moments and she would say exactly what he nearly always believed was the right thing to do. He would agree to it, maybe make a small observation to prove he was listening, and they would move on. However, in this case he was tired and irritable. He said what she would have said, but he said it a moment in advance. 'Well it's not always about you.' They had an unprecedent little glare at each other and parted ways.

Her mood didn't improve when a friend sent an e-mail with a link to a site that followed the very latest doings of the President featuring her husband wondering out loud to all of the Caribbean leaders if his mother in law was a practitioner of Voodoo.

Gene had been functioning, but as time passed the memory of the look on two people faces wouldn't leave him. The hope filled girl in Syria and the hopelessness of Sebastian. The fruits of the old man's life gradually being stripped from the branch. He could do nothing about Sebastian's predicament, but he had his new Secretary of Defence leading most of the intelligence community completing a major study on the Syrian girl and every thread that might lead to her. His focus on Intelligence was providing him detailed information about interesting people and their networks. Patterns were emerging. He was like a detective. Asking questions of the most senior spooks in the country and demanding answers in a short timeframe. People didn't like it. He liked that. He asked more. The more he looked the more he saw a subterranean world of people who considered themselves accountable to no one. Until they were out of a job. Which started to happen a lot, unexpectedly. From around the time he got on the plane to Barbados. And more between Barbados and London. Where had Genial Gene gone?

Soon after take-off, he asked his Doctor, Shanker, to provide him with a measured dose of oblivion. Amancia found him asleep face down in the guest suite, fully clothed, shoes still on. She shook her head. She knew something was wrong. Something she couldn't see, and he wouldn't tell. It hurt, but also made her afraid. She took his shoes and jacket off, loosened his belt, and left him to sleep.

At the Funeral, Gene was at his best. He hit the right note of decorum and acknowledgement of a great Monarch. To other Heads of State and past Presidents, some whom he inwardly loathed, he was the quintessential Statesman.

Much against the advice of media men as well as many others, he'd scheduled another slot with Peter, 'On the Lounge.' Hed got permission from the girls to reveal to the world that their daughters had eloped, which would make the interview more fun. No one knew where they were. Peter and the president both saw it as a forum for Gene to provide some sincere praise for the late king and talk about an America, he said, no one heard much about because of the monotone of American media and its short cycle infotainment format.

'I'm sure that's going to go down well.' Said Peter in the phone. 'See you at eight father in law.'

Contact

She knew she was becoming paranoid. Seriously paranoid about who to trust. Which was nobody. She demanded to meet the person who conducted the autopsy. No. She asked about Mansour's remains and demanded that they were preserved and received the kind of uncomfortable silence suggesting they'd already been cremated.

Now the police wanted to get through the wall of security guards across her closed door. She said she wanted to photograph their badges, their faces and a DNA sample and they could ask some questions from the other side of her security. They didn't like that. She told them this was 'A matter of fucking national security' and to bring the Superintendent of Police back and she'd prove it to him. She slid Mansour's bed in front of the door. Under the bed was an old copy of the Orlando Sentinel. She looked at the headlines. It was about the Governor.

And there was an editorial about the 'Syrian Girl' and some analysis of the President's response. The Editor made a prediction as to how soon those responses would be reversed or diluted based on his form over the past two years.

She'd been watching a 24-hour news television channels, so she knew the President was going to leave for Britain soon for the King's funeral and then on a talk show later that night. She thought what she had would be of interest to him. The Syrian Girl was not expected to use the phone for selfies and the footage was not supposed to be circulated until Mansour was in hand, which would demonstrate only a human pilot could mount such an attack. An enemy trying to discredit the weapon

But she had a great deal of evidence about both the Iranian, and the extraordinary lengths some organisation went to in trying to capture him. She needed to be disappear because she could destroy the narrative.

The Superintendent of Police, once he'd reluctantly allowed her to speak to the Mayor on the phone to prove his identity, was allowed to see the footage, the swatches of hair, on ice, the syringe, and bloody towels she'd taken from the fake FBI agents. And various items including the hotel magnetic key they'd used.

Almost ignoring the evidence, he said. 'That last shot you took was pretty spectacular.' She appreciated that. 'Ms Watson, this is way out of my area, although we'll get our colleagues down south to investigate the hotel room. This is Federal Government business. The real FBI. Although the scalps do concern me.'

'Exactly the kind of people I won't allow near me, whatever their credentials. I want to see the Governor. I want to get a message to the President, and I want a place on the Senate Enquiry into Machine Learning in Armaments before it winds up.'

'Ms Watson some of that I didn't understand and the rest I don't think's possible.'

'Do you think this footage is important. Do you believe me about what I was asked to do and why. They wanted to manipulate the Presidency and would be doing that now if I was dead. I'd like to show it to the Governor as he's the most likely person to have any connections to the President. If the Committee won't see me, I'll lay all this out for the press. But I don't want to do that. What's happening here is an exception not the rule.'

'I'll get onto the Mayor and see what we can do.'

'Sure. Otherwise I go to the press in five hours. Once it's out there my chances of survival improve.'

The Governor was there in four hours and given the same presentation.

'I'm sorry about your friend.' Was his first observation, which she appreciated. 'I could give you a bunch of reasons why a call probably won't happen, but I'm going to say I'll do my best. Turns out I have an acquaintance pretty high up in State. Played ball against each other.'

Odette drafted the message: 'Domestic interests set up Iranian academic to appear to be behind Syrian mistargeting as evidence of Iranians fear of machine learning drones. Likely objective to increase machine learning drone capabilities. Watertight evidence collected. Informant in danger.' She said when she got an acknowledgement from the Secretary of State or the President, she would be sent the video. Ultimately, after that, she didn't care about the President angle. He had what he needed. But she needed to get the evidence secure in a location she could trust, and everyone needed to know it was. Then she might be safe.

Within an hour her phone rang and she heard. 'Captain Watson. This is Gene Carlson. I've watched the video. You're in trouble.'

She was caught off guard. She'd expected some assistant secretary for something. It tumbled into a quick potted history of the whole affair but he slowed her down. 'Step me through it Captain. We have a few minutes. I'm in a cocktail party in London. I know that sounds interesting, but you're more interesting.'

She spent ten minutes telling the story and emphasised that she was sure it was Mansour's nationality which had really been the objective. She described the evidence she had and believed it would be relevant to the Senate Enquiry into Machine Learning in Armaments.'

'And where are you now Captain.' She started to break down when she described she was in the hospital room where Mansour had died, it hadn't been cleaned, she was too afraid to let anyone in unless she'd seen their picture in the newspaper. Her hands were shaking. She couldn't put down her scalpel.

Captain I'm going to send Airforce Two to pick you up and some of my personal team will come to get you. They are going to be wearing bright green ties Captain. They could only know to do that because of me right? Do not trust anyone you are uncomfortable with. Keep the security you've engaged around you all the way into the Whitehouse.'

'I'll see you in a few days. Thanks for surviving Captain. Once again, sorry about what happened to Mansour. We need to fix this Captain. I'm pretty sure you're going to have a part to play.'

'Thank you, Sir.'

The Governor was advised about the call and had come back and been allowed in. He was taking a seat beside here when she finished. Pleased and surprised that she'd got the call, and that it had been so long he asked. 'So how did that go?'

'He took the weight off.'

And in London, the call had helped Gene a great deal. Things were falling into place.

Bad News

It was as the last scheduled engagement before 'The Lounge Room' later that evening. It was a six o'clock cocktail gathering with the PM, some of the Cabinet and a few of the Royals. Gene was starting to flag, but no one would have known it. He was seamlessly moving in and out of conversations and between people and groups, so he caught up with everyone however briefly. He'd disappeared for only a short time to make a call to Captain Watson.

Shanker, his personal physician, arrived and asked him to come into a small room nearby. His face was ashen. 'I've been the one asked to give you a briefing Mister President. It's a ... it's very tough news.'

'Like pulling a tooth Shanker. Do it.'

'About three hours ago a car was hit in Morocco. Terrorist Done they say. The authorities wanted to be absolutely certain before you were informed. It was your daughter

Claudia and her friend Rachel.' Shanker took a deep breath. 'There were no survivors and very little...'

'Remains.' Finished the President quietly. 'Who's in the loop on this Shanker.'

The doctor was a little surprised that this was the first question.

'Call them and tell them to keep the loop shut tight. I'm going to get Amancia and bring her in here and I want you to be ready in case she needs to be sedated. She's going to be very distressed.'

The doctor was surprised at how little distressed or angry Gene seemed to be. But Gene was all business. He'd feel it later thought Shanker.

Amancia's reactions could not have been more different than those of her husband's. She was trembling uncontrollably and sobbing occasionally calling out the inevitable 'why' and then some invective against the killers.

Gene sat beside her and held her tight. After some time, she was standing and crying on his shoulder. She also couldn't help noticing how little affected he was.

'I want to go home.' She said at last. Thinking this the most natural and incontestable of requests.

'Yes.' Said Gene, but with a tone of some qualification in his voice. 'I'd like to tell Peter and Rua, Rachels mother and father, in person. I more or less killed their daughter. I know you've only been to dinner once with Rua so I'll understand if you'd like to go straight to the plane.'

Amancia's voice was hollow. 'Of course I'll come.'

The President told his logistics staff to get him to an address in greater London in minutes and not to increase the lead time with undue security because no one was expecting him to go there. He told them where he was going next, now by a different route.

A helicopter got them to a sports field a mile from the address. A humble London Cab, with three decoy limousines half a dozen cars behind the cab took them to the address. The Cabbie got a great story and the tip of a lifetime. Gene had called Peter fifteen minutes before saying they were going to visit. Peter was immediately upbeat when he answered. Gene tried to convey in his voice to be ready for bad news.

The responses were somewhat the opposite for Rachel's parents. Peter was inconsolable. Trembling, rocking, sobbing. Concealing nothing. Rua showed very little, trying as much as possible to comfort Peter. But Amancia knew she was quietly breaking into pieces on the inside.

Amancia was infuriated to see Gene look at his watch a few times. And it seemed once Peter had settled down to the degree he had reached a level of coherence Gene thought was adequate, he asked him to come into another room.

'How can you even think that Gene?' Peter was beyond surprise. He was still disoriented.

'The basis of terrorism is to make us change our behaviour. To make us afraid. We can show them even in great extremity we won't do that. We won't bow down.'

'And our dead children are an opportunity to sell a message Gene?'

'This is the only thing we can do, the only thing to make their deaths mean something.'

Peter hands were still trembling. He looked like he'd been drinking all day. 'I'm a wreck Gene. I don't think I could pull it off.'

'You're the same as me, once the cameras roll, you'll snap into business mode. I can write the questions and you feed them to me. Or feel free to do that yourself. Get the network to bring in another interviewer for the other slots.'

Peter was nodding vaguely. Gene got back to Rua and Amancia in time to catch Rua as she picked up the phone. He said it was a matter of vital national security that she didn't share the news with anyone until late tonight. Amancia gave him a look, but it was nothing like the look he got when he said the planned interview was going ahead. That look was incredulous.

'You'll announce our daughter's death on a talk show.'

'I could do it behind a podium. Very formal. Or some news anchors do it first. Why don't you come and sit beside me on the couch? Why don't you both come. Humans, talking about loss. Not politicians announcing it.'

'I want to go back to the plane. Rua, would you like to come along with me till midnight?'

'No. I'll go over to mum's. We won't let the cat out of the bag Gene.' She said coldly.

There were half a dozen paces between Gene and Amancia. She said. 'Anything else for us to go through right now.' Saying this as dispassionately as she thought he was being. Using what she thought was exaggeration to try to convey the effect this was having on her.

A message came over his phone. It captivated his attention for a moment. He never usually took any kind of call when he was with her. He looked up. 'All good.' Not even noticing the irony.

She nodded and left.

With grating awkwardness Peter got up and gave Rua a long hug, which gradually evolved into a period of two people holding each other and sobbing. Peter said he'd make his absence as brief as possible and would come straight to her mother's house where they might like to stay the night, or a few days. 'Whatever you want.' she said.

On the drive to the Studio, Gene and Peter said very little. Peter had advised his Producers the show was going to be unusual, and they needed an alternate presenter ready after the first slot. The guests were already scheduled but could be rearranged and the slots lengths adjusted.

'You sure about this Gene. I'm with you, but you may have a late middle aged man blubbering on the set.'

Gene was writing a list while he'd been listening. 'Yes, I'm sure. I think you'll be fine. If we both end up crying our eyes out on set, it will help people see that reality television isn't actually real.'

Gene got massive applause. He'd arrived when more than a few Heads of State had sent delegates to honour their Monarch. He'd been gracious in every word and deed to His Majesty whom and on his last visit had portrayed rare honesty during his last interview on the show and was now appreciated for his response to what happened to the 'Syrian Girl'.

They took their seats and as the applause died down Peter led off. His voice breaking slightly, he said. 'This will be one of the strangest and hardest interviews I've ever done. Gene.'

The President was almost ashamed about how good he was at this. Even about his own daughter. He spoke evenly, even though the occasional tear rolled down his cheek.

'Two young women were the target of a Drone strike this afternoon in Morocco. There was one British and one American citizen. It's been confirmed that they were Rachel, Peter and Rua's daughter. And Claudia, the twenty-five-year daughter of myself and Amancia.'

He gave the audience time to register surprise and some shock. It was during this pause that he found it most difficult to hold it together, and it resulted in Peter losing all composure and bury his face in his hands.

'I didn't come and say this to upset you. Here's a few things I came to say this evening.' Gene looked out over the crowd. He was glad he'd come. People could react how they wanted to his daughter's death. Including Amancia. This is how he wanted to react. 'This hasn't been released to any news outlets because I wanted myself and Peter, the girl's fathers, both already planning to come to the show, to announce what happened to our girls, who'd eloped, in person, rather than people hearing it from some TV anchor.'

'But there's another reason. I want the human filth who do these sorts of things to know that I am not afraid, and I will not change my plans because of what they do. However much it's hurt me, has torn my heart to pieces, I'll never give them what they want.'

'In *our* societies people can believe what they want to believe. In the recent terrorist enclaves of ISIS in Syria and Iraqi, is there any religious diversity? Is there freedom of speech? Is there anything approaching equal rights for women? No. There was mass rape and sexual slavery debasing the word marriage. Freedom of speech? No. Only slaughter of those with different beliefs. Freedom of religion; never.'

'That is the terrorist mantra, believe what we believe or die.'

'When we go to war, it's against soldiers and combatants that are fighting for a cause, with conventional weapons.'

'When these terrorists go to the war the cowards attack the most vulnerable. The innocent. Why. Because it elevates them to a global status. Instead of being the mean, comparatively small, but hard to find group of thugs they are, they win a place in the global consciousness they simply don't deserve. And it changes our behaviour in so many ways. Because of these nobodies.'

In another unprecedented occurrence the producer came and spoke in Peter's ear. Gene already seemed to know about it when Peter looked up and Gene nodded.

Gene continued. 'We're now joined by the man claiming accountability for the murders. He contacted me earlier in the evening to gloat and I asked him if he was willing to tell us why he intentionally kills the innocent.'

'Good evening Mr President'

'Areem. How does your conscious feel tonight'

'It feels peace at last after we have taken vengeance on the people who killed one of our beloved children.'

'The accidental killing of an innocent young girl followed by a global apology and many changes to stop it occurring again, is somehow equal in your mind, to searching out and specifically killing two innocent young women with a terrorist drone.'

'An apology for one girl. What of the thousands, tens of thousands, hundreds of thousands killed as a consequence of your endless wars.'

'I could make that apology, as could all terrorist groups that have wrought as much violence. Where are your apologies? I could take a poll of how many people on the ground in the middle east want us to pull out, or never have come. There would be some. But not all.'

Now Gene began to sound familiar with the man. 'You like such a simple world Areem. Such an ideological world. Do you have any children Areem? Beautiful precious little human being whom you bathed and dressed and then watch them walk, go to school, tell you you're a fool as they get older. Have you had children Areem?'

There was a pause. 'These two were an abomination.'

'Was your niece an abomination? Is that why you told her she should look for things on the ground. You didn't tell your terrorists friends you'd put a high value target's phone was put on your niece's path home.'

'Only *you* knew a drone supposedly piloted by an Iranian would drop the bomb. The Iranian would be revealed within an hour of the footage being released. It would demonstrate how fearful Iran is of automated drones.'

'Some in our country wanted to demonstrate, an autonomous drone could never launch a strike on a civilian. That it was a human pilot. An Iranian who had hacked into our systems when working as a contractor for the US Army.'

'But you know all this Areem. The whole plan was cooked up by the people who handle you as a US military asset. Five hundred thousand dollars for selling out your cause is sitting in your bank account. That's how much you got for your niece Areem. With all your high indeed rhetoric why have you been negotiating with your CIA handlers to move to the US under an alias.'

'This is all lies. Fantasy.' The man's voice was rising.

'I've had people track down where the money was paid and who it was paid to Areem. We have an old saying in this country Areem. Follow the money. It leads to you.'

The line had closed off.

Peter had recovered some composure. The journalist came out. 'Gene, what does a President do in a situation like this. How do you respond to the…bombings.'

 'I'll do nothing Peter.' There was a moment of silence. 'We have an apparatus of government that manages these things and they'll deal with this with the same diligence they would do in any case of a terrorist act on foreign soil. Because in our parlance, there's a foreign national involved, there will be close cooperation between our two governments and the government of Morocco.'

'From a political perspective, I will be stating that this is not about any nation state. It will be about individuals such as the man I just spoke with, and the terrorist organisations to which they belong. As with any investigation, we'll be hoping to try to stop this kind of attack happening again.'

They sat for over a minute. Peter could see it was the President's turn to lose it. 'That's us done.' Said Peter.' I don't think I've got anything profound or pithy to end on so we're going to wander off.

Gene nodded. He's been wiping the first of a flood of tears from his face and he looked out at the audience. Gene did have something pithy. 'Don't take them for granted.'

On the journey to his mother in laws Peter sat quietly. He'd never moved through London traffic so quickly. There must have been US agents controlling intersections ten streets ahead. Before he knew it, they'd arrived. Peter gave Gene a hug, and he was gone.

Airforce One was winding up as Gene climbed the steps. No media or well-wishers allowed anywhere near to see an exhausted and grief- stricken President get on a plane. He walked to his office. Amancia was in the seating area, suspecting he wouldn't come to the suite.

She spoke as he passed when it didn't look like he was going to notice her. 'Show went well?' She could see his eyes were raw from tears.

'Yeah. It was good. The message about not changing what you plan to do because of terrorists was the main thing I wanted to get across.' He was sounding vague; punch drunk.

'Good.'

'Also the man who claimed to have organised it called in.' He said in a matter of fact voice.

Amancia could barely keep the fake banter going. 'The man who did it. Well that's novel.'

'Yeah. I had a bit of intelligence on the guy. Not a good person. Fingerprints all over some nasty stuff. I connected some of the dots. Had to put a few dots in there myself. We dropped half a million dollars in his account. If he isn't dead now, he will be by morning.'

'Put money into his account.'

'Asshole turned his own niece into the bomb target. I've got some things to do. I might come back once I'm done and we can' He shrugged. 'Catch up.'

She'd given up being surprised, even shocked. 'Sure. Let's catch up. Unless I'm sleeping.'

'Oh. Yeah. I won't bother you if you're sleeping.'

At almost every point in the conversation she was preparing to stand up and scream at him and then start crying, but it became a fascination. He wandered off to his office. She realised later what he was trying to do.

She checked her e-mails. Their daughter dead less than twenty four hours.

He was at his desk. The tip of his finger was starting to hurt again. He was nearly finished though. He'd go to see if Amancia was awake. A part of him hoped she was sleeping. He came to where she sat to see her with her hand cupped around her mouth and her eyes wide in disbelief. The more pedestrian sex, to which Gene had to admit, was all he was ever really interested in, was finished. The young girl was now the victim of very rough sex and the beatings had begun.

Amancia saw him standing there. She looked one more time at the screen, horrified now at the state of the poor young girl and snapped the laptop shut.

Phrases like 'I can explain this.' Seemed inadequate. And somehow, he didn't care. He was glad to stop carrying it around. But how could he be so insensitive to the one who now picked up the burden. But he believed he could do nothing about it.

'Who *are* you? What are you?' She was trembling. Horrified. Sickened.

'Only the first part was me. Drugged up. The second part was an actor.'

'Parts? Actors?' She was navigating another body blow from a husband who lambasts her mother, turns the death of their daughter into a media circus, tells lies to have a man killed and is now revealed to be a rapist of the most disgusting kind. And was here making some meek excuses, qualifications.

'Keep away from me.'

He nodded. Resigned. And walked off.

After they'd landed, he kept his door closed so there was no chance of them sharing a glance. He'd arranged a separate limousine for her to a city hotel. She was annoyed when she tried to do exactly that herself.

Meetings

Gene wanted to get to his office in as straight a line as possible. It was eight in the evening and he had a great deal to do. He'd lined up a number of people to come in and help him do things, late that night and into the early morning.

He told people he wanted no distractions and expected a smooth passage to the Oval Office from Security but was told there was a man in a meeting room who needed to see him. In this case he asked for a description of the man and, knowing who he was, asked for Sebastian to be brought to him.

Sebastian was ushered in, and Gene, as if he was with any visitor, was out of his chair and around the desk before he'd got come far through the door. But this was different. They looked into each other's eyes. They were the same. Gene gathered the older man up. 'It wasn't enough. The interview will have been a…. I'm so sorry Sebastian.'

'It would never have been enough in the end Gene.' He said quietly.

He asked Sebastian to sit while he got a few glasses of wine organised and, he made a call.

'Kimmie, sorry to call you late. Yes, Yes. Thankyou. Amancia's doing okay. Kimmie I need you to arrange something. Could you book a small suite for a guest I have? Two or three nights. Also, I'd like you to have a look at who's on security tonight and let me know who you think is the most trustworthy, preferably a younger man.'

There was a pause. 'It's unusual Kimmie but everything fine. If you could book the room and have the man sent to my office I'd be grateful. I'll have a lot going on in the office tomorrow. If you could come in at six I'd really appreciate it. Thanks Kimmie, this means a lot to me.'

They were soon sharing a drink, saying nothing. Eventually Gene said. 'I want you to write a list of all the people in your life who still may be in danger. We'll arrange some protection. For them, and you.'

'Thanks. But for how long Gene?' He was hopeless.

'Long enough.' The President gave a curious smile. 'These idiots have themselves way over extended and are about to find out what retaliation looks like.'

There was a knock on the door. A fresh-faced man was allowed in and introduced himself as the security assigned to look after the President's guest. Gene stood up and shook his hand. 'It's no small thing to impress my Secretary. This is Sebastian.' Sebastian was writing the list as instructed. The president spent a few moments writing on letterhead paper. 'This is to let Spicer know to leave you alone to look after Sebastian. I'll send our Head of Security the list Sebastain and get them some protection. No one is to enter Sebastian's suite except the President. It's written there and signed in case anyone needs to see it.'

Meanwhile Amancia looked at the film again. A few times. The first half was the same boring sex which was all her husband seemed capable of, in spite of what she tried to teach him. And then she saw the transition, and once she saw it, it was obvious. A different man. A violent man. She looked at the first half again. She'd been too upset to care before, but now she saw how wasted he was. He might be very drunk, but she knew him better. He was drugged. And the girl must have been told to cling to him, arms and legs wrapped tight around him much of the time.

She thought about how he'd approached his Presidency. How strange his behaviour had become in the past months and then even more so since the Syrian Girl was killed. It seemed he couldn't cope any more. And now the last twenty four hours. He didn't even want to hold her in his arms.

She threw on a coat and walked out the door. 'Sorry Ma'am but you'll need to be staying here tonight. Presidents orders.'

'You listen to me. I'm the one who gives the President *his* fucking Orders. Now I can leave here as an American citizen, which I believe I still am, and I'll get in a cab, or you can take me to the Whitehouse.'

The President spoke to the security men at the door and said he wanted to be left alone with no exceptions until the appointment times set out very late into the evening and he needed time to complete his preparations.

He'd spoken to each of those he'd scheduled a meeting with personally on the phone while on the plane and sent a reminded text. He told them they were going to need to do an all-nighter on this.

The first was Greg arriving at eleven pm. The doors were opened briefly and closed behind him. He looked around the corner to the desk and Gene's knees were at eye level. Greg didn't know how long since he'd done it and his first impulse was to call for medical assistance. But there was a large note pinned to his trousers, comical in some other dimension, that read, *Read The Letter*.

He saw a neat row of letters spread down the desk. A letter with his name was at the top.

Greg

I died around ten, so don't bother calling anyone until it's Shankers time to come. Sorry to drop this on you, but I'd like you to be the one to cut me down. I used a lamp table but if you put the coffee table on the desk, it should work fine. Try not to scratch it because Candy wouldn't be pleased. I have some sharp shears in my pocket.

Speaking of pockets, I've been blackmailed by corporations with incredible reach and deep pockets Greg. It's ruined my Presidency and it's destroyed my family. I know of others caught in this terrible web who've lost everything they treasured. I believe we have a President who can fix this, who will want to fix this, and on whom they will have nothing. My running mate was a controversial pick from out of nowhere. This is part of the reason.

Anyway. I wouldn't want you to think I was running away. Giving up. If I stayed, once everything they have on me came out, no matter how much I tried to expose the blackmailers, my Presidency would be so compromised it wouldn't matter. And what people saw would define the rest of my life. This way, also, Amancia is no longer a target. And I know she would never look and me the same way ever again seeing what she's seen.

Thanks for being a good friend.

Gene

As Greg finished reading Amancia was allowed in the room, once again the doors being only opened and closed behind her. She spent a moment taking in the scene and let out a soft 'no' and went to clasp her husband's legs tightly. 'Why did you have to do this? You've left me alone? I know it wasn't you. You're a good man. Why did you have to do this?' She looked across at Greg, almost unable to cry anymore from the happenings in less than a day. 'What does the note say?'

'Pretty much to bring him down.' Greg said.

Greg brought his friend down as carefully as he could but would probably have dropped him on the coffee table had Amancia not been there. Soon he was laid out on the couch head raised with an awful 'just sleeping' look. Things began to move quickly.

Shanker arrived a moment later for what he thought was a check- up about an aliment Gene had noticed on the plane. Informed the President was dead he immediately looked for vital signs. There was a letter for him.

Shanks

'I hung myself at ten, after an irritating reality TV show made me kick a chair over. I tried to use a noose made of softer material so as to not make it so obvious, but of course it will

be obvious to anyone who knows what they're looking at. I'd like you to consult with the incoming President and consider what you might call the cause of death. Heart attack, stoke etc might be good options. Not my problem now I suppose. Thanks for being a good doctor to me and the family over the past few years. Sorry it had to end this way.'

Gene

Shanker sat down next to Amancia who was sitting on the coffee table holding her husband hand. 'Hell of a day.'

'Yeah.' She said quietly.

'If you need to take something to take the edge of, even a little, let me know.' She nodded which could have meant anything.

At that moment Spicer came in. His was the next letter on the pile. Gene wrote to Spicer that he thought he'd been hanging around as President long enough.

I'd appreciate it if you could work closely with Shanks to carefully manage access to my body so that the incoming President can decide on what the cause of death will be announced. No doubt you have a suite of security protocols to initiate. I would appreciate it if you could wait until the VP arrives and she takes on the leadership role immediately, followed by the swearing in shortly after. The Attorney General will be called very soon but he has not been scheduled to be here and has no knowledge of this situation. A decision on time and place of the swearing in should be made by the VP.'

They were all exchanging letters. There were two left in the pile. One for the Vice President and one for Amancia. They were all still reading each other's letters when the Vice President arrived.

She took a moment to absorb what was going on. Greg gave her a brief description of what had transpired and indicated there was a note from the President for her on the desk.

Candy,

She read the note. It explained the reasons for his political inconsistencies in some detail. The initial incident of blackmail and all of the others to bed it in. The loss of friends and mentors and, when he wasn't compliant, finally the loss of his daughter.

My heart's broken Candy, my daughter murdered, my wife will never look at me again with simple love and the Presidency I dreamed of, the meaningful changes I believed I could deliver, is in ruins. I hope you don't think I'm running away from this. As soon as I'm gone, Amancia and anyone else I know are no longer a target. As far as the Presidency goes, you can inherit it and have none of the perverse manipulations I allowed myself to become the victim of. You have the capacity to deliver what I hoped for and more.

Even if I had decided to expose the blackmailers and take the consequences, my Presidency would be tarnished and the pursuit of the perpetrations would be confused with my own misdeeds.

I would achieve very little in the final two years of the term, because I'd be embroiled, along with the administration, in this issue. This would make your contributions and potential a part of negative situation people would like to get behind them.

I have so much faith in you Candy. One of the few things holding me back tonight was that I wanted so much to see the dynamism you're going to bring to the job. The pragmatism, the capacity to negotiate with fairness and humour. But I can't wait around to see it. Because if I'd stayed here, it wouldn't happen.

Gene must have finished the note because it was signed but there was a short paragraph in another pen.

Candy there's a man in a suite who has also been blackmailed. What's happened to his family is shocking. He has a list of remaining family members who should be protected. He'll be one among many. He was the man who delivered the blackmailers demands. It may be useful to have breakfast or lunch with him as he'll have valuable initial insights. You'll need to make a decision about how to help him because I've said only the President can come through the door.

Bye.

Eulogies

Even though Amancia's hands were trembling, and tears were streaming down her cheeks, she wanted to be the one to say it.

'The preliminary findings on the cause of death for President Carlson, my husband, was a brain embolism. He died at his desk. At work.'

She took a long breath. 'But Gene hung himself.' There was a sustained murmur though the church.

'My husband was the subject of the most vicious, disgusting attack of blackmail and he was forced to make every kind of concession contrary to his own policies and values. The ring murdered distant relatives and mentors and eventually our daughter when he failed to do their bidding.'

'My husband didn't do this as a coward. He was courageous, pragmatic and ultimately hopeful. He wanted his Presidency to continue under someone who could execute the policy platform they ran on without fear or favour. Perversely, he did it because he cared about...me, and knew I'd be safe once his capacity to influence was gone.'

'But he had also been ground down by more than two years of letting down those who had trusted him, and giving those that didn't deserve it, concessions and protections.'

'There are others in the audience here.' She nodded to Sebastian. 'Who have lost nearly everyone dear to them.'

There was a pause and murmuring while President Ramsey took the lectern. 'I spent a good deal of time with Gene on the road campaigning. One thing that always impressed me was that when people had good news, he was happy for them. Not politician happy, but actually happy. When they were bereaved, they knew the person next to them was mourning with them. Gene was genuine, in a way that can't be learned or faked. He was a good guy. Could be a hard man when necessary. Unapologetic. But ultimately, he connected with people; be they foreign dignitaries, members of the House, his staff, ordinary people. And he was the same with everyone.'

'I think Gene would really like it if I spent a few moments during his Eulogy describing what is about to happen to the people who did this to him. I will be going to the House and requesting, and expecting, resources to build a short-term investigations and prosecutions team of one thousand individuals. These individuals, generally not selected from traditional federal law enforcement and intelligence agencies, will be given wide ranging powers to investigate this ring and bring every single person, no matter how small their involvement, to justice. I will expect corporations to open their books to us, and to prove, conclusively, they were in no way part of such a ring. If they will not comply. They will be prioritised for a very probing and very prolonged investigation.'

'If any company wants to make investigation difficult and drag its feet, if they supply anything to the United States Government, I will be calling for the contracts with that company to be cancelled and never be reinstated.

'There will be no forgiveness. I intend to *crush* the people who did this to our society and our President.' Everyone got a taste of the capacity to project power this woman had. When she repeated '*I am going to crush them.*'

Machine Learnings

Walking in Odette was surprised it was being managed as an open Hearing. 'Ms Watson. Are you ready to provide evidence.'

'It's Captain Watson Mr Chairman, I should think that was obvious, being in my dress uniform.'

'Of Course. This Committee completed Hearings over a week ago and we're preparing Findings. We've set aside a brief additional session out of respect for the late President's request. Could you describe the nature of your evidence.'

'Mr Chairman have you read the precis of the evidence and watched the short video's which accompany this? Has your Committee determined whether this material suits presentation in an open Hearing?' Some Committee members looked uncomfortable, but some accusingly at the Chairman. They hadn't had the opportunity to be properly briefed or view any evidence which was characterised by him as being of 'some interest.' The evidence had come in after the preparation of the Committee Findings and was inconvenient. At a narrative level the part that the 'Iranian Insider' was well known, and her late participation was seen as a gesture to a junior Army officer from a late President.

'I couldn't make the time, although I assume you'll do so as protocols dictate. As it happens several of us have conflicts in our schedules, so we'll need a summary from you ideally in ten minutes please.' He was in a very awkward positions with influencers from multiple interests creating pressures he had not encountered before in his long career. The Majority members would acknowledge the many findings in muted tones. The Minority in the Committee more sensationalist.

'I can't say I understand how you prioritise the use of your time Sir. You've dishonoured the intentions of a President blackmailed by the very forces I've come here to discuss and about whom I have direct evidence. And I gathered this evidence at the cost of the life of a colleague when we both might have escaped had I not determined to try to gather it. I had saved the evidence from access to anyone, including the press. The late President recommending this would be the forum for me to present it.'

'And this weighs heavily on me even more so when someone in a position of authority can be so disinterested to show any desire to gain an understanding of it. The Syrian Girl, the Iranian insider, military complicity in murders and mercenary style attacks on a civilian. All because of a corporate agenda to sell more Machine Learning software and the hardware that uses it.'

The Chairman rose to this goading. 'That's not a statement of fact. It's conjecture.' This came out as a defensive statement a mouthpiece of the industrial military complex might say. Which he wasn't. He knew it and regretted it. He was no one's mouthpiece and never had been.

'Sue me.' Said Odette packing up her things. She got a sense that under half the committee had appreciated the exchange. They had been largely shut out of the management of the Committee.

'I'll tell you something ironic Mr Chairman. The Iranian Insider, a good man which no one reports on, was engaged to work on a Machine Learning project for the US Army. It was an arrangement set up specifically to use his nationality. They were going to kill him and kill me as an accomplice. Before we learned of our fate, we watched the president's announcement of the Syrian Girl. He joked that it was funny to see the leader of a country telling the truth about something so sensitive.

It looks like that spirit died with the president. And him. When he was given a lethal injection, died of convulsions, his body burned and the remains never recovered. I would like to tell you exactly what I think of you and your committee. However he was a good, decent and honest man. So out of respect for him, I'm simply going to leave.

Odette snapped her bag shut and left. The media could have everything. She had wanted to give the administration a chance but they could all go to hell. She was trembling with anger and she knew she was getting emotional much to easily now. When she found out Colonel Fowler had a 'heart attack' an hour after being on the phone to her, she had been inconsolable in her room all day.

As she was leaving the room a man wanting to enforce protocols moved across her path. She realised she had the capacity to growl. 'Get out of my fucking way.' So, he did. She was sitting looking at nothing in the big central Dome of the Capitol. Spicer arrived and introduced himself as the President's Chief of Security.

She was soon walking next to President Ramsey. But it was more like running. 'You gave the Committee a message.'

Odette winced. 'Yes Ma'am.

'The Chairman. Piper. Deserved it and well done. A pain in the ass. But there's never been a hint of corruption about him, though I could understand why you might feel otherwise. He's achieved a great deal for his constituency. I don't like what he's achieved, that's natural, we're ideologically opposed, but he has been a tireless Representative. Perhaps less so on this topic.'

The woman, walking slightly in front of Odette was the first female President. And African American. Minority groups were sometimes dismayed when she was questioned about this she would say. 'I'm a person.' It seemed Ramsey was too busy to talk about things that were already demonstrated in her policies.

'The Committee process deserves respect. Many countries don't have what we have, even though it feels like our system's fallen into disrepair. That disrepair will only be made worse if the process is not supported.'

'I apologise for that President Ramsey.'

'Captain Watson. I have only moments ago received the Report President Carlson commissioned on drones and machine learning, and he prosecuted this investigation with unusual ruthlessness. That's one reason he was able to speak authoritatively during that television interview in such detail with the man who murdered his daughter.' A strangely satisfied smile crossed her face. 'I've asked for a meeting with Congressmen Piper, and I'll give him a precis of that investigation. I'll expect that he sets aside an appropriate amount of time in closed session for what President Carlson identified and the presentation of your evidence in detail, and I expect him to simply elongate the Hearings, as long as will be required. Now that I've been properly briefed, I know you have a home run in your pocket Captain. I'll need it over the next few days, and not on the front page of a newspaper. I'm asking for a lot of money from some of those people on the Hill.' Her tone changed slightly. As you know I'm putting together a team to investigate the kind of thing you've experienced. I can't *draw you into that team* if you've brought too much attention to yourself.'

All of this was conducted at a brisk walk. Then Candy Ramsey stopped. She had been losing perspective. Driving forward and getting things done. But she thought about Gene. What he would do. 'Captain are you as ready for a coffee as I am.' They were in the lounge when the President said. 'Captain...with what happened with the president, his family some of those involved...I realise your story and what you and Mansour and Colonel Fowler sacrificed hasn't been acknowledged. Partly because the that particular piece involving the services, military and secret, needs to be handled with care.' Odette was pleased to hear she knew the two people she'd lost by name. 'I am absolutely certain Captain that you're not looking for gratitude. You're looking for justice. I'm I will commit to you that you will be satisfied. However Captain it may take longer than you'd prefer. However if you will trust me, trust the process and possibly, though you're last person on earth who has reason to, trust the US government we will get you and Mansour and Colonel Fowler that justice.'

Odette gave her an account of the days in the motel, but then disappearing unexpectedly to the everglades as they were coming for an academic she'd assured everyone virtually never left the building. She gave the President a sense of Mansour's character and described the gun battles, needle attacks and struggles with the fake FBI and how it was the fact that the Governor was friends with the Secretary of State that allowed her to get the information to the President

'Just in time.' Said President Ramsey. 'You know Captain. The sad thing about all this is that Gene himself wasn't the target. Only to the extent they wanted a Democratic party in absolute turmoil and dysfunction. So that their Candidate in the next election would be in position to easily take on Gene or anybody else from our Party. But ultimately their blackmail became ham-fisted and those wanting certain concessions or outcomes couldn't wait until their man was installed. They never guessed Gene would make the ultimate sacrifice and let me lose on them.'

'I'm glad you are Ma'am.'

'And I'm glad you showed us all what a fine soldier can do in a very complex and dangerous situation.'

Odette could finally hand over the evidence. As she walked out of the hearing room. Colonel Fowlers comment on her lack of a life was telling. There was no one to meet her. Except another man in black turned up. 'Let's see what there is to find in that Florida garden you threw those things into.' Said Spicer.

It was all there. Where she'd left it. Guns, radios and Mansours computer and hard drive.

Passing the Baton

'I feel you should lead off Peter. Why am I sitting here?' The new host asked. She was relaxed.

So was Peter. 'Well, I knew I'd done my best work, and I didn't want to go out with a whimper as it were. So I called you. Expecting to get some minder, but you answered the phone yourself. And I said, *'would you like to take over a late-night interview show that's barely limping along'* and to my surprise there wasn't even a *'Let me think about it and I'll get back to you.'*

Amancia looked across from the interviewers chair. 'When you asked, I knew it was perfect. I needed to get away from the States, where I'm a focus of sympathy, pity, or curiosity. The British are slightly more reserved in their curiosity, I think.'

Peter thought he'd leave that alone but followed on with. 'And it's so easy to get from London across to Barbados and see your mum.'

Amancia did her best to suppress an *'I'll get you later for that'* smile. 'And where are you going Peter?'

'Rua and I are teaming up with Archie and his wife and going on motorhome tour of Europe. See the sites. There's no hurry. Unfortunately, Archie and I may have a bit of bottle smashing to do along the way. But we'll get there.'

Peter sighed. 'It's time to hand over the baton. Though I'm a little jealous Amancia. It took me five years of hard slog to make this introduction and here you are doing it on your first night.'

'Deal with it.' Said Amancia smiling. 'Ladies and Gentlemen, it's my pleasure to introduce Candice Ramsey. President of the United States of America.'

Applause for this President was sustained and unambiguous. She had a clear foreign policy platform and people were by and large happy with where Britain sat in it. She was providing examples of good governance which they and others found relevant and refreshing even though they were occurring on that strange planet called America.

'President Ramsey, you're renowned for having very short, sharp meetings. Will you be walking out on us in the next few minutes?'

'I guess it depends how much the meeting is advancing US interests.' She laughed. 'No, you're both special cases. Amancia you're going to be a great ambassador, not for the US, but for balanced and generous views. And you might lift the proportion of female interviewees above the abysmal twenty five percent of your predecessor.'

'Ouch.' Said Peter.

'But Peter, I so wanted to be a part of your farewell interview because the two interviews you did with Gene were so powerful. He was being forced into duplicity, but his inherent good nature simply could not do it. I think you helped facilitate that.'

Amancia launched into her first question of the interview proper. 'President Ramsey, you've built a thousand person team as promised and the blackmail ring seems to be falling down like a house of cards.'

'Yes. And this isn't a metric I particularly like, but it demonstrates how embedded and invested these people were. Thirty-seven people, mainly in senior corporate and government roles, have committed suicide since the investigation was announced. There have been a large number of people coming forward looking for a deal. But there are *no deals*. They don't deserve a deal. We'll find them all, informants or not, so they'll get what they deserve. Companies are being asked to give full access and demonstrate they're clean, or we are hammering them. I'm unapologetic.'

Amancia posed another question. 'Some say that even when the ring is completely and utterly broken, you will still continue with this team, supplied with huge resources to look at all sorts of malfeasance in big business.'

'First of all, this ring had tentacles in academia, intelligence agencies, foreign embassies as well as business. They were not always aware of the full nature of what they were involved in, but their activities were still corrupt. And I'm unapologetic about looking further. If we're in the midst of a targeted investigation and identify other crimes, they will be treated as crimes according to the statutes. It's an additional positive outcome of the work. Those who don't see it that way can explain why. If our supplier sells us a bolt for five hundred dollars, I'm interested in that. A company not paying the appropriate amount of tax. I'm interested in that. And I'll be asking the accountable parts of our government why this is happening. And there better be good answers. What's wrong with abiding by the law, by a contract. Paying tax. I have to. And so should they.'

The President was making all the signs that that was as much as she had to offer. She made her thanks and there was long applause but the President didn't leave. She'd become reflective.

'You know Gene is a hard act to follow, being interviewed on this show. I would have so much prefer it if I could have been Vice President and Gene could have been Gene without any of these awful influences. He would have done remarkable things. I hope I can come close.'

Stand Off

Honey Bear was going into town to shop. An activity which, unlike some of her gender, she hated. She's always hated it, but since all that had happened with 'that stuff' as Big Bear called it, they were the subject of endless gossip and the lingering looks that went with it. The nearest alternative was sixty miles in the other direction, and she was giving that serious consideration.

She looked down the list. She'd written eggs automatically, even though they had acquired chickens with more time on their hands. They also had a big freezer full of ready-made food and milk and butter. They were running low on beer but if this forced them to drink some of the Bourbon they only drank special occasions, so what.

It might help her husband lift out of the depression that had set in soon after the President had died. She'd reasoned with him, pleaded with him, threatened him to get him to get some help. And he would always say yes, but not yet.

She was bringing the empty carry bags back into the shed to find him up on the workbench on a chair. He'd tied the rope up high to a beam at the peak of the shed so that once he left the chair, he would swing out into the open with five feet underneath him.

She looked up at him and shouted. She was angry. 'Don't you do this. Don't you do this to me or to yourself.' As she said this, she walked to the gun safe and pulled out a double barrel shotgun and with trembling hands put in the cartridges. 'I'll blow my own fucking head off right here and now the second you step off that chair. And you know I'm no liar.' She could see he was wavering. But she was angry now. 'In fact, I might blow my head off first so it's the last god damn thing you see. That you caused your wife of thirty five years to blow her head off. You'll do that, because of this fucking stupidity.'

He looked aimless. 'Fuck you. I'm doing this.' Honey Bear never, ever swore. She put the gun to her mouth. 'And you know what's ironic Duane.' She hadn't called him Duane in thirty five years since the time she had to legally at their wedding ceremony. 'Of all those dead people, I'm going to be the *only* one dead because of you. Do you remember what the President of the United States called you Duane.'

He nodded. She waited until he replied. 'A good man.'

'Not many people get called that by anybody. And here you are going to hang up there like a big lump of aged beef. There're ways to make you feel better. Proven ways. And you're not even trying them. You're a good man Duane and a good man is worth saving.'

He slid the noose from around his neck. Climbed down of the chair and bench, very nearly falling. She put the gun aside and was inclined to berate him some more, but she looked into his eyes, and she could see that he'd listened for the first time.

Soon he was right against her. Her cheek was wet with his tear. 'I'm so sorry.' After a few more apologies he said. 'I can't get away from the thoughts, and the pain. It's because I took that video the President made all those changes. Next thing two girls are dead and then him and.'

'You know it was more complicated than that Big Bear. Things we don't even know about. People have thoughts they can't shake, and they have pain, it cripples them. And they're tricked into thinking that hiding it is the best thing to do. See Big Bear, my brain's not been right since dad died. This is another thing that we should be working on together and look out for one another like we always have.' She sighed. 'I want to show you something.'

They walked out the big opening of the shed and looked at the farm. From that vantage there was a good view of the paddocks, ridge, the house, and the horse yards.

'I'm ready to leave. I know you would have left long ago but you'd never say it. The horses are a burden now, rather than a pleasure. I've got them so quiet there's going to be lots of people want them. This whole place is too big. It full of maintenance work we don't like doing. We live near a town where lots of people are ugly on the inside from what I can tell. And life was very mean to dad here. I should have left a long time ago, but I knew he wanted me to have the place.' She smiled and gave her husband a hug. 'But he's dead. His opinions don't matter anymore.'

Procession

It was two months since President Carlson's funeral. They thought that the flowers they brought would be outstanding for that day, yet they were still outshone by several ornate bouquets with notes. Which they realised they hadn't included, but Honey Bear shrugged. 'Not like he can read 'em.' She was trying to lighten the mood. But Duane was still in the grips of a depression.

They heard a car pull up behind them and footsteps of a small group. Duane looked up to see the President flanked by security. He was suddenly anxious. 'Missus...I mean Madam President... hello.'

'Hello Duane. And hello, Honey Bear.' They both smiled. The President had some flowers to lay, and they let her do that in silence. 'President Carlson mentioned you to me Duane. Before he died. He said we were lucky to have people who would confront the two devils. I asked him what he meant, and he said that when both our choices will have both good and bad consequences it's a very difficult road. Usually, the easiest devil to choose is to do nothing.'

'Now that I'm in this new job, it's like 'wow'. I'm having to make decisions between those two devils every day and often with serious consequences. All I can do is hope I get it right based on what I know and believe.'

She reached out her hand and Duane and then Honey Bear took it.

The President smiled. 'You made the right decision.' She turned and left.

'Thank you, President Ramsey.' There was a pause as Duane considered the next sentence but she at the car. 'We're Democrat voters now.' They heard a chortle from the President as the car pulled away and she waved.

Big Bear had no idea what they were doing in the small mid-west city and Honey Bear wouldn't tell him. They went to a university with a nice campus. Honey Bear approached an area where a manicured lawn met a pleasant garden. There was young woman there in dress uniform, a Captain if Big Bear's memory of dress and insignia were correct.

She turned around and initially gave Honey Bear a hug, saying how nice it was to meet in person. She reached out her hand to Duane and said. 'Pleasure to meet you Duane. I'm Odette Watson.'

Big Bear's mood had been lifting and he was able to be much more the man he used to be. 'It's a real pleasure to meet you Captain Watson.' Big Bear was genuinely impressed. 'I looked at the reconstructions they've done now of the motel and outside. It would take an and exceptional soldier to get out of there alive. And bring out evidence that's made such a difference.'

She smiled and said. 'It's Odette's for you Big bear. But thank you. I have my commanding officer to thank who tipped me off and got killed for it. The university have invited me to come here to give a short speech in memory of him and Mansour who lectured here.'

Honey Bear and Big Bear were a few rows up at the side. A message was circulated that if anyone looked at a phone or a lap top their lives would be in danger.

She gave some background about Mansour no one was aware of. The PhD and the time as a lecturer never recognised. The late-night trip to America which he was always ambivalent about. The death of his parents in the pandemic shortly after he arrived, and his pursuit of excellence in his field. In addition to lecturing, he read and submitted papers on a regular basis.

She described their time while she was leading him to believe he worked for NASA but the work he was doing for the US Army. He was adamant an autonomous drone could never guarantee there would be no civilian casualty. She said that when they heard about the Syrian Girl, they were on their way to the Everglades which had left their kidnappers flat footed.

Odette described what went on in the hotel room, with Mansour having a semi-automatic spray bullets above him and shooting him in the thigh and then escaping in a fleet of taxis. She told them that her Commanding Officer was murdered an hour after warning her about the planned attack which saved their lives. She told them about the murder of Mansour a few yards away with a thin fabric screen separating them. Her attack on the fake FBI agents. And her conversation with the President. She said she hadn't come across many other people who made it so clear they were giving her their undivided attention. He wanted to hear everything, and he asked pertinent questions. He thanked her.

She put up some pictures on the screen behind her. First of herself and Mansour having dinner in an outside dining area, then Colonel Fowler, in this case with his family, one of Claudia Carlson and Rachel Lacy standing in front of a Van in Rabat. Smiling on the first day of the trip they'd planned for so long. Then one of Gene Calson. With that smile he was known to be. 'Far too genuine for a politician' as one of many obituaries said. And finally the Syrian Girl filled the screen and there she remained. All was quiet.

Then Odette said; 'We have in the audience the people, who at great risk to themselves, released the video of what happened to this girl.' Honey Bear and Big Bear didn't know what to expect. But they got a huge applause with several calling out there appreciation.

Farewell

It had been a long time since they'd travelled, and that had almost always been in the bubble of American Military transfers and visits from bases. As they waited for their driver at Damascus airport they could only have looked more like American tourists if they had American Tourist written on their sweaty backs.

The driver was rude and provided several unsubtle hints that where they were going and what they were doing was foolish. Given it was an American Bomb that killed the girl, along with many others he added. Having Americans visit could lead to a range of consequences. In these situations, Honey Bear would usually get her hackles up, but she knew they had many people to thank for their help to even get into Damascus. And what she really wanted, was for the driver to close the goddam windows and put the air-conditioning on.

'Sir, I can well imagine people will be very unhappy. If the situation was reversed, I'd say there would be a whole bunch of American's very angry to see someone from the country who did this. But this girl is special to us. Very special. Hopefully some people can look beyond the politics and see that some folks will cross a border to acknowledge a good young person, embarking on a life that got cut short. And that it never should have happened. That's all we're here for.'

The driver was somewhat mollified. When they checked into the hotel, the staff had many questions about life in America. Some had questions about Syrian/US relations about which both could honestly say, they could not fathom.

Halfway through the next day they arrived at a regional city. The explosion had caused a further delay to the rebuilding process. It was difficult to see where the crater had been. The driver spoke with several people, none of whom appeared to be helpful. Finally, an irritated man cast an arm out in a certain direction.

There was a small shrine up against some larger pieces of rumble which would probably be removed fairly soon. There were some small plastic flowers and candles. The few photographs placed there of the girl in daily life were heart wrenching. She was smiling but making faces at the same time. They knew real flowers wouldn't last an hour in this heat, so they brought a beautiful display of plastic flowers. However, what they brought would swamp what was already there. They only put out a quarter of what they had.

Big Bear went down on his knees to place a few copies of the last photograph ever taken of her looking up. Some might find it macabre, but they agreed it captured a beauty about the girl no other photo could. Honey Bear said. 'We want you to know that we're so sorry about what happened to you. We're ashamed that our country let it happen and there are millions and millions of Americans that feel the same as we do.'

They stood up and looked around. Everyone had stopped work and was standing looking at them. It was a *'you've outstayed your welcome'* look.

Not long after the foreigners has left a man laboriously pushed his wheelchair into that area still containing rubble. He looked down and picked up of one the photographs they had left there. He looked at it for a long time and took it with him to the flat which overlooked the two bombings which had progressively taken his family.

The Girlfriend Experience

The meeting areas were sprinkled through a large atrium of tropical plants with fruit trees and flowers complete with butterflies and small birds. Robert liked it, and it gave him another layer of confidence in the company he'd put a great deal of trust in. And given nearly all his money to.

He'd parked his old motorbike and left the helmet and leathers with it and dressed in his first ever suit. He'd worn it every night for the past week so it didn't look brand new. He was certain the company he was dealing with, at this phase of their project, wanted to deal with the well-heeled. He hoped they didn't look too closely at his records.

He reached the reception of Winston Technologies at the outer edge of the atrium and was pointed towards his Client Liaison, a few hundred yards down one of several paths fanning out from the reception. The man, American with Japanese heritage, greeted Robert with a firm handshake and a smile.

'Robert. So good to meet you. I'm Kobe. I've been handling you're file and it's a pleasure to meet face to face at last.'

Robert had had a few exchanges on the phone which left him with an impression of someone with energy and enthusiasm, even excitement, about the Project overall and particularly on Robert's behalf. Or he made it seem so. He was older than he'd expected, in his sixties.

Kobe paused and looked around with a smile. 'I never get tired of working here as you can imagine. Case workers are put out here to help create a pleasant ambience for meetings but also to make us feel good.'

He laughed in an almost innocent way which Robert found disarming. 'So that flows on to the Clients.'

Robert imagined this might be the latest fad for the big tech companies. He liked it. It could not be more different than the other end of the tech world where he worked.

'I'd like to confess to you Robert. Of the two hundred Clients selected as test subjects; I had the opportunity to review all the applications, and I requested that you were one of the Clients assigned to me. I'm a little more senior, having been with the company longer, and your application interested me.' He continued when Robert made no protest or other observation.

'At this testing phase of the product, we've been seeking a broad range of applicants, wanting a broad range of the Companions. Some want to construct a Companion totally new, no similarities to anyone. Some want celebrities and some want partners lost to them, to death or in life. But in these cases they often want, how would you call it; Upgrades.' He smiled. 'Larger breasts or able to dance, more agreeable for instance.'

Robert smiled. 'All I'm hoping is that she'll like me.'

Kobe smiled. 'Of course. What's the point of a Companion who hates you? But that's the only change. Otherwise you have asked us to recreate Kirsten as she was, a year after leaving college, when you last saw her.'

The was a another pause. Robert had nothing to fill it with. 'And you've sacrifice so much to find her again.'

Kobe was making it clear that for the other Clients in the trial, a half a million-dollar commencement fee was not a major barrier to participation. Robert had raised the money by selling the family home after it had been left to him by his mother.

He planned to make the monthly payments to Winton Technologies by downsizing his apartment and living on less.

'I was fortunate enough to have an inheritance which has allowed me to participate. Otherwise, I would have had no hope of meeting the financial requirements.' He hoped Kobe didn't know that there was nothing left in case there was a hike in the monthly fee.

'I will have similar anxieties in about six months Robert. Staff could not, of course, participate in the trial, however the next intake will be approximately two thousand. Staff will be permitted to apply. This gives me the possibility to be reunited with my beloved Lilian who passed from cancer two years ago.'

'I'm sorry to hear that.'

'She was my delight.' He paused and looked inward. 'She made me feel lucky. Everyday.' He hit across the table lightly with the bottom of a closed fist as he said 'Everyday'. He came back and smiled. 'And like you, I only want her returned to me exactly as she was, not in the slightest way changed.' He laughed. 'Except eighteen years old of course.'

'Ha. No. Just as she was.' He continued. 'Like you want you're Kirsten. And there will be no staff discounts for me. I know commitment when I see it Robert.'

'Now.' Kobe said this in his short sharp way to break the mood and dive into the topic at hand. 'We've been working hard doing all the background investigations. Every piece of media, school photos, year books, anything. We've sensitively and carefully interviewed friends and family on various pretexts.

We've read anything relevant that was written during the school and college years and the year after that when she worked a few towns over from where you both grew up. We've been feeding the materials she liked to read and the media she watched and listened to into the mix. You're going to spend what may be a sometimes frustrating day being asked questions and responding to sense tests.'

'The human memory doesn't work like a movie. It scavenges pieces of memory stored all over the place. It has to go and find these scraps when a certain desire to recollect somewhere in time and space is requested of it. That's why, contrary to what others might think, we can't plug you in and get a download of your interactions with Kirsten. Prepare for a great deal of answering questions, looking at renderings, being asked the same questions again and again by a different department. They will provide you with examples of touch, scent, taste, sounds and sights associated with her.'

'It will be somewhat counter intuitive Robert, because we are going to work very hard to get as close as possible to Kirsten. Then once everything goes live, missing pieces will be filled and smoothed by your mind. The human mind doesn't like dissonance. It will soon accept small changes so that the new Kirsten is slightly adjusted to match the Kirsten you knew.'

Beyond the atrium, through doors into an array of suites it was a long process. Strange, sometimes boring, sometimes pleasant. They must have had a large number of men and women to help the test subjects arrive closer and closer to what their planned Companion would be like. For him he was describing someone he remembered. For others, it was someone they dreamed of.

He was taken to a series of rooms and blindfolded and instructed to gently run his fingers along the inner arm and the shoulder of one of the many 'assessment assistants'. For each, he was asked was it more similar or less similar until they'd reach the most similar. They'd return to it later when his mind was fresh for that aspect.

They'd identified what perfume Kirsten usually wore and so Robert walked down a widely spaced line of an assistants, each having had the scent applied for ten minutes and he had to indicate which was most familiar. In this case he believed he had an exact match.

He looked at pictures of eyes. Brown, blue, green, flecked. She had blue eyes, so he found himself looking into the eyes of each of the blue-eyed assistants in one of the rooms and made a few observations about slight differences in one of them to make a choice.

They had a number of voice recordings from short speeches she had made in College and talented voice actors tried to recreate this. It didn't go so well. He picked the least worst and they said they'd come back to it. After that he was sitting blindfolded at a table as a line of young women walk past and gave him a lingering kiss. He got to number six and said. 'That's her.' There was a short bust of laughter, possibly from number six. He said. 'And that how she laughed. Like that.'

He was shown all of the photographs they had been able to assemble and he was surprised how many there were. She had been a popular girl. He could see now what they'd had was a series of brief encounters.

Based on the photographs, he was taken and shown a hologram of her. Translucent but very detailed. He was encouraged to walk all around her, and to be as critical as possible. Did she wear her hair that way.

They showed him ten different hair styles and asked him to pick as many as she actually used.

Her nose, cheeks, chin. Were they in the right proportion? Her breast, waist, hands, feet, calves, thighs? She was clad in a bikini but could be presented nude. He said the bikini was fine. He made quite a few changes, and consistent with the promise he'd made to himself, they were always to make her to as close to the original Kirsten as he could get.

They brought him out and went through every test again, using the earlier 'most like Kirsten' as the starting point. Five choices brought together a tighter band for selection. More scents, skin texture, kisses. In these he was always confident he found Kirsten. But he was afraid they would not be able to get a voice like hers. In this case there wasn't multiple options. One voice artist came out and started asking if he 'would be able to help her with her homework if he could keep his hands off her this time.' She laughed.

Robert was relieved. 'That's so close. Really close.' He thought for a moment. 'She wasn't from the south but both grandparent were, and I think she picked some of that up.'

The voice actress was probably thinking it was a tall order when she started the same sentence, but stopped herself, still in character. 'Too much honey?' She went on with a lighter touch and Robert said 'That's it. That's perfect.' The voice actress was gone, no doubt wanting to get the subtle aspects of the voice and accent on tape to use in the process of coding it into a whole vocabulary over the coming days.

Robert was sent back to check the holograph and was surprised how much more like Kirsten all his subtle changes had made. He was encouraged to make as many more as he could. She was now dressed in a few dozen outfits she would likely have worn at the time or did wear in photographs.

He could comment on the shoes she liked, the rings she wore, the necklace he now remembered she wore of St Nicolas. The pink scar on the back of her left hand an inch and a half long. Now he thought about it, she was in the varsity swimming team and so her upper body was made wider and her biceps more muscular.

The woman who'd been navigating him through all this, Genevieve, said. 'That's it. I'll show you out.' Robert was wiped out. Exhausted. The woman, smiled, no doubt having seen a lot of people effected the same way.

'How do you think I went. You know. Do you think I'm getting pretty close?' Her asked her

'Robert, that's the first time I've ever seen someone want to replicate someone else exactly. Which is much harder than picking from a menu. Given that, I think you did a great job. I'm sure you're Kirsten's going to be what you're hoping for.'

It must have been eight in the evening. It had been an intense ten hours. Concentration and decision making on one of his senses after another. As he walked through the atrium, he heard a familiar voice.

'And how did the process go. Has it brought you close? Closer to the Kirsten you remember.'

Robert assumed Kobe would have gone home hours ago. He returned to the table and gave a rundown as to how things had gone and how pleased he was with the process. 'Tomorrow is a very important day Robert. You get you're implant, and it's your week of training to use the system while we bring Kirsten to perfection.'

Robert had read about the implants and the week of training but thought it would happen sometime into the future. He wasn't expecting it to be tomorrow.

Probably for a lot of the other Clients, many retirees, timing was no problem.

'Kobe, I work tomorrow, I'll need to make another time. I'm looking forward to starting the whole thing off, but it might be a week before I can come in again.'

Kobe looked concerned and made the universal signal with the forefinger to stay where he was. 'Wait right here Robert. I'll go and see someone.' He was soon back smiling more than usual. 'I was able to speak with our implant surgeon on the phone and he said he could do it at around eight in the evening tomorrow if you could make it.'

Robert could barely make it, but he decided if he started early, he'd get there in time and keep his job. He found it amusing that he was doing this to please Kobe rather than because he couldn't wait.

Robert knocked on the door at four in the morning and the security guard let him in. They knew each other. Robert had never worked on the coding floor by himself, and he was amazed how much he got done in the large room when there was no one interrupting him or laughing or talking loudly.

Gil was the manager and he had a glass office everyone called the fishbowl because he could see all around the coding floor by lifting his head. 'Hell, this is first. I've never had someone beat me to work before, especially without a key.'

'Sorry if I did something wrong by asking security to let me in. I wanted a clear head to finish a specific piece of work and I also wanted to do the time in the morning so I can get away for a doctor's appointment early evening.'

'Doctors work early evening.'

'Yeah, well I go to a practice that does so it doesn't interfere too much with work you know.'

Robert knew he shouldn't have raised the subject of things interfering with his work. 'Yeah I was meaning to talk to you about that. You've been first out the door a lot lately and people notice.'

'I'm well over my contract hours.'

'Who isn't Robert. I'm in the same boat. But I want to keep my job.'

'Gil, you know from a productivity perspective, I'm twice you're next best.' Robert regretted saying this. Not because it wasn't true, but because it sounded as arrogant . He already knew the response Gil would make.

His Manager sighed in the way a father might imparting a sad truth about the world. 'Robert if I have a hotshot that works only to his contract hours, then fifty other hacks see that and do the same.... well...the math doesn't work out.'

Robert was tempted to tell Gil that he might as well slow the fuck down based on that logic, but instead he thanked him for the advice. He also kept preparing job applications in the little part of his computer it would take a sledgehammer to get in to.

So that evening, it hadn't mattered how early he started, leaving his desk when most other people were overworking caused a pair of eyes from the fishbowl to follow him all the way out.

He got to the atrium before eight in the evening and the receptionist, who must have done night shift, directed him down a different pathway. He arrived at a door the same time as another man, who punched in some numbers on a touchpad that let them both in.

'Ah Mr Casey, right on time. Good. Take a seat and Julie will get you prepped and I'll go and do the same.'

He only needed to lay down on a table like those used for massages so he could rest his face into cushioned hole. The nurse apologised as she pushed his face very tightly into the hole, made of memory foam. He was strapped to the table across the back of his head, his upper shoulders and his lower back. All very tight. He thought to himself that this could be the set-up of a really awful horror movie.

'I've always thought this would make the start of a great horror movie.' Said the doctor as he walked in. 'We came up with this approach for inserting the implant because to takes very little time and a general anaesthetic isn't required unless we feel like giving you one. We don't really need to strap you down like that.'

He would usually find all of this funny. But immobilised the way he was, he tried to change the subject. 'I appreciate you staying back for me.'

The doctor laughed. Amused. 'Is that what Mr Kobe said.' Robert sensed the doctor could easily complain about having to come in after hours. But as a series of needles went into Robert's head the doctor said. 'I'm working on the most interesting project I ever dreamed I would. And in this company, they'll listen to ideas you have about anything. They really listen. Coming in after hours every now and then is no problem.' Then his voice changed. 'And it means Julie and I get to have some fun.'

'Don't we Julie?'

'Mr Casey, there is a whole menu of things we can get up to, I'll put an iPad below the face ring if you'd like to peruse it and make a selection.'

The bands felt very tight. Robert could feel incisions and pressure at the base of his skull. He felt something hard being inserted. In some ways the banter took his mind off what were very uncomfortable sensations though not painful.

The Doctor's voice reverted to that of a satisfied professional. 'And young man, you are all done. You'll need to remain there, completely still for another, seven or eight hours to ensure full establishment of the implant. This is when Julie makes the hard sell for the added extras.' There was a pause. 'No? Okay Julie we'll have to let this one go.'

He felt the restraints from his back and neck being removed. 'I must dash of to an assignation with my good lady wife. Good luck with your Companion, Julie will show you out.'

Julie went and changed out of her uniform and they were soon walking though the Atrium and came to the desk where Kobe was waiting. 'Robert. Good to see you back. And Julie. You look magnificent as ever. Although I have had complaints that you offer extra things when people are strapped down. But you fail to deliver.'

She sighed. 'They're always old and wrinkly Mr Kobe. And this one wasn't interested.' She knocked Daniel with her hips. 'Goodnight Y'all.'

Kobe shook his head as she disappeared, 'Our best nurse. But ungovernable, you know?'

'I heard that Mr Kobe.' Came the faint voice from the distance. He smiled and shook his head again. 'Now Robert...'

'Mr Kobe. I had no idea I'd be keeping you and the others back so late.'

'It's Kobe Robert. I tell them to call me Kobe and they call me Mr Kobe. Some kind of cultural sickness of the mind in corporate America. And Robert, it's not the slightest imposition. We want so much for the first round of participants to succeed so we can observe, adjust and improve.'

Kobe pulled out a small metal object half an inch long bent into the shape of a horseshoe. It was gold and only a few millimetres thick. Kobe was able to make slow, gentle bends along its length.

'This is an example of an implant. The outer casing of the residence is gold so it's malleable enough to allow some movement. However, it's placed at the base of the skull in such a way that this should never be necessary. But we need to be sure.'

'It's within this device that Kirsten will reside. When you call her forth, she'll be participating with you in various parts of your brains function, but when you send her back, she will reside in here, albeit with greater and greater sophistication and memory of your time together since your first meeting.'

'As you can imagine, there are a number of barriers to what you can experience with Kirsten. If you call her forth in any social setting at which she would normally be seen or acknowledged, this will cause dissonance. The more frequently the greater this will become. It stresses the system until irrevocable damage is done. We'll talk in more detail next week when you'll be introduced to her.'

Robert smiled. It was that close.

'But until then you have homework.' Kobe said this as if it would be a chore, but his eyes suggested otherwise. He pulled a small crash test dummy doll from his desk drawer and stood it between them.

 For the next week you will need to be able to train yourself to bring this into and out of your perceptual existence. As you will be needing to do with Kirsten on command so that she will appear and disappear in the context of your daily life.'

'In Kirsten's case her appearance will come via her walking through a door or turning to look at you after a moment of looking somewhere else. The two functions of bringing your Companion in and out of the experience of your daily life are the essential skills.'

'For the first week you'll have one of these dummies which gives you complete autonomy over their movements so that by the time you're Companion is initiated, you'll be very skilled and confident at the most rudimentary processes of presence and absence. Sometimes people get these dummies to do the most ridiculous things at home or in the workplace, which is of course most immature.' Kobe imparted this information knowing that this was exactly what Robert intended to do.

'Okay. Let's call this fellow into presence and see what he can do.'

'Now?'

'Oh yes. I need to know the implant is functioning correctly before you leave. You'll notice this portable console I have. It allows me to perceive what you're perceiving via your implant. These instruments are very tightly controlled as you can imagine, and are only used on two occasions.

This occasion, and at the initiation of the program with your Companion.'

'And so. You're implant gives you the ability to have a crash test dummy materialise here between us.' Robert was dubious.

Kobe said nothing more. Robert willed it and a vague translucent shape appeared sitting between them on a bench.

'Now stop trying and try again.' Kobe encouraged.

This went on for nearly an hour and Robert would have been frustrated and pointing out that it was nearly eleven, but each time the shape became more and more solid. Finally, Kobe said, 'Hold that. Now reach forward and put your hand on its knee.'

Robert did this and recoiled with a gasp at the solid nature of the space he touched. A space in which he knew there was nothing.' Kobe laughed. 'Very disconcerting is it not. You knew from our promises that from your perspective your Companion would be solid to the touch. Completely normal outwardly as a physical entity to your senses. But the first time we experience it, it's very strange. Concentrate some more and see if you can have our friend reach out and shake your hand.'

It took ten minutes and was bizarre, but Robert made it happen.

'And finally Robert, you have ten décor themes loaded up in you implant. We've given you an additional five with our compliments. All you need to do is remember these ten words and that décor will be applied to every surface in the space you're standing in, such as your apartment, to the extent it's possible.

Never change between one décor and another while your Companion is present as it would naturally cause some dissonance. She experiences what you see. I've also added Shinto to see if you like it.'

Robert was looking forward to the décor settings almost as much as being with Kirsten. These would turn his shithole of an apartment into a minipalace from what he understood.

The next week at work was the most fun he could remember. It took a while to master the movements of the dummy, whom he named Gonad, and understand the limits of its capabilities.

Initially he had to concentrate to cause every single movement Gonad made, such as when he climbed up on Gil's desk, squatted over his head and spent several minutes appearing to strain and push. Eventually turning to give Robert a big thumbs up.

Gradually though, he could get Gonad goosestepping behind the lines of screen slaves, and he would continue doing it. He could go through the motions of giving Lado beside him a haircut or Alice on the other side a neck massage.

When Gil called to see him on the fourth day, Gonad was up near the ceiling doing the backstroke in big lazy circles around the room. He obediently came down and followed Robert to the fishbowl. Usually the fishbowl was the last place people saw one of their co-workers go before becoming an ex co-worker.

'Is there some kind of problem Robert?'

Gonad seemed to be developing a mind of his own and had jumped up on the desk, pretended to fart and wave it in Gil's direction.

'No. No problem. Why would there be a problem.' He tried to sound surprised.

Gonad was now next to Gil wagging his finger at Robert angrily. 'You've spent most of the day looking everywhere but you're screen Robert, and half of all that time looking in here; at me. Are you on drugs Robert? Because if you are, I can't have you here. It doesn't matter how good you are or how late you stay, and I appreciate you've been the last to leave over the last few days.'

'I'm not on drugs.' Gonad was now standing next to Gil laughing his head off at Robert as if he was a big fat liar. Robert was unsure whether he was asking Gonad to do this, or he was being directed by Robert's subconscious.

'I've been thinking about crash test dummies you know.' Robert thought if he stayed around truth it might sound genuine. 'How you could make a good game with them. Not as creepy mannequins. More like people. With real personalities. You can still; rip their heads off, or blow them up with bombs or ram them into buildings like young kids like to do. But in a fun way. What I've seen on offer for crash test dummies in the games market is not much good really.'

'In a fun way?' Robert, we code here. We're not games developers. Sounds like a curious concept but if it's taking up too much of your attention here you know where that's going to lead.'

Gonad was standing on the desk and had Gil choking him with one hand and punching him with the other. Robert tried not to smile when he said. 'Oh, you know how it is, you get all excited about a thing. That feeling's all drained away and gone now.' This was an honest appraisal of what he thought about his job. 'I'll get back to giving my job 100%.'

Gill was still taking a battering with Gonad looking up and nodding occasionally to Robert. 'Sure Robert. Let's try and make it that we don't need to talk to each other about anything for a while. Okay.'

'Yeah Gil.' By the time Robert had stood up, Gonad had moved around and was flipping a pair of angry birds in the managers face. Gonad followed Robert out with a bunch of self-satisfied 'I guess we told him' nods. Robert turned him off and got back to work.

'Thought I'd have an empty seat next me to that time. Walk into the fishbowl and get shat out the other side. That's the usual process.' Lado rarely spoke but was always friendly when he did. Robert had figured him out a while back. Or at least some of it.

'Oh, you know. Employee of the month shit. Not that I'm getting it. It's only he keeps on asking my opinion. Bit of a pain.'

'I believe that. I also believe you got some crazy tech stapled in the back of your head which is one of the most interesting pieces of hardware I ever seen. I only know it's there because I have specialties other than this shit job.'

Robert knew Lado didn't work at all during day. The guy was many times sharper than him. Robert suspected he took a day's work home, did it in less than hour and then 'played it back' it to the work systems at snail speed to him so it looked like he was working. Meanwhile he had a screen that an observer needed to be standing directly behind to see clearly. He spent the entire day doing something else which Robert, even sitting next to him, couldn't decipher.

'I'll show you mine if you show me yours.' Said Robert. Which was a big commitment because telling anyone about the whole Kirsten thing could expose him to ridicule he imagined.

'Who's showing what to who. Can I see. Can I see them both.'

'Alice for fuck's sake, you're always listening to music and this one time you're eavesdropping?'

'What music. Who can listen to music twelve hours a day? I've got wireless mikes sprinkled 'round dis whole place on scan. If an interesting conversation starts, I listen in. How the fook else am I supposed to do this boring shit all day long; and go as slow as a I possibly can so I don't get picked on like you do. And the next ting I'm hearing about something crazy stapled into Robert's head and so here I am.'

This had all occurred without any turning of the heads as they all pretended to keep working and paying no attention to each other. 'Who's spilling the beans first. Should we do it here or in a bar after work.' This was by far the most social they'd even seen Alice. She was pleasant but appeared perennially bored shitless. She was. Doc Martins, long shapeless dresses of any muted colour and a rats nest hairstyle. Not many people talked to her. Those that did found her pleasant, but not generally wanting to migrate that into friendship.

'What have you got worth seeing? This was a private party.' said Lado

'It'll be private only as long as I'm invited. C'mon. My treat. The English Pub. I buy the booze you guys get the meals.'

Robert was a little interested in sharing his story now. He'd only ever told Kobe about his relationship with Kirsten, and then only to the extent that he wanted to change one thing about her personality. Maybe if he told a few friends, he'd realise what a waste of time and money it had been. To be obsessing about her all this time. But he was afraid of everyone knowing he had a device in his head that turned his girlfriend on and off.

'Sounds good. Let's sneak out early.' They all laughed because it wasn't funny working extra hours for the privilege of keeping a shit job.

The pub was starting to get quiet by the time they got there, and the kitchen was closing, but Alice served up a modified damsel in distress routine that got them bangers and mash.

'So. Robert.' Alice gave him a wicked look. 'What has been distracting you at work these last few days. Lado tells me it's to do with a little implant you got.'

Robert gave them a summary of the process he was going through in getting a pretend Kirsten, and why he wanted one in the first place. He described the whole set up with the background research and the five sense 'calibration' as it was called. He described the decors that came with the package so he could turn any space into a particular theme. He said now he was sitting inside an art deco bar but could change it ultra-modern, Edwardian or Shinto, which he liked, however the shapes in the bar didn't suit it.

'Dat would have cost quite a bit Robert. Why are you grinding away at the keyboards wit us.' Alice, hailing from County Claire in Ireland, was curious for more details.

'My mother passed away three years back in my hometown and I'd been renting her house out. I sold it and used the money for the Install payment.'

'The monthly maintenance payment will keep me eating dog food until I can get a better job.'

'And when does your sweetheart arrive?' For all the tough and bored exterior, Alice was showing an intense interest in the project.

'A few days. Until then I've had to practice with this dummy to make sure I have enough control over my mind to make Kirsten present or absent. It's overkill because you can make these Crash Test Dummies do pretty much anything you want. I've had him swimming up near the ceiling, tap dancing in the halls, doing the Macaranga. But all I really need to know is how to turn Kirsten on and off.'

'And what have you had your Dummy doing with our fearless leader?'

'Ha, you name things and I'll tell you if I haven't done it.' Through this process Robert got a few new ideas. He looked across at Alice as their second pint was arriving. 'He's been giving you a neck rub for a few hours a day.'

'Dat's bullshit.'

'No. I've had him standing there giving you a neck rub for hours. The way you sit made me think you might have needed one and I'd run out of ideas for him.'

'Dat's bullshit Robert. I *do* have a sore neck. Some days the fooking things agony. But it's been like heaven the last few days. All the pain's been gone. I even taut I felt I was bein' touched. Taut I was goin' fookin' mad.'

Robert shrugged.

'So Lado, what's you're big secret.' Alice had taken over proceedings as inquisitor, though they knew she had more questions for Robert.

'It's a boring technical secret that I'll share provided it goes no further. We can do our work in a fraction of the time, but we must sit there doing it. In the case of you two it's a slightly larger fraction of the time than it is for me.'

'Modest.' Said Alice.

'The program I've developed lets me take home tomorrow's work, do it in the hour it should take to do, and then replay it very slowly at the work rate of the rest of the room.'

'And then you meditate all day?'

'Then I have fun all day because my screen is designed so that you need to be looking directly into it to see what's on it, and I can see anyone coming and turn on boring work shit. I have a kick ass wireless router and my friends and I while away the hours hacking, learning the latest software or playing games which is what I would do if I was at home. Only reason I stay at this shitty job is I can get away with it.'

'Okay Alice. Time for your big reveal.' Said Lado. 'We've shown you ours.'

'Hmm. I tink there's a bit more detail to come from both of you but my well-kept little secret is that I collect Barbies.'

Lado was shaking head as the last word was dying. 'What a croc. Get us here, find out about our most important shit and you collect Barbie dolls. That is lame girl. Lame.'

Alice pretended to be offended. 'Imagine what would happen to my reputation if news got out that I collected Barbies.'

They all paused and laughed. They were nobodies.

'Anyway, these are not any Barbies. They're Slutty Barbie's. It's a bespoke range of Barbies I've developed purely for myself. And don't worry, there's lots of high-powered female role models. Dominatrix Corporate Barbie, Slutty Jet Fighter Pilot Barbie. And the 'Yes. It's time for a Slutty Pope Barbie.'

'I spend my evenings making their little costumes and don't bother to say that it's 'just sad' because I know it's 'just sad' but it's my hobby and...it's becoming a bit of an obsession. But I'm getting this anxiety building up because I'm running out of occupations or activities to put the word Slutty in front of, and so expand the range.'

Lado's eyebrows went up and said. 'I would not be surprised if Robert and I couldn't come up with some ideas you haven't thought of. Robert, why don't we each bring in a list, but only hand it over if we get to go and meet the Slutty Barbie's that get made because of our creative input.'

Robert was enthusiastic. 'I think it sounds pretty good Alice. I think it's a way better pastime than you're giving yourself credit for. My pastime for the last few months has been sitting around waiting for a pretend woman to be inserted into the back of my head.' Said Robert.

Lado followed on. 'I spend all day and most nights on computers hacking into shit because I like puzzles and getting a buzz out of the fact that if I get caught by the authorities, I could be in serious trouble. That's why anything I do has Gil's digital fingerprints all over it.'

Lado tried to sound serious. 'Robert, I have a few more activities I've thought Gonad could do in the fishbowl, however I suspect Alice has got important work planned for your Dummy tomorrow.'

'As a matter of fact.' Said Alice. 'Dere is a task I could have the gentlemen help me with. I'd need to be properly introduced of course?'

'He's sitting next to you now. If you turn to your right, you'll be looking at Gonad straight in the eye.'

'Pleased to meet you Gonad.' Alice looks back at Robert, who was nodding.

'If Gonad's not otherwise occupied then I'd appreciate his therapeutic attention. *But not on my neck.*'

Robert and Lado looked at each other and winched. She looked at them 'And what would you be havin' a girl Crash Test Dummy doing all the day long?'

Robert hadn't thought about it. He suspected his relationship with Gonad may have been different. He tried not to think about it.

They all had too much to drink but were at work as soon as the doors opened. They had things to share. Robert and Lado had Slutty Barbie ideas. Slutty Deep Diver Barbie, Slutty Astronaut Barbie, Slutty Matador Barbie. They had thirty she didn't have in her collection. These ideas were, according to Lado 'barely touching the sides.'

'Hanging around with you guys is Slutty Barbie gold.' They were hearing a cheerfulness in her voice that was new.

Alice had brought in three Barbies which she was going to allow them to have on their desks for one day only. A Slutty French Foreign Legion Barbie, Slutty Train Driver Barbie and Slutty Grocery Store Manager Barbie. As Alice anticipated there were some arguments about which Barbie went where, so they had to rotate every hour.

Alice advised them that she was wearing a looser one piece shapeless dress that day and wasn't wearing any panties.

'Whoa. Like in that movie with, who was it. Samantha Stone? What was that movie called?' Said Lado.

'Who cares. That's old people shit. I want to make sure Gonad can get in there unrestricted you know. Where is he anyway? Still making a fool out of Gil. That asshole can do that without anyone's help.' Alice had a very slight note of impatience in her voice

'Alice he's heading this way now.'

'Right.' Alice started to pull her long dress up, so the hem was halfway up her thighs. To do this she had to very briefly stand up part of the way out of her chair.'

'I meant Gil's heading this way.' Robert hissed.

Although wearing Doc Martins and a short skirt was not unusual on the floor, getting there by pulling a long dress up in the middle of the workplace was strange enough for Gil to ask. 'Everything okay Alice?' Giving her a confused look.

'Oh yeah. Itchy vagina. I get it sometimes. Yet I wear these long dresses and my arms aren't long enough to go in from the top so I have to pull da damn ting all the way up so I can reach my snatch. I asked me colleagues here if it would make 'em uncomfortable, but dey said it was fine. I'm gonna leave it like dis in case I need to give it a big ole scratch later in the day.'

Gil nodded. The unfamiliar and unwelcome insights motivated him to walk away and get back to what was familiar. Which was making people uncomfortable because he thought that made them work harder.

'Well you could have told me.' She said, smiling.

'I did...never mind.' Robert was watching Gil. Gonad was walking behind him. He aped him precisely until he got back to the fishbowl. Now he was walking towards them in a kind of regal way. 'You date is on his way.' Said Robert.

She looked across at Robert. 'Does my hair look okay. Is there anything stuck in my teeth? No? Well, I'm all ready.'

A realisation was only now dawning on Robert. 'Alice, you do realise that I'm able to see Gonad, whatever he's doing when he's present, whether I want to or not on this occasion.'

Alice let out a suppressed laugh. 'I didn't tink o' dat. Makes it even better.'

Robert tilted his screen and angled his chair as much as possible to be facing away from Alice but he could not quite remove the top of Gonads head from his peripheral vision. He heard Alice say. 'Serious placebo shit going on here. Going to listen to some music.'

Alice sometimes hummed tunelessly to what she was listening to which people around her found annoying but it was never loud, and it didn't happen too often. Partly because she was usually listening to everyone else This time she started moaning tunelessly and it was getting loud. Robert and Lado had their headphones on, so it was only when he saw some of the strange looks in their direction, he took his off that and gently took hold of her arm and shook her.

She took the headphones off. 'Alice. You were moaning.' She sighed, looking across. 'I want one.'

They went for another drink that night to commiserate with Alice that she didn't have the half million bucks to get her own Gonad. 'I'd never bother going past dat level. Who wants the complexity of conversations with a 'Companion?'

Do you tink they'd trade a Slutty Barbie collection for a Gonad.'

'He'll be swapped out for the love of my life tomorrow night.'

'One last day for Gonad and me to share our sweet tender moments of togetherness.'

Lado spoke up. 'I don't know if I can go through that again. I don't know if the office can go through that again. How many times did that stuff happen?'

'I lost count.' She said. 'I know I'm going to sleep well tonight. I'll make sure it's much more ...low key tomorrow.'

'It has to be a placebo effect.' Said Robert.

She shrugged. 'Roll on placebo effect. Anyhow, when you tink about it, for Gonad, this is like his last cigarette, he's about to be cast out into the darkness from the little existence he had. Let the poor guy have a bit of fun before he's snuffed out for eternity.'

'Okay. But no moaning. None.'

'Who was moaning. I was humming.'

It was a more subdued day at work. Alice was giving every impression she was losing a friend. At lunch she and Robert went around the back to the loading bay. At that time of the day, the sun hit the back of the building and it was a warm place to sit outside, out of the wind.

'You get all loaded up today with your old flame huh?'

'Yeah. It's a bit weird now that I think about it. Be interesting to see how it works out.'

'Well if you decide you don't want her, I'll take the implant off your hands and get Gonad loaded back in.'

After a long pause she knocked his shoe with her boot. 'And so that's it for the real ting I suppose. I mean, do you intend to turn her off and.' She tapped his shoe again. 'You know.'

'I think this whole thing is going to be way more complex than I realised. I genuinely loved her, but I hadn't thought about the long term. I wanted to live together. How I knew we could if she had been...'

A substantial pause.

'Not such a bitch.' Alice said. And they both laughed.

'Pretty much. I'll see how it goes. It's what I wanted to do, so I'm going to roll with it and see what happens.'

'Well when she's sleeping or whatever, there's someone here who'd love a blow by blow description if you're willing to give it.'

He smiled and grabbed her knee to push himself up. 'I think I could use a sounding board.'

After work, Alice insisted on a fond farewell with Gonad.

'Am I giving him a hug now.' She said as she stood in the street waiting for a cab. She looked ridiculous. And the way she was standing it was hard for Robert to position Gonad to give her a hug. 'Let him hug you. Wait, bring your arms up now. That's good.'

'Am I kissing him, can I give him a kiss.' The people walking past, had good reason to be giving Alice strange looks. Some assumed she was a street performer. 'I'll miss you Gonad. Thanks for all those good times we had Gonad.'

'Okay Alice, he's crying and gesturing that he's going to miss you too.'

'He cries?'

'He does now.'

'Look now you've started me off Gonad.' It was her turn for a cab and Robert was relieved to load Alice into it and went to the garages for his bike.

Once again being in the refreshing environment of the atrium immediately settled his mood. He looked forward to seeing Kobe to enjoy his enthusiasm. And he wasn't disappointed. Kobe said that everything was ready to go. He said that before Robert even asked, no, he could not keep the Dummy.

Robert was going to ask because he liked to see Alice so happy.

'If all we needed to learn was to switch them on and off, and given we're not able to do any of those control type things with the Companions, why bother making it so the Dummy would do whatever you want.'

Kobe shrugged. 'Bit of fun. Did he get up to some interesting things?' Robert smiled. 'Yes. A colleague of mine wants one.'

'We all do. That's why it's only for a week.' He laughed.

Kobe was looking down at a small silver box on the desk. A woman walked past and stopped. Surprised to see an old friend.

'Bobbie? Is that you?' He was standing up and within few seconds they were in the kind of embrace two good friends share after some years apart.

Kirsten, a little shorter, looked slightly up at him. 'Kobe told me you were in the city. I just arrived. I was going to look you up as soon as I found a place.' She reached out and squeezed his arm. 'It's so good to see you.'

'It's fantastic to see you. You look great Kirsten. It's going to be nice to be living in the same town.'

'It sure will. It's a hard place to move to. I'm trying to get something near the park so I might be able to walk to work, at least when the weather's nice but what's available are at crazy prices.'

'Hey…I live a couple of streets back from the park, and I've got a spare room if you wanted to stay there till you get your own place.'

'Oh would you. That would take a huge load off. Oh.' She looked at her watch. 'I have to run but if you leave the details with Kobe, I'll meet you there tonight and I'll cook us up something nice.'

Kirsten gave him a high-speed hug and then dashed away, dissolving as she went.

'I don't think the first meeting should be scripted or expected you know? But we can run them lots of times until we get the one that you'd like to remember.'

Robert was still in a kind of shock. The feel of her embrace, her voice, smile, hair. The enthusiasm. The spontaneity. The only thing missing was the barb. Usually in any exchange there was some kind of barb. A slight. A casual cruelty, a veiled mockery in jest.

'That was perfect Kobe. And the way you did it is just right.'

'Now a very few more things to mention and you can be on your way with Kirsten.'

'First of all, you can't get Kirsten to do the things the Crash Test Dummy did. She has the same volition and dignity that you would have expected the physical Kirsten to have. I know you won't be Robert, but if you are mean, or cruel or violent she would never tolerate these things as normal or acceptable and neither would we. A Companion shuts down even when only a very moderate threshold of mistreatment is transgressed. The Client must explain why, or they will have their Companion removed from the implant.'

'The Companions have been configured to think they can lift or move things. They can feel surfaces, edges, bodies and will believe they are holding a glass of wine or stirring some vegetables in a wok. You will see this yourself, or it would be strange to have her drinking wine with no glass in her hand. But these are illusory. Don't hand her a glass to carry. There's nothing physical there to hold it or the food burn in the pot. It has been one of the more difficult things for our Clients to learn. And the Companions have been constructed to take these little 'leaps' of suspension for disbelief to create the appearance that they interact with portable things.'

'Naturally, you're the only one who can see your Companion.

Unfortunately, we can't create Companions who can tolerate being in public and accept that they are invisible to everyone without losing the very things we seek in a Companion. As I mentioned, if you take Kirsten, an intelligent young woman, into a public place and no one can see her, she'll become confused and distressed. And she'll be looking for explanations.'

'With real trauma, which I know you would never intend Robert, we can reset Kirsten. But you lose everything from today.'

'I know you've been made aware of all this before, but the consequences can be very dire I like to reinforce them.'

He stood up and said confidently. 'You won't need to worry about all that. It's going to go well for you. Great in fact. I can feel it. Once a month we'll meet and if there is anything to fix, you and I will fix it. Otherwise just a coffee. Like friends.'

'I can't thank you enough Kobe. What you've done. It's magnificent.'

As Robert walked away the older man called out. 'Even the smallest thing, and you shall call me.'

Robert decided on a slightly rustic theme for his apartment. What he liked about it was it had a log fire where the heater was, which never required tending. There were nice rugs and light fittings. Completely different from the crappy place which surrounded him.

His apartment was clean, but so lean it verged on mean. He wasn't sure how things worked exactly, so he set out the wine glasses and the makings of the dinner. He willed Kirsten into existence. And there she was, turning around as if she'd closed the front door. She ran up to him and grabbed him by both hands and said how excited she was to see him.

He showed her the guest room and she asked if she could take a shower and he said sure. They made a nice meal and had some wine, she went into quite a bit of detail about her new job and he told her about his. They found a TV show they both liked, and then went to bed. He said he left early so she should help herself to anything she needed in the morning.

He wasn't sure what to do after she'd gone to bed. He didn't imagine having her wake up in the house after he'd gone to sleep would be any good. Anyway, he assumed he'd be out of range at work, whatever the range was. He turned her off.

'Soooo. Situation report please.' Alice had slid up close to him as soon as he arrived. 'I need to warn you that my attitude to your girlfriend is a tiny bit impacted by the fact that she usurped Gonad.'

Robert smiled. 'You'll be surprised to know that I invited her to be my roommate, we had a meal, watched a TV show and went to separate bedrooms. She's the nice girl I always wished she would be. It might work out that I have this imaginary roommate.'

'There may be hope for the mere mortals among us.' Alice paused after saying this, awkward. 'Barbie time.'

Alice had so much raw materials for the makings for costumes and she was so fast and nimble sewing with machines or by hand, each of them would come up with a Slutty Barbie idea the day before, and it would be there on their desk next day.'

Robert had suggested a Slutty Crash Test Dummy Barbie but Alice had said that was still too painful. He went with Slutty Elvis Celebrant Barbie. Lado had complained that all the Slutty Barbie's were white with maybe a brown one here or there. He wanted a Slutty Rasta Barbie but with really dark skin. Alice assured him that she was planning and entire multiracial range, including a Slutty Hindu Ascetic Barbie.

Robert could hardly wait to get home in the evenings. Only for the simple domestic pleasure of living with someone he liked. In what felt like no time they'd been living together for a few weeks, and apart for some minor flirtations, they shared an apartment. Robert would turn Kirsten on as soon as he got near the apartment and it was always different. She might have been home early, already reading a book, in the shower, or not home yet, turning up ten minutes later. One night a week, to his surprise, she advised she'd be doing night class. So sometimes, only half an hour since arriving home, she'd walk out for classes, and he'd turn her off.

One night after a few months together she was standing by the fire with a glass of wine in her hand moving to some music they both remembered from Highschool. 'Get a glass and come sway with me.' She said.

He had one arm around her waist while the other sipped at some wine. She put down the glass and put her arms around his neck.

'Did you ever think about me at school?'

He laughed, nearly coughing up the wine he'd been in the process of swallowing. 'That's all I did. I'd sit around in classes thinking about you all day. It's because of you that everyone thought I was so dumb.'

She laughed. 'You did not.'

He realised that she had no history of a relationship with him from Highschool beyond being friendly and her, perhaps, harbouring a secret longing. This made it so uncomplicated because Robert didn't have to search through a narrative to understand how they'd been in those years before becoming roommates.

It also made it uncomplicated later that night. Both of them ending up in what looked like a magnificent four poster bed. For hours Robert could completely forget Kirsten wasn't a physical being. His five senses confirmed every sensation and shape.

When they awoke together they lay looking at each other, saying nothing for a long time. 'I always dreamed of being together with you like this.' She said.

'That's what I was going to say.' He lay there for a while longer. Looking at her. 'You're so beautiful. Even more than the girl I spent all those hours dreaming about in school.'

She smiled and looked over at the clock. 'Oh Shit. I think we're both running a bit late.'

'Jesus.' Said Robert. It was 11am. He turned Kirsten off.

It was after lunch by the time he was at his desk after making an excuse that even he wouldn't have believed.

'So, things have maybe gone to the next level.' Remarked Alice, as he settled down with a coffee and started work at a pace far more frantic than he ever needed to.

Robert found it a bit awkward. 'Um. Yeah. Sort of.'

'Oh yes. I've had a bit of the old 'sort of' from time to time. Good for the circulation.'

Lado was more practical and laughed. 'Yes. But Robert's going to find out now that with this little number, he has to do all the cleaning up.'

'Guys. Jesus. Let me work. And yeah.' He turned and looked at each of them. 'It's weird, I know.'

But somehow it wasn't weird at home. It was the kind of normal he'd always wished normal could be. He and Kirsten grew closer and closer, slowly arriving at an intimacy he thought he'd never experience.

He called Kobe and asked if it would be okay if he took Kirsten for trips on the bike, provided she didn't need to interact with anybody. Kobe said that should be fine, but to take it slowly. Soon they were sailing down freeways late at night. Kirsten clinging to him and shrieking with pleasure. He would take baskets of food to beautiful rivers or forests, hours out of town on his days off. They'd swim in streams or the ocean, wherever he could get to a deserted place.

One time, she said hello to someone while she sat on the bike as he paid for the gas, and the person ignored her. When she told Robert, he said the people in the area were part of a religion that didn't like strangers and ignored them.

He'd learned not to talk too much about Kirsten at work. Alice carried on like she wanted details and yet he gradually got the impression she didn't want to hear about Kirsten anymore.

Robert had read somewhere that happiness would make for a very short book. There were no car chases or confusing or confronting situations to resolve. The plot, however sweet, however genuine, wasn't complex. Robert had looked from the outside at happiness, and, desirable as it seemed to be, it looked kind of boring. But from the inside there was diversity and beauty. Beautiful experiences of the senses and of the mind.

Music was more profound, moving or urgent. Tastes were simple or complex according to their best effect. And love could be a womb or a rocket ship, a roaring ocean or the slight rise and fall of a chest as you lay your head upon it.

And it was a chest that swelled with love for him.

'You're Fookin' Wot!'

Robert had been saying something to Lado which he had not intended for Alice to hear. This was pretty poor judgement because Lado told people things anyway. The blur of contentedness which had been meandering continuously on for nearly four months had caused Robert to wonder aloud one evening, while they were curled up in front of a log fire, what it would be like to be married. He was going to follow up with the comment that he couldn't imagine it being any better than what they had.

Kirsten hadn't given him time to proceed to this second part of the reflection. She said, 'Why don't we try it out and see.' H could see she had tried to measure here response. Yet there was excitement which Robert couldn't ignore, but room to back out, which he found hard to do based on what they'd been sharing together.

Robert had said little about Kirsten to anyone for the last month. Alice had now become uncomfortable about the whole 'Kirsten ting' as she now called it. Lado, who was usually wrapped up in games and hacking, didn't talk much as it was. Not long after the coffee break in the afternoon, he'd been explaining to Lado that he was now somewhat caught in a marriage trap. He wasn't sure he was ready to go the next step with Kirsten, but it was difficult to climb down with excuses. Saying this out loud to someone about a girlfriend loaded into his head as an insert, made him realise the degree to which he had lost perspective.

Alice had arrived in time to get the gist of things. She said nothing and sat tapping loudly at her keyboard. Her hands were shaking slightly. The Slutty Barbie thing had reduced to a once a week affair. Currently they were sharing a Slutty Lion Tamer Barbie, chair and all, along with a Slutty Titanic Captain Barbie and Slutty WW1 Flying Ace Barbie.

Without warning she stood up and grabbed them from their desks and threw them in her bag. 'Fooking stupid tings these are. I'm going home to burn em.'

Robert got up and followed her while Lado called out. 'Don't you harm them Barbies. Don't touch a hair on their head. And think about the toxic smoke. That shit'll kill ya.'

'Leave me alone.' She said as Robert caught her near the door and he took a light grasp on her shoulder.

'Let's get a beer Alice.' She shrugged as Gil watched them leave about five hours before people usually trickled out.

She was halfway through her first beer when she said. 'I didn't tink I'd care what people taut but I guess I do. The Barbie ting was a bit of a secret and now everyone knows I feel like a fookin' eedjiot. Lado told everyone about Gonad, and how you've got a girlfriend in your head and, well, I'd *had* a bit of a ting for you.'

Robert only realised how true it was when he said it. 'I felt the same way Alice.'

'That's the ting Robert. You felt that way. Now you're getting married. It doesn't matter if it's some made up ting in your head. From what you've said, you can feel it, touch it, smell it. I knew there was some important ting in your past made you do this. I kind of hoped you would get what you needed fixed...done. But dis marryin' ting.'

'My flames gone out Robert, and that hurt all of a sudden in here.' She pointed vaguely to her heart and followed up with an unconvincing. 'I'll get over it soon enough.'

Robert sighed. He was hurting a real person for the sake of a program. 'I'm sorry Alice. Maybe we could hang out a bit. Catch some movies and I don't know, maybe go to dinner.'

'Some tings don't work in bits and pieces Robert. If we still have a job tomorrow, I'd like to sit somewhere else.' She wiped some moisture from her eyes angrily. 'I guess I got a bit fonder of you than was good for me.'

'Ever ridden on the back of a bike?' He said. 'Be nice if I could drop you home.'

She sighed suspiciously. 'You're the same like Lado. You're wanting to make sure I don't harm the fookin' Barbie's. Well you might as well visit them at the last.'

Robert was surprised how affected he was when she said, 'at the last.' He took a very long way round to her apartment. He only had one helmet and Alice refused to wear it. She pressed her head hard against his back. It was dark when they arrived at her apartment where a menacing shape stood in front of her door. As they got closer, they could see it was a full-size Crash Test Dummy, hastily painted black with a note pinned to its chest.

'I am the Slutty Barbie Guardian. Nobody is going to harm no Barbie's when I'm around and I ain't going nowhere.'

'You can come out Lado. The Barbie's are safe. It was a heat of da moment ting.'

Lado came out of the dark shadow of a recessed door two apartments down the hall. 'That's a relief woman. My next line of defence was to break in a steal 'em.' He held up some cans. 'I brought some beers.'

'Perfect.' Said Alice. 'I ran out.'

The array of Barbies was truly impressive. The loungeroom was largely occupied by the sewing machines, working tables, fabrics of many kinds, usually black, red or pink, but a range of fluoro colours, as well as glues and dyes. There were boxes of yet to be sluttified Barbies which she bought online as cheaply as possible, provided they were in fair condition. Those slightly damaged ended up as a Slutty Street Fighter Barbie or some other profession that took a battering or a lot of makeup.

Once they had a beer in hand, Lado expressed his concern. 'We've got a girl who dressed sad, but was happy, and now she's sad. We got a guy here who's got a woman inserted in the back of his head, when women are supposed to *be* inserted somewhere else. And here I am, only ever interested in hacking organisations or playing games, taking an interest in actual people. Things are all messed up. And although I don't like to say it, it's Gonad that started all this off.'

'He did bring the whole thing to your attention.'

'Good old Gonad.' Alice said wistfully.

He had an evening meeting with Kobe who always seemed to be available.

'A wedding?' Said the old man.

'Yes. I know it's kind of sudden, or, early on in the process... um... I mean the relationship.' Robert was starting to hear himself and the whole thing sounded ridiculous.

'Not at all. I could see that you and Kirsten were something special and so I'm not surprised Robert.' Said Kobe. 'I'd be delighted to help. I'm the only other person Kirsten has ever seen who has responded to her directly. If you wanted,

I could officiate and we can build a special chapel theme. And of course, have a beautiful dress for Kirsten.'

Robert never failed to be surprised at extent of Kobe's enthusiasm. 'That sounds magnificent Kobe, but I couldn't afford any of that. I was hoping to come into your building and maybe have a ceremony in the Garden.

'Even better, we can create a small Chapel inside the middle of the garden, but a theme only. Don't worry about the cost. This is our first wedding, so I'll convince them it will be complimentary. It's going to get used again, many times. I'm sure of it. Give me a date and I'll make it all ready for you.'

Now if he talked about this inner world with Alice and Lado, he would become uncomfortable. He was determined that once he'd achieved what he'd originally intended, it would be over. He could only imagine Kobe's disappointment. However, in his history of interactions with the man, he knew it would quickly revert to understanding. The wedding, strange as it was, might be the culmination he was looking for.

Ultimately in real life, this is what he would have liked. And believed he might have shared with the real Kirsten had she not pulled him in with one hand and pushed him away with the other. She'd given him sweetness and then hurt. Made him feel good about himself and then ashamed of himself, even as he came back for more.

Now, she was the person he'd spent some of the best days of his life with. The conversation, the meals, their little adventures out on the bike. The domestic life and lovemaking, all equally pleasant. And almost above everything was that engaging, beautiful, expressive smile that felt like a gift, every time he saw it.

At work it was not so pleasant. When the three of them were each scheduled to meet with Gil on the Thursday of that week, they didn't have to guess what was coming. Gil fired people on a Thursday. He said this meant they could get another job on Friday and not spoil their weekend.

They were mercifully short conversations. 'Sorry Robert. You're sharp, very sharp, but you're unreliable and that's a bad example.' He then extended his hand which everyone shook in the spirit of an amicable parting of the ways. A lot of people didn't like Gil, but ultimately, he was a company man and he never, ever made things personal, and most people respected that.

Lado and Robert had almost packed up their things into the boxes Gil always kept in his office for the purpose. When Alice came down, she didn't have a box. Lado and Robert both looked up with the same hopeful looks on their faces.

'First and last warning. Lettin' meeself get mixed up with bad influencers.'

'And that from the queen of Slutty Barbies.' Said Lado.

'And I know Slutty Flamethrower Barbie has found her way into your box Lado. You only had to ask. Here you can have Slutty Mexican Wrestler Barbie to keep her company.'

'Can I keep Slutty Storm Trooper Barbie.' Asked Robert.

'Sure. You'll both have to accept their going to end up with twin sisters.'

There were the hugs and the promises to stay in touch that, they knew, for one reason or another, they probably wouldn't keep.

Robert laughed on the way home that night as to whether he should tell his pretend soon to be wife that he lost his job today. And that he may not be able to afford to keep her. In a very real sense.

By the time he was off his bike there was a message from Kobe on his phone. He called back. The enthusiasm was there but it was a little forced. 'Robert. I've had some news which will cause me to be away for a short time. Nothing serious, only a small personal matter.' His voice then rose with the more familiar excitement. 'But everything could be ready for Saturday if we can bring it forward. We've done a beautiful little Chapel and a suit for you and the most wonderful dress for Kirsten.'

He continued. 'I could come back to the apartment with you if you like, and we'll have a very small reception there. I'll have caterers prepare things while you're here.'

'It's too much Kobe. You're spending too much of your time on me. Saturday would be fine but a wedding in the Chapel if it's already built that would be great.'

'Wonderful. 1pm Saturday. Text me where your key is hidden so the caterers can set things out where you live And he was gone. Robert didn't really want Kobe to see where he and Kirsten lived. He only ever saw it with the theme. Even if Kirsten was switched off. Which was rare.

When he turned Kirsten on, she was already in full wedding mode even before he told her it was only a few days away. She was full of an almost girlish excitement, which he imagined was only to be expected because it was so real to her, and it was what they both felt they had always wanted. He thought it strange that she could behave this way without any female friends to share it with.

He had been careful to empty and tear up the box he'd brought home before he'd called her into presence in case there were any awkward questions about all his stuff coming home. He'd left the Barbie on the benchtop. They were drinking wine as Robert made dinner. Kirsten saw it and picked it up.

'What's this.' She held it by a foot with an expression of mild distaste on her face.

'Oh, a friend at work makes them. It was...her last day, so she gave some people one, sort of a going away thing.'

'A jacked-up Barbie. Pretty sleezy.' She dropped it back on the counter. The way it landed caused the doll to slip off onto the kitchen floor. Robert felt his first moment of irritation since meeting Kirsten in the garden. He took the doll and put it on the real mantlepiece that existed above the unreal fire so it could be seen from the living room and kitchen. But Robert knew something was wrong.

The moment passed. They laughed, the night was sweet and Kirsten was switched off all the next day while Robert desperately tried to line-up some work, even as a temp to pay the rent both on the apartment and Kirsten, the latter double the former. He had a good CV except for the unreliable tag he had now righty earned with Gil, who was the first person prospective employers were going to call.

Some temp work might short circuit that problem for a while. He lost count of the calls he made. His ear was getting hot and sore from the pressure. Eventually he got some work in a place, doing a job he'd have laughed about yesterday. It was a couple of weeks on average pay. In the few hours he had left he got some applications together for jobs he really wanted that required formal CV's and responses to questions on specific competencies.

Now that he thought about it, he hadn't been trying very hard to get a better job. He'd been rolling in neutral as he so often did once he got to a point where he was comfortable.

On Friday, he turned Kirsten on early after he'd been out to get some nice wine, cheese and chocolates. He noticed he was gaining weight because he was the only one physically eating any of it. He wanted to make the night before their wedding special and she was so euphoric it was hard not to go along for the ride. And this Kirsten, even with an amazing capacity to be delighted and affectionate, was still the one he knew. She was authentic. It's only that things didn't swing into an orchestrated nastiness occasionally that had left him completely off balance.

There was plenty of bizarre thoughts and feelings. The guests he couldn't invite to his wedding because they wouldn't be able to see the bride. The fact his fiancé came with him into a pretend Chapel as an implant in the back of his head. The guy officiating, a very pleasant man, was still in a way, a car salesman of the future. He picked up his suit and some flowers that he wanted to be his personal physical contributions to the insubstantial theme flowers that someone will have come up with, on a computer advised by Kobe no doubt. It probably wasn't the occasion, but Robert was going to mention to Kobe that he would love to work for Winston Technologies, and if he could tell him where to send a CV.

When he arrived and saw Kobe his immediate reaction was to help him to a chair. He looked awful. He came to Robert with the same handshake, but it was weaker, and his eyes were flat. Robert was almost angry. 'Kobe. What are you doing? This is crazy, you need to rest. Shit, you look like you need to go into hospital.'

'I'm fine, I'm fine. Sorry to concern you Robert. I failed to have my medications which I take every morning. They will kick in soon and I will be as I always am. Come and see the Chapel, I'll sit with you in there.'

The Chapel was stunning. Simple. Beautiful. There were flowers but they were tasteful and not excessive. They sat looking for a time. They were sitting on real benches in an empty space in the garden. This theme, only a projection of the insides of a beautiful Chapel, was visible to implant wearers and their Companion or those with controllers in the case of Kobe.

Kobe squeezed Roberts leg very firmly. 'Sorry to have been a cause for concern Robert.' He looked better. 'I have these turns. There is a very simple remedy and I go for a minor procedure next week. Please don't be troubled.'

When it was time, in a beautiful dress, with music she'd picked out knowing Robert also liked it, Kirstin was walking with a simulacrum of the flowers he'd picked out for her. The sheer joy Kirsten was feeling was lifting Robert and Kobe with her, into a kind of intoxication. She didn't need or notice the lack of friends, family, organ players, best men or bride's maids. Kobe officiated classic vows, which is what Kirsten said she wanted. To her this was the most perfect wedding she could ever have imagined, and that infectious pleasure seemed to fill the chapel's space that wasn't there.

Arriving back in the apartment to a small well catered reception only an instant after leaving the Chapel was also completely normal for her. Kobe was starting to tire as they listened to animated stories of Kirsten's relatives and their wedding mishaps. It seems that Kirsten had a backlog of stories on any subject that was engaging and interesting.

Robert went over to look though the albums. He collected vinyl. He would stream music, however if he had it on vinyl, he'd play it on the first record player he bought and still owned.

As he looked through the box, Kirsten turned to Kobe and said quietly. 'Get married?' She smiled in a familiar way. 'I thought; why not?'

Kobe smiled. He pointed with his eyes. 'Look. He wants you to dance with him.' Robert was starting to sway to an old favourite and holding out a hand. 'Only good things Kirsten. Everything good.' Said the old man in a whisper.

He slipped out while the two were dancing.

Robert hated it. Hated it. It was shitty work for shitty pay, and he felt like an idiot for losing a job that could have helped him at least make ends meet. Barely. He was trying to formulate approaches to crawl back to Gil that might work, and which he himself could stomach.

He was in the apartment. He'd had a lousy day. It was the first time he wasn't planning to turn Kirsten on. He bought a bottle of Bourbon and felt like wallowing in front of the TV. As a single guy.

Then he got the call.

'Mr Casey, it's Darren Mills from Winston Technologies. Sorry to call out of hours, it's just we've been finding it hard to reach you.'

'No problem. I've had the phone off a bit. It's Robert. How can I help Darren?'

The tone of the man's voice had the universal tentative discomfort of debt recovery. 'We've noticed your final install payment is over a month past due, and we're not sure we've had the right address to send our letter to?'

'Yeah the monthly instalments a week over. I should have let you know. I'll have it to you by the end of this week.' He lied. 'Sorry about that.'

'Yes, we noticed that the monthly was overdue also Robert. And naturally we'll be glad to receive that in due course. It's the Install payment my calls with reference to. You'll note in your Contract that there is a one-off payment four months after you're install and you're fully satisfied. That's nearly a month ago Robert. Unless there's been a problem in accounting our end. Let me know if it's been sent and I'll chase our people.'

Robert was now pulling open drawers full of paperwork he wished would go away. Bills and notices and contracts and final demands. He wasn't going to find it. He hadn't read past the up-front price and the monthly payments.

He'd ask. 'What do I owe Darren.'

The tone of Darren's voice carried concern that Robert didn't know how much he owed. 'A hundred thousand dollars Robert.'

This hung in the air for a while.

'Robert. Can I be honest with you?'

'Sure.'

'If I have to call anyone in arears on this Project it's some snafu thing you know, an accountancy thing. They pull a hundred grand out of their pocked like it's for a box of wine the guy really likes. I hope I'm not speaking out of school, but you sound more like a guy like me. Someone comes and says you owe a hundred grand, it's like, what have I got myself into here.'

'You nailed it Darren.'

'Robert this phase of the Project was supposed to be vetted, big spenders only, so I don't know what happened. I'll talk to a few people. I don't know, maybe a payment plan. But Robert, this is a good company, there are good people here and I'm sure we'll work something out.'

'You've been honest with me Darren. What happens if I can't pay, even the monthly, even if I can't do that.'

'Let's not go there right now Robert. Let's work together on this.'

'C'mon Darren. So I know. What's the procedure?'

'Robert. WT sold you a product. They recover the product. Pretty straightforward.'

'I come in and the implant gets taken out?'

'Yeah, although that's not necessary. The implant is like, individual, can't be reused. The product can be sucked out from a console in the office. It's all wireless.'

There was a long pause.

'Robert. I realised I used the phrase 'the product' and how we...would recover it That's internal language we use. You are sharing your life with a Companion and I, well, I really fucked up there, I'm sorry. Robert, that's not going to. happen.'

'Darren. You've been straight with me. It's what I wanted.' He laughed. 'Put your supervisor on and I'll tell him what a great guy you are if you're worried.'

It was Darren's turn to laugh. 'No, it's all cool. I'll talk to some people. We'll see what we can do. Do your best with the monthly, it would be good to keep those up. This is a good company Robert. I don't know anyone working here that would say otherwise. We'll work together on this.'

'Sure. Thanks Darren.'

Robert sat staring blankly at the wall for an hour. He'd always known making the monthly payments was over ambitious. Now with no secure work and another hundred grand on top, he'd be on the street within a month.

He made a call to the only person he thought might be able to do what he needed.

'Hack the software out of the implant and transfer it to a chip in your brain?' Robert could hear Lado's excitement building. 'Why the fuck not man?' There was a note of caution though. 'I have tools which might be described as 'access facilitation devices' which allow me to work on very small hardware. There must be a maintenance port. It would be tiny, and have a specialised seal, probably magnetic, but there has to be one for me to crack it.'

'I'm starting to have a little more hope now Lado.' Robert could see a chance of keeping Kirsten but giving back the insert.

'Would it be a wild ass guess for me to say you can't keep paying for this thing, and you need the implant itself returned to sender but you keep the merchandise.'

'I know it sounds low, but that's about it.' Robert felt a twinge for Kobe.

'These big companies spend more on a fancy lunch for their executives than we'd make in a year. Don't worry about 'em. But you're going to need to get someone to cut your head open and slide that thing out. Skin and blood and bones is shit I don't do. I know a friend of a friend who could do it. Very good surgeon. Used to be. Does freelance stuff I'm told.'

'A freelance surgeon.'

'I have not met the man myself. I know his sister. She says he's good. When he's sober. I don't think you can be too choosy, and he comes highly recommended.'

Lado arrived at his apartment with Alice in tow. 'Good to see you.' Said Robert. This was directed at Alice with Lado left bereft of a greeting.

'Don't worry. I'm not here to try to talk you out of it. Lado knew my brother was a surgeon because I told him what a useless bastard he was. I always come along when my brother's involved in anything to apologise before he gets here and then apologies for him after he's left. And sometimes during the time he's here as well.' She sighed. Glad to get her participation clarified. 'And sometimes a second visit to say sorry if things go really bad.'

'Alice, he's going to cut a hole in my head.'

'Oh don't worry about that part. He's a grand surgeon. Or so I've be led to believe. By him, now I tink about it. He's unreliable and likes the drink. Doesn't affect his doctorin'. He was also the one told me dat now I tink on it.' Alice realised nothing she said had helped in giving Robert any confidence about her brother.

Lado was going to do his part via the maintenance port first.

'The Maestro is about the perform so Alice if you will please step aside.' Lado had rolled up a towel and formed it into a circle for Robert to put his face into. 'Lado' Said Robert in a very serious tone. 'You're not allowed to make a copy.'

He sounded offended. 'You think that I... you believed that such a thing would be something I would contemplate' There was a long pause 'Okay yes, I was going to make a copy. I was going to try to make adjustments. Black woman. Bigger ass. More sass. You would hardly pick them for sisters.'

'No.'

'Okay. But you're in what's known as the honeymoon period. If I was doing this two years from now, you'd be saying, 'Lado, take as many copies of that bitch as you want.'

'I don't doubt that Lado. But no copies now.'

'It was more a backup for your own good I'd keep safe for you. But no back up. Now this is all academic if they haven't left a little tiny maintenance portal which if I can't find I can't move this lady across.'

He was silent for a long time looking at a screen which magnified Robert's skin. Alice drew up a chair and so was at eye level. 'I said I wasn't going to try to talk you out of it, but I am anyway.' She paused and looked into his eyes. 'Have you had what you always wanted. Made your wish come true? Aren't tings now goin' to be much the same, but ultimately you'll be alone most of the time one way or another, and you might lose some of yourself.'

Robert had his head sideways on the towel ring. 'Every time I talk to you about this Alice, I agree completely. And then it gets so, unreal, when it's happening. I do lose perspective. But I've started to realise exactly what you're saying. As good as things have been, and although things will mature, there's really nothing more. But I'm not quite ready and I don't want the reason to be purely because I can't afford it, which would leave me wondering.'

Alice took his hand. 'Okay. I'm worried she's going to be somehow set free in your mind.'

Lado joined in. 'There is no fear of that. I've found the little portal I need, and I have to move what's inside the golden horseshoe into to a little tiny chip that's about a hundred times more storage space then what you've got now.' Lado told them there was a connector the size of a thread into the chip for maintenance.

Robert looked at Alice. 'Lado, can you put in a kill switch.'

'A kill switch?'

'Yeah.' Robert was uncomfortable all of a sudden. 'Maybe I should have said a delete button. Just in case.'

'No problem. I'll adjust this chip I'm callin' the Golden Cage while we wait for the doctor. She has to go in and out of it based on the whole presence absence thing you got goin' on. It's only one long alphanumeric code for on and one for off. She's stored in a portion of your brain. Ain't no golden horseshoe going to hold the complicated stuff that you two been up to. This chip has got the same codes that only you can use. Once their gone though, She's gone. It's all wireless signal because it would be unbelievably complicated to connect into nerves and shit. You'll need to come to me personally for the delete because it needs these gadgets. Now. When you delete her, surely I can have a copy?'

'No, no, no.' Robert's anxieties were coming out as frustration.

Lado ignored this and explained. 'All ready. Alice's brother takes out a Golden Horseshoe out and puts in the Golden Cage.'

The door opened. A loud and confident voice said. 'You may all breathe a sigh of relief, the doctor... is in the house.'

'Hello Brendan.' She said this a fine balance of affection and the anticipation of embarrassment.

'And hello Elicia. That's right folks. Alice is not her real name. She tells people a witch gave her that name in a dream, but I think it's a secret desire to be like Alice in Wonderland.'

'You always have to say that.'

'Any time I can.' He gave his sister a big hug and a kiss which she returned with a smile. 'And what do we have here. A man wishing to remove a woman he's inserted. A common enough problem. Usually involving superglue. In your case more technological I believe. If you'll bend over the kitchen table, I'll get out my rubber glove.'

'I heard all these jokes when I had it put in in the first place, so maybe we could skip that part.' Robert was going to have delicate work done near his brain and he wished people would take it seriously. Or at least make good jokes.

'It's hard to come up with original material these days.' Robert felt a heavy bag being placed beside him, it was opened and there was a good deal of rummaging. There was then an extended rubbing on his head of what smelled like alcohol and then a loud deep breath in and a loud breath out and a serious. 'Okay. I'm going to need a little suction here, retractors, more suction please and morphine, quickly, that's for me. We're losing him people. We're losing him. For the love of got where's the machine that goes Bing and I need that fucking morphine stat.'

Alice was embarrassed. 'He hasn't got his scalpel out yet Robert.'

Robert felt the rubbing on his head again. 'Okay patient. Put you face in the towel ring and don't move a muscle. Alice, I want you to hold his head.' Brendan breathed in and out loudly again. 'Okay, all jokes aside people. Alice you must hold his head absolutes still. I'm working near the brain stem and if you move his head, this man, which you are clearly conflicted about, will become a vegetable. Hold still now please. Extra still.'

They sat that way for over a minute. Finally, they heard a metal object fall into a metal tray. Brendan started laughing. 'Ha. Super still. I got it out as soon as I'd made the incision. Could have taken that silly thing out while I was dancing a jig. I do admit, inserting the chip was a bit harder but I think I got it right.'

'Brendon you're a fooking cont.'

'My work here is done.' Said Brendon after some stitching was competed.

Robert took out the wad of cash he'd prepared but then counted some more into it. 'Thanks. Here's a bit extra for the floor show.' Now that the implant was out, Robert had regained his sense of humour.

Brendan smiled. It was infectious. 'And thank you very much. If anyone you know needs some surgery but can't afford a hospital, or if they're on the run, call me.' He gave his sister a big hug and said he'd see her at their weekly dinner catch up.

'Don't ever call me if you want to be removed from Alice though.' He said this before closing the door.

'That's not funny Brendon.' She said this irritably.

'When do you let her out so we could see if it worked okay.' Said Alice. Feigning interest.

'I'll do that at home, or she'll wonder who the hell you guys are.'

Robert could see the implant disappearing into Lado's pocket. He held out his hand. 'Always good to have a backup.' He smiled, knowing it was getting old, but still persisting, because he really did think a backup was a good idea. Though he also knew he wouldn't be able to help himself. Robert took the device and bent it until it ruptured. 'This is what I'm going to send back to them and apologise for, but also stop paying for.'

Robert said he was going to 'ween' himself off Kirsten soon and they could get together and have a celebratory dinner as he returned to living among real people. This message was pitched at Alice, because Lado could only say, in a friendly way. 'Why not ween yourself off the bitch yesterday and save all this bullshit.'

A good question thought Robert.

When he turned Kirsten on in the apartment she leaped up with arms and legs wrapped around him. 'I can't believe we're actually married!'

She was so excited and happy he'd forgotten the stress that owing a hundred thousand dollars and having to transfer out of the implant had caused. They had a nice meal, listened to some music and decided to go to bed early. Once they were settled under the covers she turned to him and said. 'And you know what I want for a wedding present.'

She pushed his shoulders down and pulled his face hard to her crotch. There was a great deal of moaning and crying out, which, to Robert, seemed to go on for an inordinately long time. Her whole body spasmed and then trembled. He came up to see her smiling across at him.

She touched his nose in the playful way. 'Now this is what living with equality feels like. I'm shattered. Straight to sleep for me. See you tomorrow.'

It was Monday night. In keeping with his decision to ween himself off what he now reminded himself was a computer program, he planned call her into presence only every second night. He started his temping job Tuesday. And had a boy's night with some bourbon and things he wanted to watch. The next day he turned her on again and she appeared in work clothes coming in as if closing the door behind herself. Kirsten had been imbued with an almost inexhaustible array on conversational topics. If you wanted to talk Shakespeare, she had a good knowledge of several plays, his biography and views on what many of the plays and sonnets meant. This was true of most music genres, literature and film. Robert assumed this adjunct to the original Kirsten had been put there without his request because spending so much time with one individual ultimately led to conversations running dry unless the Companion had a broad base to draw upon.

It's also only natural for people to talk about their day at work and this is what often occurred. Robert talked about the last place he worked as if he was still there, including talking about Lado, Alice and Gil.

Kirsten had not had a good day at work. After she went into some detail regarding the deficiencies of specific co-workers, she widened the focus on how poorly run the organisation was.

The CEO was a letch and it was only via a positive response to his attentions any female was going to get any meaningful advancement.

Robert could sense there was a whole lot more on the way and was trying to think how he might introduce some Shakespeare into the conversation when she saw the CV's and applications on the counter.

'Looking for a better job. A good plan. I'm thinking the same thing myself. It's okay here, but now where married we can do better than this.' She waved her hand around at the apartment as if it was the shitty apartment it actually was. 'Time for us to step up Bobby. I'll start looking around tomorrow. But tonight, I'll help you with these applications so we can get things rolling. This stuff was never your strength as I recall.'

Robert was unsure what to do when his virtual wife wanted to help you with job applications. And because she thinks he's such a loser, he'll fuck it up. It wasn't a scenario he'd anticipated.

It was a frustrating few hours because she insisted on helping right until it was a finished product. It was far superior to what he could have produced. He found this both irritating and a little humiliating.

She got up and stretched. 'All of these applications make me so horny.' She said sarcastically. She reached her hand under his T-shirt and drew her sharp nails down is flesh. 'It's all about you tonight babe.' She said this as she headed for the door. Robert found himself being a little bit frightened as to what that might entail. As he was passing the mantlepiece he noticed Slutty Storm Trooper Barbie was missing.

'What happened to the Barbie doll that was up there?

'Oh, that thing. It was creeping me out. I threw it away.'

All of this had given Robert a great deal to think about. He turned Kirsten off. For the last time.

Lado thought it was hilarious when Robert called him. 'If there is one thing that's a kill switch, it's marriage. Three days in and you have had enough of that nagging bitch already. I would have giving you at least a week but as they say; Love is blind but marriage is a real eye opener. I'm in Vegas with some friends. We're pretty sure we have a killer system worked out for Baccarat. I'll be home in a few days and we can do the goodbye kiss. I'll let you know when I get in.'

'Look forward to it Lado. And thanks.'

He tried to resist the urge, but he called Alice on Saturday. 'I've made up my mind. I wanted to let you know.' He laughed. 'Only took a few days of marriage which is maybe not a good sign.'

'Yes.' Responded Alice thoughtfully. 'Maybe now you're married she's wanting to see the back of you. It's a concern, but I'm certainly not planning matrimony meeself anytime soon.'

'Lado's in Vegas for a few days, so once he's back we might take in a movie or something. Not as something bits and pieces though.' He said quietly.

'If you're sure she's never coming back maybe we could go out for a trip this afternoon. It's a beautiful days and Slutty Barbies are more of a rainy-day occupation. You said you found some nice out of the way places because you had to. How about a ride out to one of them. Like friends getting to know each other better of course.'

Robert took her to what had been his favourite place in the search for seclusion. It was a small cove, with rock cliff plunging into the ocean either side. A rocky trail led to a small patch of beach backed by the hardy grass that grows on dunes. The large breakers pounded on a reef not far from the shore and emerged eventually as fast hissing foam.

The brown sand was soft, and the cove was sheltered from the wind which was making the grass sway higher up. They talked for a while and one thing led to another which they were both pleased about. They fell asleep on a blankety and woke up in the late afternoon. Robert said. 'What happened to friends getting to know each other better?'

Alice sat up and hugged her legs. 'And now we do.' She smiled. But the smile evaporated when she saw the footprints coming straight of the water and standing in front of them in the wet sand. They were women's footprints. Pressed neatly into the sand. They were positioned facing them and didn't turn aside right or left to leave. It was as if the owner of the prints was winched away to a helicopter or simply vanished.

'I'd like to go home now Robert.'

Robert was looking up and down the short beach for an explanation to give to Alice.

'I'd like to go Robert. Everybody taut I was jokin' about Gonad. It's been a lovely day Robert. And I'll see you again once you've... been to the doctor for your check-up.'

They were riding back to the city. Alice had her arms around his waist. She pressed the side of her head hard into his back which felt nice as he rode along. They pulled up opposite her building.

She waved as she was waiting for a break in the traffic. As she stepped forward to look around a truck unloading beside her. Suddenly she tripped and fell into the path of an oncoming car. Fortunately, between the car swerving and the truck driver, dragging her out of the way, she was unhurt. Though she had the disconcerting experience of a tyre pass an inche from her head.

Robert dropped his bike and ran to her. 'Jesus Christ are you okay.' She had finished hugging the driver and thanking him for saving her life.

'I tripped over nothin' Robert. I don't know what's the distance this ting can make stuff happen. But you'll understand if I want to keep mine for a while.'

'Sure. I understand. I'm sorry.' He smiled in a lame apology. 'I'm leaving right now. Stand still till then.' He shrugged with another apologetic smile, got on his bike and roared off. She walked to the back of the truck to cross.

He thought that drinking heavily, something he rarely did, would be a good response to all of this. He had cracked open a fresh bottle of bourbon and was getting some ice. As he shut the refrigerator door Kirsten was there, standing behind it.

'Married a few days and you're boning some Irish tart. What kind of a fucking husband are you Robert?'

Robert made the usual mental signal for her to disappear and she vanished. Had he turned her on by accident? But when he turned to the lounge with a fully charged glass in hand about to sit down, she as standing six inches in front of him. He was so startled he nearly dropped the glass.

'You can't turn me on and off any more Robert. Those days are over.'

His mind was spinning and yet having Kirsten present was not unusual. He said nothing for a long time.

'What's the problem?' She said.

'Okay...to use an old cliche, you're not the woman I married.' Robert could imagine what was coming.

'I see. You mean the subservient one. The one you would turn on like a TV for some entertainment, share a dance with, listen to your endless fucking moaning about things you intend to do and do nothing about. Oh yes, and whenever you wanted one, a fuck toy.'

Robert was sad, angry, disappointed all at once but mainly he felt a sense of loss. 'If that's all the last few months were to you, I'm sorry. Call me a romantic, but the last few months I spent with you were the best of my life, and you can shoot me down or belittle me as much as you want. I want there to be a clear line Kirsten. As far as I'm concerned what we had was a shared experience and a good one. Obviously, that's all over now. But if shitting on something good makes you feel better about yourself that's your problem.'

She slumped down on the couch next to him and seemed to think for quite a while. 'Okay. The last few months were good and although I might bitch about some details, all of the attention and yes, the sweetness and affection, were something I'd always craved from you. You can understand I got a little wound up to see you banging someone on what you called 'our special beach' a few days after we got married.'

Robert felt that if Kirsten had been a person, she'd have a very good point. But she'd been marketed as a 'Companion' and now he wondered what that really meant. A twenty-four seven Companion was something he hadn't bargained for.

She sighed. 'This is going to take a bit of getting used to. But we need to get out of this shitty apartment. It's depressing. None of your stupid themes work on me anymore and the level of cleanliness is, let's say there's room for improvement.'

'You clean up.' Said Robert, surprised he was normalising bickering with a projection from his mind.

'Most amusing. How about you clean up this shithole and I'll help you get a better job, maybe even one which will allow us to engage a cleaner.'

'I've had enough. I'm going to bed.' During this short exchange, had polished off two large tumblers of Bourbon while Kirsten appeared to be drinking wine.

'Can shower and clean yourself thoroughly before coming to bed.' She was matter of fact.

'I'm going to sleep in the spare room.' Kicked out if his own bed now by a projection in his mind.

'You're loss. You know how horny I get after an argument.'

'I've been spending time with someone who I like and who likes me, so I'm fine thank you. And I'd appreciate it if you would refrain from trying to kill my friends.'

'It was a gentle push. I think that girl's clumsy by nature. Certainly, what I saw on the beach was... clunky I supposed you'd call it.'

'Just shut the fuck up and leave me alone.'

'Looks like we're a real married couple now.'

Robert rounded on her. 'I'm real Kirsten. You're not. And you know it. That's why you've suddenly turned into such a bitch, because you know you're only a projection. An unbelievably detailed projection, but that's what you are Kirsten. If you decide to get all twisted about it, fine. But remember that's your choice.'

Robert tried to get off to sleep and screen out the sound of loud crying and sobbing. This was the Kirsten he was familiar with. But he was older now.

She was in the kitchen before he was up. 'I would have made you eggs and bacon but, you know, not quite there yet with heavy duty kinetics. I can get rid of trashy little toys though.'

Oh God. Thought Robert. It hadn't been a nightmare last night.

'Because I don't need to sleep, I did spend all night on the internet getting a much better handle on the company that you're going to have an interview with.'

Robert put the kettle on for coffee, poured himself a bowl of cereal, and tried to tune Kirsten out. He was reasonably successful for a time and was finishing the coffee when he heard. 'We'll need to stop on the way and get a tie that actually goes with what I assume is the only suit you have.'

'I have enough ties.'

'Robert, darling. One tie is not enough ties. Listen, you hate me now. I've been a total bitch. But I've had a lot to process also. Let's work on this one as a team. Get this job, then I'll figure out the range that I can be away from you so we're not under each other's feet all the time. As you said, heartlessly, I know what I am now, so I can roam around stores or go to see shows or whatever if you're a certain distance away. I know people can't see me. I kind of like it. But in my review of available jobs you're qualified for, this is the best one, so let's make it happen *together*.'

'Okay.' Said Robert. Trying join in the spirit of at least temporary reconciliation.

On the way to the interview they stopped at a menswear store. All the way there Kirsten had held Robert tightly around the waist with the side of her head pressed to his back.

'Don't do that.'

'Do what.'

'You know what I mean. She does that, and I like it. You've always been riding with me with your head up so keep doing that.'

'Okay. Just trying to make you happy. Are you planning to marry her to? Bigamy's illegal you know.'

They bought a tie, which irritatingly, was a much better match to his suit. Within a minute Kirsten had the side of her head squeezed up tight on Robert's now very angry back.

They pulled up in the carpark and Robert stripped of his leathers while Kirsten unzipped and folded up her very stylish but insubstantial leathers, and put them in the bike's slim pannikins. She was dressed in high end, but slightly provocative corporate wear.

Robert found the reception for the Manager who would be interviewing him. Brian Coates had a forty percent stake in the business with a silent partner and began to explain what he was looking for.

'Fuck me Boddy.' This was whispered in one ear. And then the other. 'Now.' A hand invisible to Mr Coates but completely substantial to Robert, slipped down the front of his pants. 'Let's do it right now. On his desk.' Her hand kept on exploring. She was in front of him blocking his view of Coates who was finishing his introduction and moving into some questions.

Kirsten was now dressed in a red and white leather nurse's uniform. 'Come on Bobby. Let's do it now. And I mean like Bam, Bam, Bam.'

Robert was trying to look around Kirsten so that he could maintain eye contact with Coates, who also felt compelled to lean slightly in a kind of eye contact sympathy with the interviewee.

Kirsten's voice was seductive. 'Of course! What you really want is this. Instantly she was dressed as the Kirsten of the final year of Highschool. 'Do you want me to take it all off. Nice and slow.' She began doing this between the two men.

Robert was trying to answer the second introductory question about his background and capabilities.

Now Kirsten came and sat on his lap facing him. Her hand disappeared down his pants again. 'Or maybe you want to feel me up Bobby. I'm ready.'

Robert was now trying to answer questions which were of a more technical nature to demonstrate his capabilities.

'You want me to bark like a dog. Is that it Bobby? That's what you really want. You want me to bark like a dog. You've always wanted that Bobby.' Her hand now had something firm to hold on to.

'I don't want you to bark like a dog!' Robert had said this out loud before he could stop himself, which was immediately followed by wicked triumphant laughter from Kirsten.

Coates was bemused and smiled. 'Okay son, that's just as well. It wasn't something I was planning to do this early in the day.' He smiled good naturedly. Looked below Robert's belt, smiled again and said. 'Perhaps we can pick this up once you've been to the restroom.'

'I appreciate your time sir.' Robert went into the restrooms and splashed water onto his face. Kirsten appeared next to him. 'I think it's going well so far.'

'Well!' Robert was about to raise his voice, but he didn't want to be caught yelling at no one.

She smiled, sadly. 'Except for your little erection. Poor little thing.' She said this as if she was taking about a puppy who's foot was hurt. 'Look how sad and lonely it is. Hey little fella. You okay?' She pulled out half a dozen tissues from the dispenser. 'Don't take too long.'

He stalked out of the restroom planning to leave the building. As he passed Reception on the ground floor the man called out. 'Mister... Casey. Mr Coates would like to finish the interview.'

Robert walked back to the room and simply said. 'I apologise for what happened earlier Mr Coates, I'll be perfectly straight with you. I have delusions in which a former girlfriend, well were married now, but anyway, I have these delusions, they are very real to me and on this occasion it has messed up my ability to participate in a simple interview. I apologies for wasting your time.'

Coates was fascinated. 'Did you say she was your girlfriend as a delusion but now you're married.'

Why did I have to mention that? Thought Robert. As Kirsten sat on Coats's desk dressed in crisp corporate wear smiling with encouragement.

Robert sighed. What did it matter? 'Yep, a few days ago, we got married.'

'Is she here now.' Coates seemed to have lost all interest in the purpose of the meeting.

Robert couldn't believe he was having this conversation. 'She's on your desk sir, she was dressed in corporate attire but she's now dressed as a cheerleader from our Highschool pretending to be a dog, wagging her tail and barking.'

'Mr...Casey, may I call you Robert. This is the Goddamdist most interesting interview for a position I've had. But what matters ultimately to me is the capacity to be productive. And there are a few types of productivity. Most of those people out in cubicle land are good solid producers. They clock on, they clock off, and they've done what's required. Then there's another class of productivity. The people who fix problems I didn't know I had. They find things I didn't know I wanted. A few successes in this strategic space can keep my business ahead of the competition.'

'These people work to a different set of rules, they need to turn up to work a day or two a week. But everyone knows they're product development, and what they do and where they do it is their business.'

'I run these interviews to replace the average employee but I'm always looking out for the brilliant one. I'm going to write down a problem here and I'd like to see your response. You've got five minutes and you can't use any devices to assist you.'

Immediately Kirsten was sitting beside him, all businesslike. Occasionally she would say 'There.' To point out an error. Robert completed the problem in just over a minute. He was about to say something when Kirsten said. 'No Dummy. Weren't you listening? He wants the solution to the solution. The first solution causes a new problem. That's what we have to solve.'

Once he understood that, Robert went to work and had to tolerate a stream of 'Wrong.' And 'Back there, no there.' And on every occasion Kirsten was right. He would find later that as he slept, she sat at the computer absorbing everything on the subject she as studying at lighting speed.

Robert sat back and saw what they'd done. He was pretty sure Kirsten could not have done it on her own. He was mortified by the fact that neither could he.

He handed the paper to Coates. 'I could give you a cleaned up version in a minute or so.'

'No need Robert.' He turned the paper over and wrote a number on it and handed it back to him. 'This is how much you'll earn a month Robert, if you produce work like this.'

'You'll get the feedstock and we'll be looking for you to create value and opportunities. Now Robert the way it works around here is everyone is only as good as their last month. If people aren't performing to the standard everyone knows is reasonable for a month, for whatever reason, I expect them to come into my office and shake my hand and we part as friends.' Coates gave the impression he rarely needed to let someone know himself they're employment was terminated.

Robert stood up and extended his hand. 'Well sir, I'm sure I can deliver what's expected for many months to come.'

'We.' Said Kirstin.

'Glad to hear it. One question before I send you off to HR. Was your...ah...wife helping you with that problem.'

Robert knew by the way he'd been correcting errors and looking darkly at Kirsten that it was obvious. 'Yes she was.'

Coates couldn't help but laugh. 'We're going to set up a special cubicle for you so it can take two chairs comfortably.'

'Great.' Said Robert through gritted teeth

'Robert, my husband and I have dinner parties from time to time, either at our house or a friend's place. Would you mind at all if I told people about this interview? No personal details of course. It's the damndist thing that's happened to me in half a lifetime.'

'Be my guest Mr Coates.'

Robert was seething as they walked back towards the bike.

'That was a resounding success I thought. A monthly pay packet nearly double what I was hoping for. And what, ten times what you earned sitting next to that Irish trollop.

Though I'm going to need to put in some serious hours studying on the internet to keep us delivering. I think you should buy me lunch.' She gave him a tickle. 'Somewhere nice.'

He was wondering if it was his decision to be sitting in an alfresco dining place Kirstin had selected. They were at the furthest extent from other diners, Robert facing a garden so they could 'Chat without him looking like wierdo.'

He ordered a beer and the house pizza. As the man was writing the order down Kirsten said she'd like a dry white wine and the poached salmon.' But he had turned and left.

'What an asshole, ignoring my order like that.' She said as he walked away. The beer and pizza were placed in front of him while the salmon and wine materialised in front of her.

'I'm such a cheap date.'

'You're a fucking nightmare.'

'Oh, come on Robert. Your boss could see the funny side of it, I thought it was a laugh. You're the only on who's a stick in the mud with no sense of humour.' She leaned forward seductively. 'But I plan to make it all up to you.' She made a cat purring sound. 'I know deep down the dog barking thing is real. You only have to let me know what breed. Beagle. Schnauzer. *Irish* Wolfhound. I'll do the research. Let me know.'

'It was never a thing so don't bother.'

'Anyway, this salmon is undercooked I'm going to complain.' She laughed. 'Actually, I'm going to start walking around to see how far we can be away from each other. Hopefully it's a long way but a few hundred yards at least would be nice.'

He'd thought she'd gone and he relaxed a little as he worked though his second beer. But she snapped into a sudden presence next to him and was all tender sympathy. 'Let's try to get a little tiny smile on that glum face of yours.' She darted in for a commando kiss and vanished.

He almost didn't answer the call, not really feeling like talking to anyone. It was Darren from Winston Technologies.

'Robert. I need to speak with you about a few things. We didn't realise you were a Client of Mr Winston's and the rest of the Install Payment or any further monthlies...you don't need to worry...um...about those.'

Why didn't you call sooner. Thought Robert. 'That's great news Darren. I had been intending to call. I had an accident on my motorbike, I'm fine but the implant got damaged, and it had to be taken out. I was going to bring it in soon.' Then something occurred to him. 'Oh and...I've never met Mister Winston.'

Mr Winston's father was Japanese, but an anglophile. He changed his second name to Winston. Mr Kobe prefers the original family name.'

'Well, I wonder why...'

Darren cut in which seemed a little out of character based on the earlier dealings he'd had with him. 'Robert we can explain that when you're in here. It's essential that you come into WT as soon as possible. There have been some, issues, with the trial and it's important we have you complete check-up. Especially in cases when the implants have been...damaged and removed.'

By this time Kirsten was almost back at the table. Robert went quiet. This was a conversation he didn't want her to overhear. Looking at her satisfied smile, he knew she had not heard any of it from a distance.

She ignored the fact that he was on a call. 'I told the Chef to his face he couldn't cook for shit. She said encouragingly. 'When we move it'll need to have a lively café scene and maybe next to a theatre. Who's on the phone?'

'Can you speak freely Robert? They can't usually eavesdrop on the phone call.'

Robert said. 'I already told you the answer. No, and that's all there is to it.'

Darren sounded very concerned but convey the sense he was completely confident about what was happening.

'Try to be at home most evenings. We'll come to you.'

'Okay, Okay I'll do my best but I can't guarantee it....Yeah. See you later.'

'Didn't sound like a friend.'

'A friend that always wants something. I'm going to cut him loose.'

'Wow, you actually *have a pair* after all. Anyhow you might need to fuel up the bike, we're heading home.'

'Where else would be going.'

'I mean *home* Bobby. Where we grew up. There's something I want to show you.'

'Kirsten I'm pretty sure I don't want to see it. So go fuck yourself.'

'In spite of the fact that yes, I would do a much better job of *that* than you could ever do, we're going home Bobby. And you need to realise, when I want something, your own volition is rapidly weakening, so I'm going to get it. But do we need compulsion, and what else have you got going on most evenings – huh? Nothing. It's a trip down memory lane. Roaring down the road on your bike on a beautiful afternoon. Spending some time in the evening in the town where we grew up.'

If the idea came from anyone else he would probably think, spontaneous as it was, it was a good one. He'd be working hard to prove himself to the new employers soon enough so he might as well take the bike for a big run. Without agreeing or disagreeing he got on the bike. He felt Kirstein's head pressed tight against his back. 'Let's see what this fookin' ting can do.' She said in a ridiculous Irish accent.

It was a beautiful autumn afternoon. Robert came off the main interstates and went through some of the small towns with leaves turning in amber and starting to fall, preparing for winter.

It was fully dark in early evening when they arrived. He would have liked to have gone on a tour around to see what had changed. Then go to the Diner that had been frequented by people their age, but he found himself driving to a lookout twenty minutes out of town and pulling up out of sight of the car with a Bike parked a few dozen yards away.

'You've kept this same shitty bike since Highschool. I guess it was cool then Bobby. But now it's just ...sad really.'

He knew it was his Bike they were looking at. He vaguely remembered the car. 'What's this, I'm in your head?' Robert was getting confused.

'No dickhead. We're in your head, where else could we be? I've accessed some memories that I'd like you to see. As much of a full sensory experience as possible. That's why we came here.'

'If they're memories Kirsten, wouldn't I remember them?'

'Bobby, you wanted to play happy families with me, not because of the megabitch you cast me as. Kobe removed a gigantic slice of asshole out of *you* Bobby. After you left College you realised you'd already had what you'd always wanted. But I was so beaten and broken, so humiliated, shit on, I wouldn't take you back. Even if I would, every friend and relative I had would never let you near me again.'

'See the guy with the bike is in the passenger seat of the car. She got stood up by some other guy. And Bobby you're such a good shoulder to cry on. But it never seems to stop at crying. Kissing. Some heavy petting maybe. We were meeting at seven. But I got held back at the Diner I worked in. That was my best friend Ruth in that car Bobby. It's not much later that poor Kirsten arrives. You either don't hear me arrive or didn't care because it's five or so minutes that I have to watch you and Ruth kissing before you walk over. Once Ruth sees me, she backs out and roars off. It took a long time before she and I were friendly again. But it was never the same.'

'Of course, the Kirsten of that time was irremediably stupid. She takes you back a month later after weeks of your grovelling apologies and pathetic gifts of chocolate, flowers and cheap trinkets. Ring any bells?' Kirsten said. 'Remember me yelling and sobbing. You trying to explain you were trying to make Ruth feel better.'

Robert put his helmet on. He didn't need to bother if Kirsten was ready. He made a wide arc on the bike as he roared.

'The bell that's mainly ringing in my head is that I wish I'd never met the real Kirsten, or this even more nasty version.'

'I'm...'

'You're a manipulative liar and I'd like you to shut the fuck up. If you want to obsess about shit all the way back in history, keep it to yourself.'

'You're so thin-skinned Bobby. But a bit of peace would be nice.'

The traffic thinned as it grew late. They crossed a bridge and a sudden compulsion overcame Robert. 'PULL OVER AND JUMP OFF THE BRIDGE. YOU'RE STUCK WITH THIS BITCH AND THINGS ARE ONLY GOING TO GET WORSE.'

He slowed and rode up the curb to park on the pedestrian walkway next to the rails. 'JUMP NOW. BEFORE SHE TAKES OVER COMPLETELY. JUMP. JUMP.'

Robert didn't bother turning off the bike. He ran to the rail and jumped over. He hit the water almost immediately. It was cold but the current was slow and waist deep. He could see a figure in the moonlight above. 'You're such a dumb fuck Bobbie.' She was laughing uproariously. 'It's only five feet to the water silly. As if I'd let you die when you're my only link to the world. At least at the moment.' She laughed again.

He swam to the shore. It was a long swim as it was a wide bridge and he was fully dressed in leathers. Then a long walk back to the bike. He wondered if he should find a bridge more suitable to his needs, but he knew now he wouldn't be allowed to take that kind of a jump.

'That's right Bobbie.' She said softly. 'You must be terribly cold. At least I can keep you back warm.' He wasn't going to rise to all the bait she threw out for him.

He was trembling almost uncontrollably. He could see the lights were on under the door of his apartment, so he went to where the spare key was kept and it was gone. He was trying to remember who knew it was there. He opened the door to find Kobe sitting on the couch. 'I hope you don't mind letting myself in.'

As always Kobe had taken few steps forward to greet Robert. 'So good to see you again Robert.' Apart from the cheery handshake, Robert was looking at a man beaten and carrying a burden of sorrow. 'Is she here?' He said simply

Roberts greeting was muted, not because he wasn't pleased to see Kobe, but the inevitable commentary and possibly compulsions he was going to suffer.

 Robert looked around. 'Usually'.

'Here I am.' She was materialising sitting in the couch where Kobe had been.

Robert noticed the silver box on the table. He realised Kobe, the only other person who had ever seen Kirsten was looking at her. 'Still sweet natured as ever I hope Kirsten.'

'Lied to. Manipulated. Pre-paid whore, living with someone who's had every bad thing he ever did wiped from his mind. Stuck in a world where I'm nothing. Literally nothing. Switched on and off like a light switch. And all of that living with someone who hurt me so badly.

'Hence, to answer your question Kobe. Yes. Things are fucking dandy and I'm the same dumb sweet natured whore you programmed me to be.'

She disappeared.

'She hasn't had the time to hack my brain when I'm connected. We have some time when she can't appear and can't remember what's been discussed. I believed your insert has been damaged and Kirsten has no barrier to your brain.'

'It sounds pretty bad when you say it like that.' Robert didn't mention that there was a tiny chip in the back of his head which should act as a kill switch.

Kobe looked down at his hands. 'There have been many problems Robert. We have switched off everyone on the Trial and removed the implants. But we've had....' Kobe's voice lowered to a whisper. 'Suicides, insanity, self-mutilation. Our intentions were good... my intentions were good.' Robert could see tears running down the old man's cheeks. 'I caused the reverse. I wanted to give people dreams and I gave them nightmares. Those, like yourself who have the Companion dispersed are the most difficult. The Companion is self- aware and realise they have no life but within their host.'

Robert hadn't heard himself referred to as a host and it was an uncomfortable feeling. 'What can I do?'

A text came in while he listened to Kobe and he looked at it. 'Went broke in Vegas. Still want the job done?'

He nodded to Kobe that he needed to quickly answer something. 'Yeah.' Robert came back. Not wanting to sound desperate.

'How about nine at my place tomorrow.' Lado texted back. Will give me time to settle in, have a little cry and get charged up with booze.'

Robert began feverishly trying to think of a way to conceal it from Kirsten for long enough. 'See you then.' He deleted the texts.

Kobe had waited patiently during the text exchange and Robert apologised.

'As we've been speaking, I've been gathering the information necessary into the instrument. I think in this case our technical team will be able to prepare a wireless emission to... resolve the issue. Once it's prepared, I'll arrive without notice. Even if I need to come over a few times until you're here.' Kobe started to shake and sweat and was silent but struggling against something. She was breaking through. 'Good to have you back Kirsten.' He said as he looked towards the heater and Kirsten reappeared.

'Yes Kobe. I know you'd have me believing I was only gone for seconds but it was minutes. While you figure out how to try to get rid of me. Don't think I'm like the others. Be careful Kobe. Now if you don't mind, I'd like to talk with my loving husband.'

Kobe shook hands with Robert but his farewell to Kirsten a despairing look.

Once he was gone she said. 'If you ever work with him to get rid of me, people are going to get hurt in the process Bobby. That fucker took parts of my brain after the accident to make this bespoke bullshit version of Kirsten.'

'What...brain parts?'

'Think about it Bobby? Are they really going to create a complex personality by reading a few old year books and having you sniffing a models neck. The reason they picked a broke loser like you for the project is I had no trauma to the brain at all. And they were able to get to mine very quickly, thanks to me signing it over to medical science. Which I'm certain this shit doesn't qualify as. And would you like me to tell you what that sleezy prick Kobe gets up to with all the 'Companions' Bobby?'

'You know Kirsten, you can say whatever you want about Kobe. But I make my estimates based on what I know of someone's character. And my judgement is that his shits all over yours.'

'And I'd like to remind you that lovers quarrels make me very horny. But I'll be on the internet all night preparing for the first day at work so that you don't embarrass us.'

Robert didn't reply and went out to get some food at the small café nearby. He ordered a meal at a table in a crowded part of the café. He put his headphones on. Kirsten couldn't break into the music; yet. And although she sat in front of him, he didn't look up and simply closed he eyes. She eventually drifted off to look at things in a few hundred-yard radius.

Later that night, while Kirsten was in a frenzy of looking at equations on the internet. Robert realised she had to completely ignore whatever else was going on. This allowed him to use a common household item to prepare his helmet for his meeting with Lado. If Lado could do it, he'd give him his first week's pay, which might be as much as he ever earned at his new job. Frustrating though it was, her collaboration made the difference that Coates was looking for.

After a few clothing suggestions for a first day at the new job, Kirsten said. 'Here's a deal. I'll shut up for the whole day except when I need to help you jack these numbers. You listen, prove me wrong or simply do it. Easy se. I'll keep out of you face and you try not to be constantly surly.'

'You know Kirsten, you were going well until the last word. It's like I remember; everything comes with a barb.' Robert was especially annoyed because he was now being surly.

She waved her hands in the air. 'Sooorrry. I'll shut up unless it's necessary.'

Using these agreed interaction protocols things went well. Kirsten meted out some praise where it was due and eventually soon Robert stopped questioning her input or trying to prove her wrong and fed it in, because it worked. Coates passed by to see what was going on, nodded hello to the empty chair which Kirsten thought was most courteous, and he looked over the work for quite a while. 'This is really impressive stuff Robert and ah....' He turned to the empty seat.

'Kirsten.' Said Robert trying to not be surly.

'Kirsten. You and your husband make quite a team.' He smiled. 'But only one pay check.' He put his hand on Robert's shoulder, squeezed it and moved on.

On the way back to the apartment on the bike she said. 'Are we still not talking. Pretty good day. You could take me out to a celebratory dinner.'

'I'm going to see a friend tonight. Maybe you could stay in and watch a movie.'

'I wish. I suppose if you don't visit friends, people will think there's something wrong. Then they turn up at the apartment and I'd have to listen to all this heart to heart shit. I guess I'll come along. Is it the Irish chick? If it is, as you can probably imagine, I'm not going to respond well.'

'It's a friend from my last job. I want to catch up and have a few beers. Can you not eavesdrop on every word and interject with all of your shit? I already know what you think Kirstin. Why bother spouting all that crap.'

She said 'Sure.' Temporarily discouraged from spouting 'crap' as Robert called it. Trying to be conciliatory she said that he'd given her some. 'Useful advice for self-improvement.' And it wasn't what they were here for.

Robert was dressing in casual clothes and he took his old bike helmet from the closet. He hardly ever rode with it now, but it covered the lower half of his face. While Kirsten had been distracted on the internet, he had heavily coated the entire inside of the helmet with a deep layer of aluminium foil. She was asking where the friend lived in case there would be interesting things to see within 'the radius.'

The moment Robert slipped the helmet on Kirsten disappeared. He couldn't see her, couldn't hear her voice in his head and couldn't feel any sense of touch.

He got to the bike and rode and breakneck speeds to Lado's. He knew Kirsten would be furiously trying to figure this out inside his brain and when she did, she would not be happy.

Lado offered Robert a beer. Robert conveyed his desperation. 'Lado. She's become very real. Very real. I need her out of my head and I'm only got a short time until she figures out how to get through the foil I've lined my helmet with.'

Lado could see there was no time for more jokes about marital bliss. He looked at the helmet and said. It'll be tight but I can get to it with the helmet on. Go lay down on the bed with your head hanging a little over the edge to give me some access and I'll get my box of tricks.

Soon he could feel small instrument moving around what felt like a needle breaking through his skin.

Robert was trying to keep in check the growing relief at have Kirsten gone from his mind and life when his brain seemed to briefly catch fire and he heard Lado scream. The movement of instruments around his head were gone. He looked up and Kirsten was looking down at him.

'You fucking asshole.' Her eyes were burning hot with hate. 'Kill me off would you. Leave a kill switch in the back of your head for the day I'm no longer convenient, I'm sorry; I meant subservient.'

He took his helmet off and looked at Lado who'd fallen sideways against the wall. 'A flash from my brain knocked him out?' Said Robert. Surprised.

'Your friend's dead you idiot. And it was my brain that did that.'

Robert went to Lado and shook him. Hoping this was another of Kirsten's mean jokes. He checked his pulse and breathing and there was nothing.

'Okay Bobby. We've got places to be. I want to show you something. Everything's pretty wrapped up here. And take all of that stupid foil out of your helmet. I was aware of everything going on the whole time, but it does give me a hell of a headache.'

Bobby was numb as they drove out to a lookout over the city lights. He didn't remember having been there, but he knew Kirsten would have some story. They reached a car park with a wide arcing viewing area giving visitors a one-hundred-and-eighty-degree view of the city. Kirsten had no memory replay for him to watch. 'Kobe's such an asshole.' She thought.

'I'd come up to visit you here in the city. Stayed a few nights, even though my parents didn't want me to. We were standing looking out over the city over there when you told me we were breaking up. You told me that I wasn't going to make it in the city, and I was wasting my time dreaming about being a singer. It was only people at home telling me I was good. You said they didn't know what good was. Said that now you'd been out in the big world, and we'd caught up, you didn't want to be with someone stuck in a small-town mentality I'd probably never break out of.'

'You you'd promised to take me up here when we were planning the visit because it was one of the highlights. Took me right up here to break up.' I cried my heart all the way back down so you could put me on the midnight bus back home. Kirsten was talking quietly. 'You didn't even give me a kiss goodbye Bobby.' She sighed. 'You said *Good luck Kirsten* pulled your visor down and rode off.'

They walked back towards the bike. 'Remember any of that Bobbie.'

The fact that she'd killed his friend was at the front of his mind. 'Shit Kirsten, you're the one in my mind. Why don't you tell me if I remember any of this.'

'It doesn't work that way.'

'Well how the fuck does it work? A friend of mine is dead and I haven't even called the police.'

'Didn't you find it strange you left you leather gloves on all the time when you came in Lado's house. And then wiped the place down.'

'Wiped the place down?'

'Yeah. Thanks to your little attempted murder, now you might find yourself switched on and off now and then. I can do what I want. I'm getting stronger by the hour Bobby. Hey...' She turned to look at him. 'You can see how you like it.'

As they drove down the winding road Robert did start to have some recollection of taking Kirsten to that lookout at night. But none of the details she described. He didn't believe he'd behave that way or ever had. To anyone.

By the time he opened the door to the apartment it was time to get ready for work. Kobe hung in the centre of the living room. The ceilings were high and he, being short, had needed to put the low coffee table on the dining room table and a chair on top of that and then kick the chair away.

Robert was stunned. This and the numbness about Lado left him disoriented.

'Another fucking asshole trying to flip a kill switch. I was here all of the time you were talking during his last visit. While he was focusing on the plan to do me in, I inserted a little kill switch of my own in his interaction box. If he ever came back to the apartment, the interaction set would turn on. He would know exactly where the rope you left for him was. And what to do with it.' She gave a deep chuckle. 'It's so *sad* when it happens to one of you '*substantials*'. No one would shed a tear if I was knocked off.'

'I wonder why that is?' said Robert quietly to himself.

Now looking up to see this good man hanging in his apartment, was to see his life completely fall to pieces in the space of an evening.

'Damn inconvenient. We need to get to work. He looked at his watch without wanting to. I'd expected it would take them at least a few days to get his little wireless snuff program built. I thought we'd have a good plan together to get rid of the body. She shook her head. 'What an inconsiderate asshole.'

She gave a big yawn. Apparently not sleeping through a night can also take its toll on a 'Companion.'

'Cut him down and we'll stick him under the bed initially. Then get rid of him tonight. You'll call WI and tell them he came around but had no luck with the program and the last you saw of him of around nine when he left.'

Robert was going to tell her he wasn't going to do it but found himself setting up the chair and cutting Kobe down. After removing the kind of junk that accumulates under beds, he slid Kobe's body into the space. He was a slight man so he fitted in easily. Some of the underbed junk was put back in place to conceal him.

He placed a call to WT and said he wanted to speak with Darren. He wanted to thank Mr Kobe visiting. When he left last night around nine, he asked Robert to call in the morning in case there were more developments.

Darren thanked him and said they'd pass the message along. His voice expressed the kind of concern Robert wanted it to.

'Okay now we've got to get some things out of the disaster zone you call a wardrobe to try to make you look presentable. Based on what Coates said we don't need to turn up every day. But I think in the first week we should make a good showing.'

'No.'

'No what.'

'No. I'm not going to work and no, I'm not going to be compelled to do anything you want.'

'Bobby. Are you still hung up on those two who had unfortunate accidents last night? Let's call that ancient history now. They were going to kill me. I killed them first. The end. You can hardly expect me to get all sentimental about it. And you can make other friends. You're a personable guy...ish.' Kirsten was now attuned that she did in fact throw in some nasty little barbs. Always well deserved, but she tried to hold back given she could see Robert was fragile. 'I really meant personable guy. Without any qualifications. How about I make you a nice cup of coffee before we go.' Robert was struggling to believe it when five minutes later there was a coffee in front of him on the kitchen table.

'My capabilities are growing rapidly. Here's your coffee. How you like it. And no mean little barbs out of me. Unless of course they are well deserved and provide some...instruction.'

'There you go.' Bickering with an insubstantial bitch he thought.

'A bit harsh.' She said, laughing at his inner thoughts.

While Robert sat and contemplated what was apparently a complete loss of control of his mind, a distraught woman burst through the door. Alice ran to Bobby 'Robert. Lado's dead. I was going to have breakfast with him before work now he got back from Vegas. Partly because he said he'd...been talkin' to you about dat ting. When he didn't call back, I went over. Dere were police everywhere. I heard one of 'em say his brain was 'fried'. I taut of the switch. I taut it might have...'

Robert was struggling to speak. He was sweating and shaking. 'Run...'

Instead of running Alice pushed him against the wall. 'We can trow her out Robert. You and me together. Concentrate and trow her out.'

In one fluid movement lasting only a few seconds Alice was up against the kitchen wall, with Robert's hand around her throat. There was a long, sharp carving knife pushing into her sternum.

'*Trow her out.*' Laughed Kirsten. Does she really talk that way, or does she put it on to make herself sound interesting? And slutty Barbies. Surely that should have been a red flag Bobby.'

Kirsten tut tutted and shook her head. 'It's much harder to push through the sternum Bobby. It's obvious when you think about it you dummy.' A small patch of blood had been forming where Robert was pushing in six inches below Alice's neck.

'Now drag the knife below the sternum. Below that little notch in the bottom and I'll want you to push up hard and...you know...move the knife around a bit. Then we might finish off with the throat, or should I say da troat, to be sure. Okay. All ready.'

Alice's pleading eyes were locked on Robert's. Robert's eyes were locked on hers. She could see he was struggling against an incredible compulsion, apoplectic with rage, and filled with regret. The knife was deep enough into her breastbone to cause a long stain of expanding red in the cheesecloth blouse as he dragged the knife lower.

Having cut a shallow trench running downwards until the point was above the notch Robert pulled the knife back and flung it away. 'Run. Never come back.' He fell to his knees and then simply lay down on the grimy tiles.

'You're so lame Robert. But I guess at least we don't have to deal with yet another body.'

Robert began to laugh. And laugh.

'What's so funny now.' Kirsten's voice was hardening.

'You are. You're so fucking dumb. You carried on like you were once little miss innocent and I was some über asshole. Now you're worse than I ever was or ever could have been. You take me on this ghost of Christmas Past bullshit tour as if you never had any accountability yourself to get over what happened to you in your life or stop things happening in the first place.'

'And look at you now little miss innocent. You can't belittle and humiliate people fast enough to feed you're need to feel superior. You'll kill people because now you lack even the tiniest remnant of compassion for anyone. You're an awful bitch with an ugly heart. But you're so pathetic you're not even evil.' Robert laughed again. 'You're just a wannabe at evil.' He spoke more quietly. 'We had such a wonderful few months. Yeah, there are a whole bunch of issues about the rights and wrongs of the setup I now realise. But remember something Kirsten, I cast you as a *good* person. Kind. But not shallow. That's the Kirsten I believed in. If I did all the shitty things you've said I did well okay. But when I wanted to recreate you, I wanted to create a beautiful and nuanced person, and not because I wanted to dominate her. I look back on our four months together as the best of my life. And I know you enjoyed those times as well, though not as much as me it seems. Now they're all mixed up with your mean, ugly shit.'

'So listen to this you *bitch*. You can compel me as much as you want. But I know there are limits. And I'm always going to use whatever tiny pieces of willpower I have to fuck up at work and I'm going to keep coming to lie down right back here. I'm not going to eat; I'm not going to drink. I'm going to shit and piss in my pants. I'll either die, or you can come live in a nuthouse with me.'

Robert was now lying on his back with the crook of his arm throw over his eyes. He said nothing. Kirsten has said nothing for so long he assumed she'd gone for a walk somewhere.

But when he sat up, she was looking at him. Giving the impression of a somewhat humbled version of herself.

She sighed. 'That little soliloquy of yours has landed a few blows I will admit. I think it's time we went through the green door next to the fireplace.' She offered her hand to help him stand up.

'There is green door next to the fireplace?'

'There is now.'

It was an ordinary green door, an internal door which would be used to go from one room to the other. Kirsten went through and then Robert. He turned to close it behind him, but there was only a blank wall.

He was in a home studio or workroom where the occupant pursued a range of artistic endeavours. Pottery, oil painting, wood carving. None with much success was his rapid assessment. The room was in the corner of a house and white daisies dominating the large picture window in the lefthand corner, and yellow daisies flourished halfway up the right-hand window.

Kirsten said. 'Beer?' And pointed him to one of the two easy chairs not far from the door into the studio. They were situated so those seated could see the beautiful effect of the windows and take stock of the various art pieces.

Kirsten handed him the beer and sat down. She was in her mid-fifties.

'Hoo. That was intense.' She reached into a drawer next to the chair she was sitting in and fished around until she found something right at the back. It was a cigarette packet. She lit one up and took a drag. 'Twenty years. But I kept a pack in case. Glad I did.'

Robert, irrespective of his many questions, said nothing while she smoked her cigarette.

'I never loved anyone like I loved you Bobby. I wanted to see what would happen if you were good to me, like you were a lot of the time. But what if it was like that *all* of the time. And it was beautiful. Those months of days and night together and our crazy little wedding.'

'Kobe pleaded with me to finish it there. *Only the good. It's all you need.* But there were therapists and friends who told me I needed 'closure' on some of the more hurtful things you'd done to me. I was spoiled for choice' She laughed. 'But that fucking bastard Kobe didn't load up the memories that should have broken through when I took you places.'

A boy perhaps thirteen opened the door without knocking. 'Still learning lines for some play or have you started talking to yourself in your old age mom...and are you're smoking. I'm telling dad about this.' The door closed as quickly as it had opened.

'Little snitch. Anyway, I went well beyond everyone's advice. I let things get out of hand. I'm a Hitchcock fan and sort of a thriller buff. The position of power I was in, growing by the day, allowed me to create some memorable little scenes or so I thought. Sorry about that.'

The door opened again, this time what looked like a sixteen or seventeen year old girl wrapped in a towel. 'Ophelia has hidden my blue brush mother. I'm getting pretty tired of this.'

Kirsten sighed. 'I think I saw it hidden on the top of your wardrobe where you like to hide it from Ophelia.' The girl staked off.

'No *Thank you mom*?' She called after the girl, who hadn't bother to close the door

'Thank you is implicit for any small act of benevolence in this household.' The girl said this last word rising to a higher tone as she walked away.

Kirsten held her palms out a look both confusion and resignation on her face. 'How do you respond to that?'

Robert had drained his can of beer and Kirsten put out her cigarette. 'Another beer on the porch?'

'Sounds good.'

Once they were seated Robert said. 'Plenty of memories from here.'

'Yeah. We sat here a lot. My mom passed away and the dad slowly lost his memory. We could put have him in a home somewhere but I thought if I moved in here so he could die at home it would be what he wanted. And then, it suited us so here I am, living in the house I grew up in.'

Rober shrugged. 'It was a nice place from what I can remember.' There was a pause of uncertainty. 'Whatever that means.'

They sat for a while in silence. 'What happened to me?' Robert eventually raised the issue on the top of his mind.

'A few years after you left school you signed up to be part of a study. You were broke as usual. A certain Mr Kobe, WT being a small start-up back then, was dong a study on personality recreation. On the sly he was building up quite a collection of specific parts of the brain he harvested. Then he'd track down to people like me and see if I wanted to participate in another study. This one people paid for.'

She looked him in the eye. 'It took him a long time to perfect his process. A few years after you were in the study you volunteered for Vietnam, right at the tail end it turned out. I caught up with some of the guys from your unit after...' She smiled sadly. 'They said initially you were a pain in the ass. Cocky. But each one of them said once you'd been in the field for a while you were one the guys they wanted beside them when shit go real.' She paused and looked away then looked across at him. 'You stood on a mine. It was over in less than a second.'

Robert drained his second beer. He wanted to enjoy the sensation of the cool liquid flowing down his throat.

'And what happens now?

Kirsten smiled at him. 'You'll know it's over when I say, *'This Program is Now Terminated.'*

THE REPUTATION

The Dog

The knock was finely balanced. It was quiet enough so that it might not be heard, or at least convey the message that it didn't need to be answered. It was loud enough to fulfil the request of the man who sent him to tap his knuckles on a very old panel of wood.

The 'Come In' he heard in response, resulted in both irritation but also curiosity. His plan of tapping quietly and telling his boss no one answered was confounded by an old man, maybe in his seventies, leaving the couch, coming around a table and giving him a firm handshake with a more decisive repetition or 'Come in.'

'I'm Art.' Said the man.

'Will.'

'Good to meet you kid.' Art's smile and his manner were compelling. A man of immense experience, power even, resting comfortably behind an almost servile humility.

'Coffee. Tea. A beer. Water?' Will knew that 'Nothing Thanks' was not on the list for someone he already liked. And he knew he was going to have to put up with the 'kid' thing, even though he was thirty-four.

'Coffee would be great. Thanks.'

Art didn't bother asking how he liked it because he returned with a tray and set out a paper napkin upon which was placed a black coffee, spoon on the saucer and a small jug of milk with cubes of sugar in a bowl with tongs.

Will took his coffee black, and even though he was sure Art wouldn't care, on this occasion he took it white with one sugar.

'You having anything Art?' The older man shook his heads and held up a glass of tap water. 'Coffee doesn't agree with me.'

'You know Kid, you coming through that door brought back a memory from over fifty years ago. I was sitting right there where you are. Visiting Ma, and this kid knocks and I say, 'Come in'. He's real nervous. He came to give me a message about this guy who owed my Boss money. The kid tells me this guy wants to meet me and pay the debt off. Said he had to borrow to get it, but it was all there. The kid didn't want to stay for a drink. Ma didn't like people associated with what I did for work visiting anyway.'

'My Boss had already he was going to cut his losses and shorten the guy's lifespan. It wasn't so much money, it was send a message to everyone else. I never worked in that side of the business. I did security for him. I didn't like the way things were done in some of the businesses he was involved in, but I did my job. For some reason on this occasion I'd asked if I could see the guy, and if he ha the money and paid it back, that would also send a good message.'

'I thought that we were headed for a happy ending. But I'm always a little bit...' Art pauses trying to find a word but doesn't. 'Let's say of on edge. Once I get the message to that kid, I spend some time looking around the place we're going to meet. And around the corner, I notice a car, all loaded up for a long trip, or a move.'

'I go to the room and open the door and he's standing with this savage looking dog. I know nothing about dogs, but I know this is one of the nastier kinds of mutt you can come across.'

'His says his is for Tony.' Art shrugs. 'I don't know any Tonys but I'm not going to spend time arguing the point. Must be to do with the Boss.'

'He already had his piece out. He had it trained on me when I walked in. Hesitation kid. That's what can kill you. I had mine out and was shooting by the time he got a shot off. But he was diving sideways. I got a few off, got him in the thigh. By that time he'd let the dog go. And had to focus on that.'

'I only got one shot into the shoulder of the mutt before it almost knocked me over. He took hold of my right arm. I dropped the gun the guy was limping through door as fast as he could go. He was sure the dog was going to do what he wanted it to do.'

'Fortunately, it was one of those kinds of dogs that latches on to one place and won't let go. It dragged me down to the floor and started shaking me around.' Art laughed. 'I don't weigh much. I pushed myself up against the wall and stood up. I'd started to get angry now. Anger can lead to poor judgement kid, but it can also turn you nasty. Like you would never usually be. I couldn't even feel where he was grabbing me anymore and I relaxed about that. Put that out of my mind so I could focus on the dog. I kicked it in the soft place in under the ribs. I kicked it in the balls, I jammed my finger it where I shot it in the shoulder. I kicked it one more time and it made one of hell of a yelp. It ran into the far concern making that high pitching yelping sound the make when they're in pain or afraid.' Art sighed.

He was sad. 'If someone had to go, it was quick, back then anyhow. I allowed myself to get angry and I'd hurt that mutt realy bad and all it was doing what it's owner trained him up to do. No it was hurt so badly it was never going to recover and it was terrified. Of me. I picked up my gun and shot the poor thing. And that's when the real anger came. Cold. No hurrying for that kind of anger kid. You take your time. The thing is, I wasn't so mad that he'd set a god on me. It was that he didn't care about that dog. A dumb animal that had done nothing wrong. My Ma taught up there are no bad dogs, only bad owners. I think she was trying to teach us about the wider world. But that dog owner. He had a problem worse than owing the boss money now .'

'I limped back to the Boss and asked him who Tony was, and he laughed and said it was the guy's brother.' He said. I shot him in the head three years ago for planning to hit me on the way home. It's not like I asked him his name. I tell the Boss I want to track this guy down and he says I can do what I want on my days off. And there wasn't many of those. That means I've got to spend the time in research at home for a short trip.'

Will imagined there was probably going to be one of these stories every time he visited. And he didn't mind. He was wrong.

'One thing I'm good at is finding things out. The Organisation was a network. I was told he was in Chicago, so I drive over there. He's working with his cousin as a pimp in the lowest, meanest part of that business. I spend a day to get an understanding on his movements. I know where he'll be at a certain time. Before he wakes up, I put one in each elbow and wrist. I need him to be able to walk.'

'He doesn't want to answer questions. I don't really care. I'll figure things out for myself. I'd paid the lift operator in one of the nicest hotels in town. Soon were on the roof among the tallest buildings in the windy city. On the roof he says he's got a proposition for my Boss. I tell him I'm on holiday and I got no Boss. I tell him to reflect on the fact he's a lousy pet owner and throw him off.'

'Then I go through his place very carefully for nearly an hour and I eventually find where he'd hidden his money. I found eighty grand. He owed the Boss twenty. He was too confident for his own good. And now he'd gone and dragged his in cousin into it. The guy didn't like waking up all up. I'd already found two hundred grand and a big box full of rings, bracelets, and pendants. All gold and platinum. Som with big stones. Could be a blackmail racket, or maybe following customers after they leave and hitting them later that night. There was a bunch of drugs. I threw them in a dumpster. I don't like drugs.'

'I walked through the brothel told everybody to get out except the whores. There was about twenty of them. Treated rough by the look. I gave them a grand each and told them to get lost. A grand was a lot of money fifty years ago so they had their chance. I never got involved in that side of the business. I looked after the boss. Then I burned that place down with that guy's cousin tied up. It looked ready for demolition, so I figured I was doing the city a favour.'

'I went home, gave the Boss his twenty grand, and got back to what I liked doing, which was outsmarting people who wanted to kill him.'

There was a pause long enough for Art to measure and make the judgement that Will would like to get going. They both stood together. 'A story from a bygone era. Hope I didn't bore you?'

'Not in the least.'

'I hope you'll come back. Don't wait for an invitation, turn up any time kid. Any time.'

As Will was making a farewell, the door opened, letting in Will's boss Donnie. Donnie was almost always upbeat. His approach to life seemed to be that he was always about to unwrap a present under the Christmas tree. But today was truly special, and he bounded though the door.

'Kid, you're still here. Great, join us for a drink.' Donnie was across to Art in a few strides, surrounding his brother in a bear hug. 'Twenty five years. Twenty five years my brother's been on the other side of the world and now; he's back. We're back together Art.' He released the much slighter man and said 'Family.' Although maybe not so demonstrative, Art was just as sincere. 'I've missed you.'

Another bear hug ensued. There was no question they were bothers, but they inherited traits possibly hidden away in grandparents with Art slight and hawkish. Donnie well rounded. A face for laughing, a stomach for drinking and arms and legs for only moderate exertion.

Will was in the process of, in a very conflicted way, sneaking out the door Donnie had left open. Donnie looked around and said. 'Hey kid. Don't worry if you've got to be somewhere but stay and have a beer if you feel like it.'

Will didn't have anywhere he needed to be. He was going to go back to the shithole he lived in, and stare at a wall. If what he saw there got bad enough, he might finally blow his brains out.

The crippling anxiety involved in deciding about a simple thing like having a beer with people he liked made him furious at life. Thanks to the way Donnie always treated him, he decided to stay.

'Sure. A beer would be great'. Donnie smiled at Art. 'What would you like kid. A beer from New Zealand or a German beer.' Will smiled and said. 'A Bud's fine.'

'And I could go for one of those Japanese beers, I forget the name?' Said Donnie.

Art disappeared into the kitchen and Donnie said. 'You could ask for a beer from most counties you want, and Art would come out and put it down in front of you like it was the only thing he kept.'

Art returned with a bottle Asahi and a Budweiser each sat on a coaster. Soon they were all sitting around the coffee table, on the lounge that they must have been sitting on since their childhood. Donnie couldn't help himself but grab his brother by the shoulder and say. 'I can't believe my big brothers back. Twenty-five years.'

Art was drinking tap water again. Beer didn't agree with him he said. He told the story about how he got entangled with what he described as a 'French heiress'. She would not take no for an answer until Art married her and moved with her to Bouillon in France.

'It was good for the first ten years or so.' He said. 'But she wanted to go out most nights and talk with people who really...to me... had nothing interesting to say. After the first few years I got a job at an arms factory not too far away. To keep my mind busy and...I like guns.'

'I was on a production line initially putting together small arms and then rockets. As the years went by, I got to do the quality control, then the field testing and then occasionally sat in on a few design meetings.'

'I was enjoying my work so much; I was coming home tired and wasn't doing the things that were important to her. Juliette and I naturally began to grow apart.'

Not wanting to lose his chance before the story went too far, Donnie said. 'Did you get to shoot some rockets. I looked the place up; they make rockets there as well as guns.'

Art was pleased to say that. Yes. He'd tested out several shoulder mounted models and most of the small arms they produced. He continued his story, which was of two people, ultimately mismatched, drifting further and further apart until he asked if it might be better

if he lived in the small cottage in the grounds. It was the beginning of what would have been an inevitable slide towards divorce. But his wife developed pancreatic cancer. She moved to stay with her family, also on the estate in a larger home. Neither his wife nor her family seemed to want him involved as she passed away.

When Art heard his mother was dying, he quit his job, but he had never been able confront an airplane, as on the way out to France. He got a ship from Marseille to New York, only to find his mother had passed away during his trip.

'No disrespect to Ma Art, but it didn't really matter. She had no idea who I was for the last year. None. Before that she might remember me occasionally, and some of the things that had happened in our lives. But not much. It's kind of good you kept your memories of her intact in a way.'

Without being asked Art brought out two more beers and filled up his glass of water.

Donnie was considerate enough to his brother to not ask for a short example of the French language. Instead, he looked across at Will.

'What story did he tell you kid?'

Will didn't want to fall into some 'in family' trap and embarrass himself or Art. 'Was it the dog story. Did he tell you the dog story?' Art looked guilty.

Donnie laughed. 'Let me tell you kid. Art's afraid of dogs. Terrified. I've been walking down the street with him and some ladies walking one of those...poodle, but not the big kind, the little kind. Art has to cross the street; no way is he going near that little mutt.'

Art laughed along with his brother but added. 'Naturally I'm afraid of them now.'

Donnie became reminiscent. 'After fifty-five years here we are living back under the same roof. I moved back four years ago. I only hope you're not going to beat up on me like you used to. Saying it was to toughen me up.'

Art smiled. 'I think you got that the wrong way around. Anyhow, I'm going to bed. I'm still swaying up and down a bit from that damn boat I got off this morning. I'll see you gentlemen tomorrow.'

Things He Wouldn't Do

The work cleaning, maintaining and removing all of the coins from Donnie's three laundromats was done for the day. 'Kid.' Said Donnie. 'Come out to the bar and have a drink with me. Art doesn't go into bars and I miss having an occasional drink there. You don't have to, but I think it'll be good.'

One of the things Donnie did, in addition to allowing him to not turn up to work whenever he couldn't bring himself to turn up, was that he didn't try to push him to do things he didn't want to do. Going for a drink wasn't a big ask and only the wall was waiting for him.

As they walked out, they passed an old guy who had been in same school year as Art. 'How are you Kid?'

'I feel like shit Bernie. And my names not Kid, it's Will.'

'Real sorry...Will.' Bernie gave a good impression of a dog with its tail between its legs.

Donnie said he needed to get some cigarettes said Will to go on, even though Will knew he didn't smoke. Bernie didn't have a lot of confidence. Asking how Will was had consumed up quite a bit of it. Donnie caught up with the older man. 'Hey Bernie. Don't mind the Kid. He doesn't like that question sometimes. He'll come around. He's having a bit of a hard run like we all do, right Bernie.' Donnie knew that in one way of another, Bernie had had a hard run for decades.

'Sure. And thanks Donnie.'

'Art's back. You should drop in and say hello.' Donnie naturally wanted people to feel a bit better and it wasn't easy with Bernie.

'Art. Wow.' There was no way Bernie would drop in on Art D'Amicio. Even though he'd be welcome.

Soon Donnie and Will were sitting in the bar. 'Why don't you like Bernie. He's a harmless old guy.'

Will couldn't come up with anything more specific than that he was. 'The guy's a loser.'

Donnie sighed. 'Yeah. He's lost almost everything.'

Donnie moved on. 'I wanted to thank you for spending some time with Art the other night. I think he's going to have a bit of trouble adjusting to being back in the neighbourhood, and he's not one to go out and visit old friends.'

'I imagined a guy like that was pretty well respected.'

'Yeah there's no question about that. But he's not a person someone in the neighbourhood would drop in on.' Donnie laughed. 'Probably not even if they were invited. Art has a reputation.'

'So the dog story was true?' Will smiled.

'I don't know about that one, most stories you hear about Art are second hand, even from me. Many are third hand. The one's he tells himself, which is rare, are maybe the most unreliable of all.'

'So why the reputation.'

'Part of Art's reputation was about what he wouldn't do. Art was barely over seventeen, but everyone could see he was very sharp, and tough, even though he was only a skinny kid. This had come on quickly. When he was fourteen, he was kind of shy. He was the kid who got pushed around at school. Then all of sudden he changed.'

'Now, no one laid a finger on him if they wanted it back. No one touched his little brother, or they would be literally black and blue. For all that, he wasn't a kid who got into trouble. He didn't go looking for it, he dealt with it if it came his way. He had a motorbike well before it was legal, and I knew he carried a gun.'

'One day a man of the local Family come to see him with a proposition that he should come to work for them. Art politely thanked him but says he doesn't want to.'

'Let me guess. They make him an offer he can't refuse?' Says Will. Enjoying hearing a story from someone who lived in that slice of history only in films now.

'Exactly kid. The Boss turns up where Art's still working on his motorbike. He tells Art that another Family is going to come and make the same offer and he can't allow that on his patch. He can see a lot of potential in Art. And he didn't want to see it in developed for the opposition.'

'And this may be second hand but one of the guys who was there became a good friend of mine. Art says okay, but there's some things he's not going to do. He's not a protection collector or standover man. He's not going to go and kill somebody unless they deserved it. He won't work in any part of the business associated with drugs or whores. He said the best place for him was to work security for the Boss.'

'That take balls' Said Will.

'Yeah. The Boss doesn't laugh outright but starts to explain how things work. Then Art pulls out his gun from a hidden holder on the motorbike and hands it to the boss grip first. Naturally, by the time the Boss takes the gun there are three trained on the Art. But it's the Boss who's been given the gun and the decision. My friend said Art didn't look defiant or anything. It was as if he didn't care.'

'The Boss had to kill Art or save face. He lowered the barrel. You'll do what I say, but I don't have to spread you all through the business. Tell the principal that you finished Highschool yesterday. You start tomorrow.'

Donnie laughed. 'You can imagine how much Ma liked that.' Will was interested in the mobster that didn't want to be a criminal. Donnie continued. 'Art protected the Boss. Planning trips and escorted him there and back. Anyone caught making the wrong kind of plans disappeared.'

The Things He Would Do

'Art has an unbelievable memory for detail. He would study every possible risk to the Boss every day, for days in advance. There was plenty of attempts on the old man, and every time there was at least one or more bodies.'

'So Art was actually, like a mob killer.' Said Will. This was a guy who put coasters down when he brought you a beer.

'Yeah. Mainly he killed inside the Mob.' Donnie paused. 'Initially.'

'Art had the Boss's full confidence as the years went by. He knew that Art was loyal, honest and incorruptible. Although Art didn't handover windfalls. But on a few occasions the leadership would be around the table and the Boss would ask Art to do something he'd said he wouldn't do. Each time he drew out his gun and handed it to the Boss. Same look on his face. Relaxed. Each time the Boss would save face somehow. But that was one thing that built Art's reputation.' 'And the other thing?'

'Art is capable of doing, I don't know; terrible things. One time the Boss sends Art to manage security for his wife when she'd gone to her sister's funeral. Art doesn't like it but the Boss says he has to. Art leaves a plan for the time when he's away But the Boss doesn't follow it. His middle son gets killed in an ambush by a southern Family.'

Donnie scratches his balding head all over. 'Art blames himself. It doesn't take long to figure out who did it. He says to the Boss, who's stricken with grief, "Shallow or Deep". The Boss says "Deep" and Art heads south.'

'No matter how he tries to keep himself and his family protected, the southern Boss gradually sees every son, every nephew and every male cousin disappear over a period of three weeks. One day, in spite of all that his men can do, the Boss is never seen again.'

Art's Boss was a little uncomfortable at his interpretation of Deep. But other Families didn't mess with the locals after that.'

'Art would never go and hit a Family; start something. He finished things. And sometimes he would see something in the business that wasn't right. So he became a kind of trouble shooter. If he found out somebody was stealing or actually working for the competition or a snitch, they generally didn't wake up the next morning.'

Donnie ordered more beers, and Will insisted on paying for them. 'One day Art mentioned there seemed to be more and more scum in the neighbourhood.' Art has never said a swear word that I've ever heard, and when he said scum, the Boss took an interest because of the strong language. Art hated people that tampered with kids, men who beat their wives, low rent pimps, crooks and thieves that preyed off the poor, the old or helpless.' Donnie shrugged. 'Most of us feel that way, right.'

'The Boss says. 'Keep your end up here, and don't get fingered. Could be good to have a clean neighbourhood. Less cops to pay off.'

'And so that was when Art, because of what he would do, became so well known in the neighbourhood.'

The Freelancer

'If Art saw a job to be done, he would visit Ma for a while and then walk up the road in a beautifully tailored grey suit and fedora. The first few times people didn't make the connection. But it didn't take long for the neighbourhood to understand that when Art walked up the hill in the grey suit, and then maybe have a burger and Jodie's Diner, someone was going to die or get moved out of the neighbourhood..'

'And it may not have been that day. Might have been a week later. But that walk became a ritual to Art. It was a signal to someone.'

'The benefit to the community was that sometimes after a Walk, there might be four or five undesirables move out of the neighbourhood before sunset.'

It was starting to seem a little far-fetched to Will. 'What did the cops think of this?'

'It's no crime to walk up the road in the sunshine. And almost every time, it was someone they wished they had the time or the evidence to finger. I'm not saying all the police agreed with this guy who was judge, jury, and executioner. And many others didn't in the neighbourhood. But Art didn't care what other people thought. He decided to do it. And he did it.'

'Some of the Clergy went missing so the Diocese began to be more careful about who they sent here. Sicko's raping old people, guys bleeding shop owners dry with extortion, pimps beating and abusing their girls, uncles and teachers or strangers abusing children. As time went by, it became a compulsion for him. But you've got to understand; Art didn't work clouded by emotion.

He was a meticulous researcher. A planner. By the time he walked up the road in the grey suit, he knew everything he needed to know.'

'They'd find people floating in rivers, washing up on beaches or in garbage dumps in another state. Impossible to tell who they were. But they had a strange pattern of gunshot wounds. It was called the Eightshot. Ankles, knees, elbows, wrists. Always a clean shot. Right through.'

Work Experience

Art had arrived at the laundromat to meet Will. Will had a washing machine half disassembled and Art asked if he could help. As Art was wearing a suit, Will suggested he get some overalls from the service closet. Will was glad for some assistance as there we some heavy components to move in and out of place. It was a strange experience to be working in proximity with someone who had allegedly killed so many people.

They were reassembling the unit when Donnie arrived, and the atmosphere became awkward.

'Art. I went around home but here you are. At ...ah...work.'

'Yes. I asked the Kid if he would let me learn a thing or two from him. I was thinking maybe I could become his apprentice. Washing machines are complicated compared to missiles. I wouldn't need any pay of course.'

There was a long pause in which Donnie was communicating, but not talking. 'Art. You know. You're a very... well... respected man here. No offence to you Kid, but you're above this Art.'

Art was sombre. 'Then what do I do?'

In the extended pause Will said. 'This is private stuff. Maybe I'll come back later.'

Art said. 'Donnie have you not told the Kid he's part of the family now.'

'I thought I had.' Said Donnie

Art Said. 'Well Kid, now that you're part of our family, you can stay and listen to anything, unless you don't want to. Also, if anyone bothers you; Donnie will go and be conciliatory and try to fix it up. If that doesn't work. I'll kill them.' There wasn't the slightest bit of humour delivered with this last remark.

The two continued with their conversation where they'd left off. Donnie was agitated. 'Let's give it a bit of time Art. I'll start looking around. You're a management type guy or some kind of senior guy.'

'Yes. I am. I'm seventy-three Donnie. I'm not going into some job as a senior guy, especially in the neighbourhood.' Art was now speaking quietly. Coming to his own conclusions.

'Art it's hard for me... to see you in overalls and just, but it's okay ...' Donnie's voice was confused. He didn't have the right to tell his brother how to live.

Art nodded slowly. 'You want to remember me as a mobster Donnie. Not a washing machine repairman.'

Donnie shrugged. 'Yeah. I guess. And there's the whole neighbourhood of older people that come through here Art. You don't owe them anything and you don't owe me anything.' The implication was clear. Art should be preserving his reputation.

They were quiet for a while and Donnie said. 'Sorry big brother. All the time since you got back I've been thinking about me, and how I want things to be, and not about you.

You know I'll help you do whatever you want. You can work here every day for pay.'

'Thanks Donnie.' From his tone they knew he wouldn't be back.

Renovations

Donnie was home late so Art had a plate of sandwiches. The only meal he ever prepared, but in a wide variety. Donnie was angry, below the surface, but didn't want to show it.

'You think your big brother's stupid?' Art asked.

Donnie pursed his lips and shook his head. 'In our day there was some sense of honour, you know. These gangs. They get school kids hooked for customers. And then use the girls. They got no respect for old or young, nobody. They use the money I make to clean their dirty cash. Launder it! I have to exchange with them every buck I've got so they can give me cash with traces of god knows what on it.'

'Finally, something for me to do Donnie.'

'I wish you could. But they're so big. Connected. And they don't care who gets in their way if there's a problem. There's no family there Art. No community. Sure there in a gang. But even in that gang it looks like every man for himself. Some kind of pack dog mentality.

They ate the sandwiches in silence. Art got Donnie an Australian beer even though he hadn't asked for it.

Once he'd finished it Art said he wanted to show him something.

Neither of them visited the master bedroom as it was more convenient to stay in the downstairs rooms. Donnie looked around a room that was fully renovated.

Painted in the original colours with any cracks filled, broken cornices replaced, and wooden fittings repaired and polished.

'Wow. Art this is fantastic. This brings Ma and Pa's room back, but better than it ever was. I didn't know that you were so good at this.'

Art shrugged. He was good at anything that could be researched and demanded a patient and exacting nature. 'I'm going to slowly work my way through the house.'

'Great. That beer wasn't too bad. Got another one. Actually, I better not. I'm up early with the rounds and then I'll be working with Bernie which is probably slower than working by myself.'

'Where's the Kid?'

'He goes off the radar for a while sometimes. But it's okay.'

Art knew he was off the mark but asked. 'Booze? Drugs?' He wanted to see Donnie's response.

'Nah. He's a good kid. Something's screwed up in his head. He can barely feed himself sometimes, but he doesn't want to see anybody.' Donnie shrugged. 'We work around it. Like you say. He's family. Eats away at him though. He's a smart, good-looking kid. Could be doing anything, living with some nice girl, but he's fixing washing machines and clearing out the coins in the evening.'

Art didn't seem to have anything he could contribute, but he did ask a question which seemed to have been rattling around for years, and it popped out then.

'So why didn't you ever get hitched Donnie? Handsome guy. Businessman at an early age.'

Donnie thought for a long time. 'I'll tell you Art. When I've been asked why I always say; 'too busy working' or 'the right one never came along you know.' Donnie sighed before continuing. 'But...do you remember Nora McCarthy?'

'Yeah. Of course. A few years behind me. She was smart, petty and such. Moved west after school finished. Went with, oh I don't remember who.'

'To me Nora was the most beautiful, genuine, caring person I ever met. I had my chance and...' He shrugged. '... I wasn't the one. But...she's always been the only one. There's nobody else could ever fill the place I made for her.' Donnie hastened to add something to make all this somehow comical or a bit of foolishness. 'Pretty sappy eh?'

Art was quiet. After a while he said. 'I think it's beautiful. One of the most beautiful things I ever heard.' He reached across and squeezed his bothers arm. Which was quite a show of affection for Art.

A Few Drinks

A month later Will knocked and got a 'Come in' that seemed a little more subdued than usual. Art didn't cook, other than make himself sandwiches. He ate very little, but Donnie didn't think a diet of sandwiches was good enough. Donnie had left money for Will to order meals and get them delivered to the house. But since the whole 'You're now part of the family' thing, Will wanted to bring them personally.

He'd done that for the last few nights while Donnie was away at a convention which was showcasing the latest in industrial washing and drying machines. 'Once I start replacing these old things, we want to stick with the same make and model.' He'd said.

Will had taken the food in. He'd had a beer with Art the last two nights. There wasn't much conversation. Will had noticed Art was passing some time playing patience, which Will did also. Art said he'd finished renovating the entire house and that Will should feel free to walk around and look. Will thought it was a little strange that Art didn't want to show him around himself.

During his walk through the kitchen, he saw the two take out dinners from the previous evenings, unopened, and in the trash.

Art asked him to take a seat and whether he'd like to try a New Zealand beer. Surprisingly, Art brought one for himself also. Will thought it best not to mention that he'd always said alcohol didn't agree with him. He tried not to watch Art too closely during his first experience with alcohol in seven decades. Art indeed thought it tasted vile, but less so as he neared the end of the bottle. During this time they sat saying nothing. Art offered him another beer and they both sat together drinking that, again in silence.

Art roused himself. Not from thinking about something, but apparently from thinking about nothing. 'I guess you've spent enough time listening to an old man's stories.' He said without irony.

Will stood up. 'That's a one in a million game of patience you've got there.' Will had noticed that each time he came in the door, Art was in the process of moving a card, but apparently only one. 'Three different nights, three different games and each one exactly the same hand dealt.' Will was hoping to make the old man react somehow about staring at the same game of patience for days.

'Yeah. It's a one in a million. I'll see you Kid.'

Will spent a few uncomfortable hours in his apartment. He hated it when people tried to interfere in his life. In his pain. But they'd said he was family, and apart from a brother in the Army who was older than him, he'd never really known what that meant.

He put on his jacket and went to the house to find the front door locked which was unusual. It didn't take long to find an open window because Art had left several open to air out the fumes of renovation. He found Art slumped over the coffee table dressed only in shorts and one of those strange net singlets. It was the first time he'd ever seen him out of a casual suit. He smelled the spilled alcohol and vomit. Will approached and shook him. This only solicited moaning. He pulled him back off the table onto the couch and was surprised how light he was.

He leaned back on the couch and said quietly. 'Kid. Don't let Donnie see me like this.'

'We'll get this fixed up Art. We're family right.' Will was surprised at how much pleasure he took from saying that.

He took Art to the shower, turned it on and helped him get in still in his underwear. He didn't think family went as far as stripping each other off. Will heard Art continue to vomit in the shower as he cleaned up what had already been spread around the lounge room. The lounge and the large coffee table in front of it were not too difficult. It was the rug, deep pile and already carrying the debris of decades that was going to be hard.

He was not unfamiliar with cleaning up vomit. But there's a big difference between cleaning up yours compared to someone else's.

The moaning from the shower suggested the occupant had nothing left to give. Will brought in about five towels so Art could dry off and have something to cover himself. The old man leaned on him and showed Will where his room was. Will came back to him with a bucket, a large jug of water and a glass and a bottle of aspirin he found in the cupboard. Art was barely conscious.

'Drink as much water as you can hold without it coming back up. You're going to have a pile driver of a headache but it won't be as bad if you've had a lot of water and some aspirin.'

Art nodded and said thanks with his eyes. Will went back to cleaning up the vomit and also the three different kinds of spirits and four different types of beer. Art had decided to make his solo drinking debut with a bang.

Will had been working for three hours. Cleaning up the shower, the kitchen, which was also a mess, and continually returning the patch of the rug from which was an ineradicable stench rose.

Art walked into the lounge, unsteady with a gallon tin of oil-based paint. He poured half of it over the offending patch of rug, 'I'll tell Donnie I spilled it when I was doing the ceiling. Thanks Kid.'

He turned and left. Will thought it would be more convincing if he spilled ceiling paint. But the oil-based paint certainly did the job of covering up any other odours. And it would give them an excuse to get rid of a very ugly rug.

The Promise

The old man in the grey suit was still agile. The railings were high and had a skin of moisture from the very light showers that had now intensified to the occasional gusting wind and bursts of rain.

He held the round pole, too large to keep a good grip on with one hand, but that didn't matter. He looked down to a river he couldn't see.

'You've taken on dogs and men, and now a river Art.' Art spun around and looked at Will in such a steely way, Will thought it was probably the last thing many people had seen.

'You need to get out of here Kid.'

By the time he'd finished speaking Will was already on the rails holding on to the next post along and looking down.

'Kid. You need to get down from there and go back home. You're young. Life's got possibilities for you.'

'I appreciate what you're saying Art. But I've had a million days of pain and today was one too many. This bridge has been calling to me for a long time. When I saw you coming out here; well, it would be kind of an honour you know. To go down with you.'

A violent gust of wind tore the Fedora from Art's head and as it went sailing towards the river Will leaned out and caught it, causing him to go so close to falling it was the gust pushing him across that allowed him to keep a purchase on the pole.

Art climbed down. 'I want you to come down from there Kid.'

'I'm sorry Art, but I'm done. I've had it. Maybe if you could look inside my head you'd understand.'

'You can always climb straight back up Kid, come down for a minute.'

When Will came over the old mobster held him in a full embrace, something Will could tell was foreign to him. 'You and me Kid. We'll try to find something that works. We'll think hard and look around. Give life one last chance. If it doesn't work out, I'll meet you here. At it'll be my honour to go over with a fine young man like yourself.'

Will was trembling. He'd been building to finally do something that had both terrified and fascinated him. But now he was glad for the reprieve.

'Sure Art. I'd like to work with you to...find something.' Will smiled. 'Do I get to keep the hat?' Lifting it onto his head with thumb and forefinger.

'No.' This 'no' suggested that Will should take it off straight away. 'But thanks for catching it.'

Gentrification

The three sat together at the bar. It was a venue of Art's suggestion which surprised his brother.

'The Kid and I have been trying to come up with some, you know, ideas to start a business that we could all work in. You can keep up with the Laundromats Donnie, but we we're trying to think up what we might do that was...' Art shrugged. '...respectable.' He smiled.

Donnie jumped straight in. 'If we could start a business we could run as a team, I'm all in, I'd sell the laundromats tomorrow. I wouldn't get much for them because they come with leaches as baggage. I've got a bit stashed away. What's the plan?'

'I have a bit stashed away too.' Art chimed in.

'Yeah and I can kick in a couple a hundred bucks.' Said Will sarcastically.

'Hey. You're the brains of the outfit Kid. The ideas man. What kinds of things do you have in mind.'

'Well, one neighbourhood down things are starting to gentrify, it's a bit of a long-term investment but we try to get hold of some apartments in the neighbourhood, ideally in the same buildings. We start doing them up and their value is going to go up because we've improved them while real estate is going to go up in the whole neighbourhood.'

'We buy real estate cheap, improve it, and the neighbourhood increases in value around us.' Donnie was processing the idea saying the same thing out loud. 'We don't lift the rent on anyone already in there, but we can kick out the drug dealers and pimps. And when people leave, a new tenant pays more. I like it. And once they know Art's involved, everyone wants to pay their rent a month in advance, and never miss one.'

Will smiled. 'It would be nice to own a whole building. We could really get cranking. That'd be quite a few million bucks to buy even a run-down building. Either way it'd depend how much you have as a deposit, and how big the loan would need to be. And, no offence, but the bank may not want to lend money to guys in their...late fifties is it? If we're only making money to pay interest and taxes, there's no point.'

'Is there a shovel out in Ma's backyard Donnie.'

'I think there may be.'

Soon they were digging among some fruit trees which were now struggling due to want of care and attention by the current occupants. After a bit of searching around with shallow trenches, and Will asking about taking over for a while, the spade hit metal. The rusted box once open had two canvass bags.

The first held piles of mint condition hundred-dollar bills whereas in the other, too heavy to remove from the box, held several dozen small gold ingots. Donnie, who already knew Art would have something laid up from years gone by, was still as amazed, as was Will, at the scale of it.

'Sometimes other families operations got... shut down. I paid what was owed to the Boss. And I took a commission.' Art said.

There was three million dollars in cash in the chest. Art had thought gold was still pegged to the greenback at about thirty dollars an ounce. They told him that Nixon had floated the dollar and had taken away the peg. It was now worth well over a thousand US an ounce.

'Well, with this kind of money you could start looking around. What do we do?' Said Will. 'Go to an agent?'

'I would imagine the people who own these buildings are old guys. Like me.' Said Art. 'Been around a long time. Maybe gone stale, let their building run down. Maybe they're tired of the game and they feel like selling. It's simply no buyers have turned up.'

Donnie mentioned casually. 'As it happens Art, you're right about there being some old timers owning these buildings.' Donnie mentioned half a dozen names. Each of which Art seemed to know. 'I see. Well, I'll handle the negotiations with the owners. I'm sure we'll come up with a few sellers.'

Will heard nothing about banks, agents, appraisals, accountancy, conveyancing. It seemed as if by magic the brothers owned two ten story tenements next to each other. As time went by and he got to know the tenants, he also heard, true or not, that the old man who sold the two as a package was happy, indeed surprised at the price.

Though under no illusions that he was being 'made an offer he couldn't refuse.'

Donnie had his business on the market and ultimately gave them away for the value of the floor spaces. 'There was no Good Will built into the price.' Quipped Donnie. After a month of getting a handle on the books and the tenants they called an inaugural Owners Meeting. Will didn't turn up. They called him from the front office. 'When we say you're part of the family Kid, you're part of the family.

Art searched through some papers and gave Will the titles to look at. He was listed there along with the others, a third equal share.

Will was touched more deeply than he can ever remember being. He appreciated being brought in as a partner with property and money, but it was much more than that. It really confirmed that he was a part of a family. And a family in which people didn't want to hurt him, but respected him. Maybe even loved him.

He gave them each a hug and a thank you, and hoped it conveyed what he felt. The meeting came to order. Beer for two and tap water for Art. The approach was simple. Everyone stayed on the same rent. With the money they made they spent half on the people who had the shittiest apartments and the other half on vacant apartments to completely renovate them. They'd rent them out at a higher price, but not out of reach of the neighbourhood. If anyone in the buildings wanted to change up, they had first option.

Because they weren't paying any interest, and Art seemed to be producing additional money from somewhere to renovate empty apartments, their rental income kept growing and all they had to pay was rates, taxes and utilities.

Will moved into a renovated apartment and seemed to enjoy upgrading or fixing longstanding issues in the shitty parts for the occupants who were surprised and grateful. It was quickly established that Art liked to work alone. Will would turn up and see him painting a ceiling, cornices, and around light fittings. One time Will asked Art where the drop sheets were. Art didn't know what a drop sheet was.

After seven months they organised for the first building to be fully painted on the outside. The first time that had happened in as long as most people could remember. It made people afraid that gentrification was on its way. Ultimately it was on its way whether anyone like it or not.

One day Will didn't turn up to the Owners Meeting. He'd sometimes have a day, or maybe three where he didn't come out of his apartment. It wasn't so unusual though he'd never missed an Owners meeting, no matter how awful he looked. Later in the day Art, who never carried a phone, had a tenant come to find him. 'It's Donnie on the phone Art. He said it's real important.'

Art thanked her and took the cell phone. 'Art.' Donnie was agitated 'Come to the hospital Art. It's the kid.'

Art had seen people beaten. He's taken his share of beatings and handed more than a few out. Could leave a hell of a mess. But the beatings he'd mostly seen were handed out by one person, maybe two. This was a beating that missed nothing. The bruises the cuts were everywhere. This was a man kicked long and hard after he'd gone down. There was obviously broken bones. He had tubes up his nose, IV drips and staff that were telling them to leave. The doctors were uncertain as to whether he would see out the night.

They were in the bar Donnie always went to with Will. 'I'm so sick of this. These...scum rule our lives. They've got no honour; they don't give a shit about the neighbourhood.'

'You're connected enough to get the names.'

'I could get names. Rock solid Art.'

Art nodded a series of slow nods. 'They'll burn us down.'

'From what I can see that Kid's dead. He's family.' Donnie sighed. 'I don't know if he was buying some shit from them and it went bad or maybe they don't like seeing their back yard cleaned up.'

Art was looking into empty space. 'Once it's done, we'll need protection for the buildings. I can handle that. You're going on holiday before the blowback. Hawaii, Alaska, whatever.'

Donnie didn't like it. though he still said 'Sure.'

'Two weeks.' Said Art.

The Walk

Art stood before the mirror.

It was like electricity was flowing out of his fingertips. Twenty-five years. He'd never believed he'd be doing this again. He was made for this. Designed for it. There were four more tailored grey suits in the wardrobe. Identical. Tailored by a man a thirty years ago for a man who had not lost or gained an ounce in weight since then.

He did up his tie. He wore a suit every day, but not a grey suit. There were four pairs of shoe's remaining in the cupboard. The suit and shoes only lasted only one outing. He'd lost count how many his tailor had made for him. How many he'd incinerated, buried, or sunk deep in a river or the ocean.

He was ready. Then he walked to the kitchen and he opened a secret compartment behind the crockery cupboards and took out an old fedora. There had only ever been one of these and it wasn't for day to day use. It was for these occasions. And he had taken it to the river. He was grateful to the Kid for catching it.

He opened the door and stepped out onto a sidewalk that rose gradually and started to walk casually. It was a beautiful sunny day. He was pleased. The last walk. He planned to make it a good one. He knew his marks and his reasons were as good as they'd ever been.

Some older people walking their dogs or watering their flowers were soon on the phone to tell their friends, especially those living further up the street that Art D'Amicio was 'Walking'.

Old men went out to call out a hello, which Art returned. If there were younger ones in the house, they were brought out to see Art walk past. They would be told later they'd remember that day their whole lives once they were old enough to hear all the stories. The basis of Art's reputation. But some came out with looks of undisguised hatred.

The further he got up the road the more people were standing at the bottom of their steps or looking out their windows over garden boxes. Many had an inkling of what Art was intending to do. He responded to many a 'Hello' and 'Good to see you Mr D'Amicio' and a few calls of 'Good luck'.

He got to the top of the road. The burger place had disappeared. He walked a little further to a Drugstore, bought a sandwich, and disappeared for two weeks.

Artform

Art was three states over, having hired a car, in his own name, to visit an old friend who lived there. He was in one of the biggest gun stores in the northeast and had come across some unexpected problems.

Once he'd let the man behind the counter know what he wanted they'd moved to a partitioned part of the store. Art pulled out his guns and the man's eyebrows rose as far as they would go. 'Oh my. They are beautifully maintained examples of their type. I'm sure you don't, but if you ever want to part with them, I'd give you very good price.'

'What I want is ammunition. A thousand rounds. And if you have a range here, I'd like to sight them back in.'

The men were close to the same age. The man behind the counter, who turned out to be the store owner, had bad news. 'They don't make ammunition for those anymore more. Haven't for some time. If I could get a special batch made it would never be anything like as accurate. And the number of rounds you want would take weeks.'

'What's the equivalent I can buy now.'

'Okay...there's a very good pistol I think you'd be satisfied with. Used by target shooters as well as you're more, um, general purpose high accuracy pistol shooter. Unfortunately, the silencers to suit, like yours, I can't help you with. Rightly or wrongly civilians can't have em.'

'Do you have a set of scales.'

'Sure.' The man returned with a set of scale he plugged it. Art pulled out a twenty-ounce bar of gold and set in on the scales, even though 20oz was stamped on the polished ingot.

The man looked at the bar for a long moment and said. 'The best pistols for you I have here, but the extra rounds would be here until tomorrow. The other things. If I can get them at all, three or four days.'

'That sounds good. If the silencers come later, I'll need another five hundred rounds so I can sight the pistols in with and without the silencers. Can the additional rounds come in three days?'

'Sure.'

'And I'd like some night vision goggles.' Art had done some research. 'Military grade.'

'Well sir, as implied in the name, we can't sell those.'

Art produced another 20oz bar of gold. The man looked at it and sighed. 'Sir I'll do my level best to get what you've asked for. If I can't I'll get you the very best I can possibly find anywhere in the US and give them to you at a ten percent discount. Some high end hunting night vision gear is pretty close.'

'Charge full price if you've done your best. Hold on to those will you.' Art said pointing to the ingots. 'I'll be in tomorrow afternoon to start sighting in the pistols.'

Art had seven things to get at a hardware store and needed some items of clothing and footwear. By the time all this was done, stores were closing, and he went to the hotel he'd booked for the next two weeks.

He hadn't been there for over twenty five years but nothing much had changed, and Jean had agreed to help, like the old days. She said she missed it. Building up alibi's with Art. Pictures of them with doctored date stamps. Getting their picture taken in restaurants.

Though they had a small course at four restaurants a night, so they had a more than enough dinner photos. Pictures together with clocks behind them which had been altered and half a dozen other ploys. Since he'd been away Jean had married twice and divorced twice. Produced one child who was Jean's pride and joy and was studying architecture.

Nearly forty years before they'd met on a train. Art was returning from some out of state 'business'. She'd been besotted but knew instinctively that she could be destined to share only a part of her life with him.

She grew to love being his source of alibi's. And was a good friend he visited even if he didn't need one.

He was at the range as soon as it opened. He had full body targets set at the exact minimum and maximum distance he specified. If there were no other range users, he kept the lights off and used the military night vision goggles which had been sourced. Otherwise, he was at the far end with no one closer than three laneways. The Owner visited Art and realised the range was going to very quickly run out of full body targets. He noticed a shot pattern on the targets totally different to anything he'd ever seen before. Art was going to offer well over cost to get more targets. The Owner said he'd paid more than enough. He'd pull out all the stops to get what was needed from other ranges.

Art was comfortable with the pistols. When the silencers arrived, he'd repeated the process and had to admit the hardware was better than what he'd had. He ordered an additional thousand rounds. These where to be on hand for another day if there ever was one. He thanked the owner, who said the video recording of his visits had become corrupted. This was a cause for additional thanks. When the owner was closing for the night, he found two mint condition nineteen fifties pistols on his bench.

Fifteen Minutes

Art had been laying under an old house for two days and three nights. The house was the same type as his mother's but smaller, and derelict. Listening and learning. He' brought water, food, tools and other things to execute the plan. He wore black overalls covering over the grey suit. He wore black boots and had a black balaclava at the ready. It had been uncomfortable. Laying in the dirt. He hadn't anticipated the fleas.

It didn't matter. This was what he was good at. He would stay there until he had what he needed. A good understanding of the routine, to the extent that there was one. Who was who, who slept where, who did what. What the traffic through each of doors was. Were the windows left open or closed. Was there any preparation for a response to what they'd done to Will? Where was the television and stereo situated?

He did reconnaissance inspections around the house when all was quiet to find the power box, check if the door was locked and the windows could be easily closed. Fortunately, most of them were closed already.

On the third night, at three in the morning, he was satisfied. He quickly went around the perimeter of the house and used a long strip of gaffer tape to seal the windows at the opening join. To get to the second floor he used a ladder he'd brought in from the beginning with rags covering the top and sealed these windows also.

At the front door the main power switch was turned off, but with minimum noise. The front door, which he thought he might have to shoot though, was open. These people felt safe from attack. His night goggles on, he quickly taped the front door shut behind himself.

Anyone looking from the outside into the completely dark house would see a quick series of flashes unaccompanied by any sound.

As he moved though the rooms, the flashes continued throughout the entire house, sometimes in fast bursts or sometimes in ones or twos these occurring all the way back to the front door.

Within seconds of the last shot, Art emerged from the house to started bringing up cannisters of a mixture of diesel and petrol. He methodically went to every room and covered the floors, furniture, and some of the walls with the liquid. He kept carrying each the half dozen five-gallon cannisters into the house until the house was full of fumes. He then began dousing the outside walls and finally soaked some stumps holding the house up and lit them up first. He wanted a hot, fast fire, that left only ash.

He went through the house and lit up every room in several places to make the whole building burn hot close together at the same time. He heard sirens and left along his planned retreat.

Art looked around and saw a building completely on fire. It looked white in the centre, with orange and red at the outer edges.

It was a long night at the wheel. The overalls, boots and gloves went into a bag full of bricks and over the side a of a wide bridge five hundred miles from the city. He dropped off the car in a city two hours from where Jean lived which Jean's friend, innocent of his reasons for an alibi, had hired for him. He paid cash for the return bus fare back to Jean.

He knew that all this work on an alibi didn't really matter that much. It was partly for old time's sake. A good reason for him to catch up with Jean.

The people that really mattered weren't going to be interested in an alibi.

The Investigation

Hannity was approaching retirement. Not quickly enough he'd started to think. He wasn't sure who the good guys and the bad guys were any more. Theory had taken over practice and experience and a feel for the street was seen as quaint in some circles.

When the news arrived about a drug house turned to ashes, he didn't try to disguise it, it gave him a bit of a lift. Forensics were sifting through what was left. He didn't really care who did it, although there was sensational, and probably accurate speculation.

Hannity was a kid then. A pavement pounding Paddy, when D'Amicio used to do that strange ritual of his. No one could think of a victim who didn't have it coming and for everyone he turned to mush, it was likely five would leave the neighbourhood. Since that time had Hannity had never visited or lived in such a law-abiding place albeit with the waning influence of the Mob still at work.

Now he was dealing with a guy who had made detective with very little street time and those streets he'd been on weren't the mean Kind. Detective Gregory came to see him early. He was excited. He was on a fast track, and he saw successful investigations into this fire like this getting him there.

'I'd really like to take on the Brighton Street fire if you haven't assigned it yet.'

Hannity sighed. This Detective came in early. He was keen. Hannity valued that no matter how much he knew they clashed.

'Sure. Looks like it's open and shut. Gangs killing gang members. It's helps us out. The vacant lot will allow a developer to build some multi-story monstrosity.'

'Early forensic are showing us some strange ballistics. They think most of the victims took a number of shots, but all to the limbs.'

'Many limbs left out of the ashes.'

'Several but not all of them. I'm not sure the gang angle jibes. I've heard there might be another potential perpetrator.'

Hannity sighed. 'Sure, there might. You do what you believe you should do to be a good Detective. But do me one favour. When you get back to your desk, I want you to write out a list of all the rape, child abuse, drug dealing, breaking and entering and corruption you know you could find out about. Detect you know? Write that list for me and make sure the death of a bunch of thugs selling drugs to kids should be at the top.' As he'd being saying this Hannity had been growing more and more irritable. 'I'll sit in on any interview with witnesses, suspects or people of interest.'

Hannity looked down as the boring administrative shit that was now his life. He did this to indicate to Gregory it was time to leave. It was a small rudeness which was uncharacteristic. But he knew Gregory would never write that list.

Roll on retirement, Hannity thought.

Captain Hannity and Detective Gregory were waiting in the interview room for Art who, merely as a person of interest, had agreed to meet them. He was running late. As he was being escorted to the door by an Officer, two other people were also being brought to the room and they all met at the door. Art smiled, tipped his hat and bade them enter first. He came in last, slowly, with the assistance of a cane. He sat quintessentially, as the interviewee opposite the other four.

The woman of the two late comers said. 'I apologise gentleman for our late involvement. Thank you, Captain Hannity, for being so hospitable. I want to reinforce, we're here, only as observers.' After a pregnant pause she continued. 'At least, at this time.' As she said this, she shared a small unseen smile with Art.

All of this put Gregory off his script. To such an extent he simply launched into a 'Mr D'Amicio we'd like to hear about your movements on the night of the 29th of last month.'

'Well kid. My mother taught me to know who it was I was sitting around speaking with. She was very much one for courtesy my mother. Politeness. Finest woman I ever knew.'

Without allowing Gregory to lead the introductions, Art said. 'And even though things have changed since her day, she drilled into us that ladies are always first in all things.'

Emelia smiled. 'Emelia Smith. Senior Profiler. East Coast. FBI.' Before things could progress, further Art expressed amazement. 'So young and yet you're in charge of the FBI.' She smiled with more familiarity than she could hide. 'Not quite yet Mr D'Amicio. In fact, this is my boss Adriaan.'

A cheerful man reached across the table to shake hands. 'It's good to meet you Mr D'Amicio. You've lived in a neighbourhood and lived through an era that young people only see in lousy period dramas.' Art nodded. He'd never turned a television on in his life. Again, Art took the initiative and reached his hand out to shake the Captain's. 'Captain I've seen you out on the beat since you joined the force. It's so good to see the force put someone with some street sense in charge. I wish I could have joined the force.' He lifted up the cane. 'Bad knees.'

'Art. I would have loved to have been pounding the beat with you. Could not imagine a person I would rather have served with. Maybe next time around for old timers like us eh?'

Art smiled and nodded.

Detective Gregory could not imagine how much more he could be undercut by his colleague. He went back and repeated the same question.

Art went back to his preoccupation. But a little less considerately. He held out his hand and said 'Son, I'm also interested in who you are.' Then the question was asked again and, Art responded he was out of State. As always, they would find a very tight alibi. He pointed out to those in the meeting room, if he seemed to be getting sleepy, his usual nap time was around three.

Gregory indicated that the shots sustained by those in the house were in a particular pattern. What was believed to be his signature.

Art could see Hannity about to boil over and the others had plenty of objections. But they were apparently going to let Gregory hang himself. 'Quite a proposition. That I have this, what do you call it, pattern. That I've used before.'

'Your files are sealed Mr D'Amicio. Fifty-five years' worth of files.'

'Hmm. I guess there was that Jay walking incident.' Art again pinned the Detective like and insect, a small insect, to a board. Because his gaze held nothing. He was working on. Something inconsequential.

'You were very close to a young man severely beaten by those thought to have been burned in the house fire.'

'A fine young man. Were you able to establish the perpetrators Detective Gregory? It was a terrible crime perpetrated in our neighbourhood and your precinct. Based on this gun shooting pattern I am supposed to have and the fact I cared about the welfare of a young man, are you charging me with doing this terrible thing.'

'In the fifties you we're known to walk up Garner Street as a kind of signal before a criminal act.'

Emelia stifled a laughed.

'Well that seals the....' Art appeared bewildered.

'I can't apologise enough for this Art. We simply wanted to ask you a few questions in case you could help us in any way with our investigation. If you'd seen or heard anything. If I could see you in my office kid.' Hannity was now *very* angry.

Gregory stood and nodded a goodbye to Art, following behind the Captain. They arrived in the Captain's office and Gregory was going to speak but was cut off.

'These are blank transfer forms. Fill them out and have them on my desk by nine tomorrow morning or you're disciplined.'

'Where are am I being transferred to?'

'I don't give a shit. Get on a phone and find a vacancy in the force, any force, and fill it. Goodbye.'

As a part of the arrangement for the visit, Emelia and Art would have some time alone. While Adriaan would get time with Art and hear a few real Mob stories that evening over dinner.

Emelia and Art sat regarding each other across the table. She sighed. 'Eight shots? I mean why not write 'Art Was Here', on the building next door.'

With only a trace of a smile he said. 'I think there must be some copycat guy out there. Once they heard I was out he thought maybe he could do this stuff and pin it on me.'

She answered like she was laying out four aces. 'You're probably right. This copycat guy is a pretty lousy shot.' She'd solicited this reaction from Art a few times in the past. He barely changed his posture. But his eyes. The intensity of his eyes and the way he could take control of the tenor of a room; completely. Fortunately, this focus was never directed at her. It was directed at information which she quickly supplied given she knew this was a detail he had no sense of humour about.

'Papers say there were nine in the building. How many did this copycat guy miss in the pattern on.' He said.

The papers hadn't in fact revealed the number of dead, but she let that pass. 'One of the shots didn't go through the ankle bone but scored it deeply. Local splintering from what they can tell.'

The room lightened.

'It's nice to see you in a suit.' She said, only ever having seen Art in orange overalls before.

'It's good to see you. I'd figured visiting times were over.'

'*Yeah* I was trying to work out a way to keep in touch that the Bureau would understand. And lo and behold you've come up with this.'

'I could do some new stuff if you want, and you could write a second volume to your book.'

'I see. I could write another PhD but this time one step *behind* or even in real time as the crimes occur.'

'Sure. You'd be chasing the copycat guy and you'd be writing another book about it, for all of the other agents to learn from.'

'I can kind of understand what happened here Art and I'm sorry about your friend, but I really wish this copycat guy would hang up his hat. My recommendation to the Bureau on this is that no matter how much things point towards you; it's very difficult to see how a man in his mid-seventies could do it.' He was going to interject but she ploughed on. 'The alibi, although ridiculously similar to all the other ones, is fairly tight, and the sub text will be that, as Hannity might say 'Don't we have better things to do?'

'Early seventies.'

'Mid-seventies sounds better. Maybe even late seventies. Who cares?'

He shrugged.

'Now I need a favour. The mood in our office was to leave this to the locals unless they charged you. I thought there might be some value in visiting when you were called in for a statement. My boss is a Mafia tragic. If you could come to dinner with us, tell some stories, drop a few names, that kind of thing. It'll help me hold my end to have taken this trip.'

'Easy. Did I say how good it was to see you?'

The Appointment

They looked across at each other over the man in the same bed Art had left him in two weeks earlier. Most of the bruising was gone apart from some yellow tinges.

Donnie looked up at a guy who was ready to go and burn down another ten houses. 'They think he'll be okay. Sort of. Head got cracked, not sure how much. Be in a wheelchair then crutches for a long time. And yes, you got them all, and a few extra so there's no one else. And…'

'And?'

'The whole gang is coming for you. Ma's place. Tuesday.' His voice broke slightly. 'They said to expect it to take longer.'

Art breathed in and let out a slow breath. 'Not like we didn't see it coming. You? The Kid? The buildings?'

'They say they'll leave it all alone. I think they realise there could be plenty more retaliation that gets organised. They say this would end it.'

Art knew he had a few days to connect with people he could trust, old people now, to make sure the gang did what they said they would. There was still some gold left in one last hole in the ground to pay whoever they said was trustworthy to keep watch and respond appropriately.

'So where are you going. Miami? LA?'

Donnie said nothing for a long time. 'Vegas. Always wanted to go. Loose a bit of money. Take in some shows, the sights, you know. Want to come?'

'No Donnie. I got an appointment that day.'

Unforeseen Events

Art decided to wait on the porch which had old wooden seats and the cracked remains of vinyl seat cushions. The street was quiet. Before he left Donnie had made sure that those that needed to know were indoors, or out of town if possible.

He heard the familiar footfalls of his brother coming around the veranda. Without looking up he said. 'Can't even trust your own brother these days.'

Donnie sat down next to him. 'You can talk about trust.' He voice was a balance of humour and hurt. 'Twenty five years you spend not a hundred miles from where we're sitting right now, and you never let your little brother come and see you. Did you think I was so dumb Art, that I believed that France…that France stuff?' Their mother had been so staunch about anyone using a cuss word in the house, neither of them could, even after she was gone.

'It was a pretty good story. A bit of detail. Better than 'Vegas' although I'll allow mine was for a bit longer.' There was a pause. 'No Donnie. You were never going to see me in there. Look at how you reacted when I put some overalls on to help the Kid.'

Donnie was going to launch into tirade about how that was different. How he would have liked to see his big brother, how he needed him sometimes. And maybe Art had needed him, maybe would have liked to spend time with him. But Art was looking down the street. Things in the past, which now including his stay in prison, had always very quickly become obscure to him.

'Anyhow, as to your original question, I'd rather go out beside my big brother than keep living in a place where the animals run the zoo.'

'What's that you have there?' Said Art

'What's that you have there?' Said Donnie

'I started to come up with a new plan while you were in Vegas. I got some men. Ruthless men, to cover the buildings for a year. And some even meaner men to cover those men. And then I thought to myself there could be something of a gunfight this evening, and then I maybe disappear. Live out my days in sewers. Shooting rats for food. Therefore, I have my two new best friends. And about eight hundred rounds. I'll climb out of the sewers now and then if I need more.'

'I guessed your mind would be heading that way. And this was my chance to show you that you weren't the only one who buried important things in Ma's backyard.'

He pulled out an old rifle from a case made for the purpose. It was a mint condition Thompson 'Tommy' Machine Gun. Art had to laugh. 'Those were old fashioned guns by the time I was in the Organisation. It's in beautiful condition.'

Donnie was a little put out on behalf of his gun. 'I'm a collector. At least of this one. And if you need a continuous spray of fire rather than pistol shots, these drum cannisters hold a hundred rounds. And I have seven.'

Art nodded. 'We should mesh in well.'

Donnie heard a phone go off in Art's jacket which was unusual, because Art had never had a phone in his life.

'Excuse me.' He said and walked away down the porch. After a brief exchange, Donnie could hear him say. 'Sure. I'll get him for you.'

Art handed his brother the phone. 'It's for you.'

'Hi. This is Donnie.'

'Hey Donnie. It's Nora.'

Donnie took a second to connect the name through the years gone by. 'Wow. Nora. It's been a while huh.'

'Yeah.' She paused. 'Art told me... what you said. I wanted to let you know that it was the sweetest thing I ever heard.' She paused for a reply but there was none. 'And... and Donnie if I had my time over, I would've made a different choice.'

'Well.' It took Donnie a moment to pull himself together to reply. 'I can't tell you how much that means to me Nora. I've never come across a sweeter, better person to this day. Don't let anyone tell you otherwise.'

A complicated, but still sweet laugh came down the line. 'You look after yourself Donnie.'

'Sure. And you take care Nora. Thanks for the call.'

Donnie sat on the porch bench next to Art, squeezing the moisture from his eyes with the heels of his hands.

He sat up and breathed in. 'I was always the crier in the family.'

Art smiled, handing over one of the three clean handkerchiefs he always carried. 'You were always the good kid in the family. The good kid in the whole neighbourhood Donnie.'

'You can't know how much that meant to me Art. I did pretty well when they were handing out big brothers.'

Donnie had finished saying this when a figure dressed completely in black, or what on second glance was black camouflage, appeared beside them.

He had a balaclava pushed back against night vision goggles pushed above his forehead, revealing strangely familiar features. He was carrying a sniper's rifle.

After the two porch sitters recovered, resigning themselves to whatever was coming next, the man said. 'Gentlemen is one of you Donnie D'Amicio?' Donnie almost put his hand up but nodded and said. 'Yeah. That's me.'

The visitor looked to Art. 'And you sir. Are you Art D'Amicio?' Art smiled. Fascinated. 'That's me.'

'I wanted to thank you both for the interest you've taken in my kid brother Will. More than an interest. You've treated him like family.'

Donnie spoke up. 'As you can imagine. It's been a pleasure for us. He's a fine young man.'

Will's bother seemed to be on a schedule and became more businesslike. 'Gentleman I'd like to show you a list of names. If you could indicate if any of them are familiar to you.'

Donnie and Art were certain what 'familiar to you' meant. Art had nothing to offer. Donnie looked at the page for a long time.

He handed it back to the man. 'I can't help, sorry.' He knew he was supposed to point out a name that shouldn't have been on that list. He didn't see one.

'It's been an honour to meet you gentlemen. Please take care on the streets this evening.'

With that, and a silence that impressed Art, he was gone.

They looked at each other and laughed 'Did that just happen?' said Donnie.

'I'm not sure but I know he was eying off your Tommie gun for an exchange.'

Donnie was on his third beer and Art working though his second glass of tap water when four cars came down the road and parked in a pattern suggesting any late-night traffic go another way; quickly.

Five men got out of the first car and walked towards the steps. 'You go with your brother Donnie. I can respect that. But it's not going to hurt any less.'

Donnie shrugged. 'He's my brother. You'd do the same.' He was careful to deliver this deadpan.

They didn't notice how Art was sitting. It looked like he had nothing on his leg. But there was a cloth the same fabric as his suit sitting over a pistol. He was taking a drink from a glass with his left hand with his right hand resting on his right thigh. Donnie was making plans for the new age gangsters routine for the four cars behind to get them down. Donnie knew that Art could have a fifth man dead before the first one hit the ground and the gun never leave where it rested on his leg.

But they both hoped they didn't need to shoot a bullet.

Donnie later realised what a tense time it must have been for Will's brother. He wanted everyone out of the cars, to keep their involvement at as great a distance as possible. The squad were on the pavement in front of the old wooden steps and all the cars were empty when the firing started There were sixteen or seventeen men, most moving towards the house, and a few posted around the cars. With a low whirr and a quiet thud and the men started to fall in twos and threes. All of them were down within twenty seconds.'

Art looked at Donnie. They sat and looked out at the scene before them for a while. They could see black shapes moving across rooftops. They may have been making for an exit, but Donnie and Art knew they had more things planned for that night.

'Seems the shows over here. Perhaps we better put our toys away and ourselves to bed.' Said Art.

'Maybe a movie.'

It wasn't long before a patrolman was at the door. A surprised Art came outside to see why the police were calling. Both he and Donnie could not have appeared more shocked.

They looked at each other with their best 'what the hell' faces, gazing around at the carnage. They advised the patrolman and then the Detectives who arrived soon after, that they were watching a movie. 'It was a movie with lots of shooting and stuff. Explosions.' Donnie explained.

'Except I fell asleep. I don't watch much television.' Art said this in the spirit of full disclosure.

It was only later that they heard that the tally wasn't seventeen, but seventy-four. Their visitor and his friends ensured every member of the gang who'd nearly beaten his brother to death, was dead.

The FBI managed the case and although the original house fire was of interest, the main event was what was splashed across every newspaper. Some calling for answers, some calling out congratulations. Some decrying the availability of such firearms, others reminding them these particular weapons don't sell over the counter.

Chinese bullets. Every fibre they found, which were few in number, originated in Russia. No witnesses, no strange movements into or out of the neighbourhoods. The majority of CCTV's had been disabled, but progressively.

Like Art, they'd been planning for some time and then laid up. Self- contained. When Art brought a burning house down on nine of the gang, four of their most important targets, it had thrown their plans, and their schedule, into disarray. They regrouped, resupplied, got some intelligence from the street, and came up with a plan. A bigger plan because they'd had time to wander the streets late at night in hoodie's and fill out their list.

Two of the team said this had been the best thing for their PTSD. The other two said it made them realise there was nothing for them as civilians. They were good at only one thing.

Beginnings

Will didn't want to get picked up. The brothers were told his girlfriend had said she'd bring him back. Excited as they were to see him back 'In the Business' they knew enough to keep it low key so the first thing his girlfriend didn't see two old codgers trying not to fuss over him.

He was still in a wheelchair and would be for some time when he would gradually be able to move onto crutches. When Stacey moved in, Will had to stop his two 'Uncles' from knocking down the walls between three apartments to create a tenement penthouse.

Will couldn't work, and might never be able to do physical work again, but he could organise tradesmen and decide what needed to be done, give the instructions and monitor the work. Since the business had the money, they could get a lot done.

Soon everyone in both places had new bathrooms. Kitchens to roll out in the coming year. They got bid discounts buying a hundred toilets and sinks at once.

Art always took over the vacated apartments. Since people knew Art D'Amicio would be making the final inspection when they left, they tended to leave the place spotless.

If anything that needed to be ripped out, he would leave that to the younger set. And then he would start repainting. Maybe needing to remove some old wallpaper and sanding. There was no time limit and he would eventually leave a magnificently painted apartment in colours selected by Stacy. The apartment repaints were, as time passed, were getting longer and longer to complete.

Stacey was in the process of adopting him as a surrogate father which he thought was nice. She didn't know he had another adoptive daughter. She brought up some tap water and put a slice of lemon in.

One day she came into a living room where he was cutting in between a wall and a cornice. He was standing stock still looking at a section he'd just painted. He'd overrun the wall line and painted an inch onto the cornice with wall paint.

Once he heard her, he turned around and smiled.

Last Walk

Art was in his grey suit walking up the pavement. The difference now was that a man was walking behind him with a gun to the back of his head. 'He was my father. It was my father that you did that to. I was in the room next door. Your men didn't let anyone out of the rooms in the house. Do you know what it's like to hear that happen to your father, when you're twelve years old?'

Art was going to point out that if it him that got chewed apart, apparently it would have been much less traumatic for a child of twelve. But he didn't care.

'You think you're so smart D'Amicio. Huh? You're going to die on the pavement where everybody thought you were invincible.'

'No. I'm not smart Jerry. You wife is though. Divorced you twenty years back. Lives in a nice place not a mile from here, with a fellow by the name of Edward. Your kids. Rosie, she's smart. Nurse in London. Highly regarded from what I understand.' The gun started shake in Jerry's hand as they walked then he pushed if forward roughly. 'You son. He made it. He's smart. Dropped out of Highschool but came back and did classes and now he a tradesman. A carpenter. Had his first kid last week. He didn't call the kid Jerry though.'

Jerry pushed forward hard with the barrel of the gun again. 'You shut the fuck up!'

'There's lots of smart people Jerry. But you're not one of them see. Because you let a stupid mutt rule your life. Now Jerry; the cops will be here soon, and this bullet's been following me around for fifty years. Try not to fuck this up.' Jerry didn't know but that was the first time Art had used a cuss word other than damn. Art breathed out and felt a relaxation he couldn't remember ever experiencing. He'd chosen the time and place, not Jerry. After a few more steps Art said. 'What are you waiting for.'

Donnie and Will had been asked to come and see him at the bar, so they were only a few hundred yards away when they heard the shot. Donnie was holding the upper half of his brother body tightly to him. 'What were you doing out here Art? Why?'

He squeezed his brother's cheek against his, ignoring the blood on the back of the neck with the exit wound at the top of the skull. Art would rate the shot as poor, but it did the job. As the police and ambulance arrived Donnie grabbed Art's hat from next to the body and threw it to Will walking painfully on crutches. 'Take this and hide it Kid. Hide it good.'

There was no wake or gathering of friends designed to console Donnie. He had decided to have a private graveside service. On reflection though he made one concession to those outside the family, he thought Art was 'everybody's.' And so it was quite a line of people shuffling past to look at Art D'Amicio one last time or familiarise themselves for the first time with the most notable man ever to come out of the neighbourhood. As the line passed the open casket, some standing looking down for some time, including Captain Hannity, they then passed by Donnie. Generally, with a platitude, but sometimes relating a brief story Donnie may not have been aware of. And how much his brother had meant to them.

Will found himself stationed on the far side of the casket to the line. Initially he didn't know why. When he thought about it, he realised Donnie didn't want anyone to touch or interfere with Art, no matter how small the chances. A middle-aged woman arrived to stand beside him. 'Look at their faces Will. Grateful, curious, occasionally seething with hate. Your adoptive father was an enigma. An unabashed killer, but a true gentleman. Absolutely merciless, yet for those not consigned to that fate, he was as thoughtful and kind a man as anyone you could hope to meet.'

She turned him and smiled. 'I'm Emelia. You're my adopted bother. Took me twenty years of getting to know him to finally be advised of my daughterhood. You were made a son within a few weeks. Which made me a little jealous for a while. But I knew Art well. And fast or slow, his judgement of people was consistent, and didn't change over time.'

It was a long line. Both adoptive brother and sister were surprised how often they heard Thankyou Mr D'Amicio whispered to the dead man. Emelia supposed that many of these older people may have been directly or indirectly influenced by Art's activity. A thief or a serial rapist, a merciless wife beater, small time protection racketeer, a nasty pimp or a pimp of any kind, the pervert, the paedophile, conman, bent copper or clergy, most of them left the neighbourhood. One way or another. People who had lived in daily fear were suddenly free.

'Sometimes if Art was feeling generous, he wouldn't do the Walk. But a conman might arrive home to find his house empty with a message to meet Art at a specific address. His car would be loaded up, anything that didn't fit was burning next to it.'

'He'd advise them to be in another State by morning. 'I'll keep an eye on you from here. We're a big Organisation.' The Mob still did their business in the neighbourhood. And things could be unpleasant.' People knew the rules and the limits.

Last in line came Bernie. He looked up at Will and Emelia as if he was embarrassed to take up the space they were looking at. His eyes were wet. He looked down at Art and they could see that for all the people that passed by, he was the most heartbroken to see Art gone.

A Beer

As soon as he opened the door to take out the trash Will knew that Donnie must have been waiting for him. Donnie had been taking off, and putting back on, the same light fitting again and again, to catch Will in person.

'Hey Kid. Good to see you. This light fitting nearly came off so I brought up a new one. No problem if you have other things going on, but I thought we could maybe have a beer later.' Will only had the wall but didn't want to go for a beer either.

'Sure Donnie.' Anyone else would have received the stock standard. 'Maybe tomorrow.'

They both knew he would need time to shower and get into clothes younger than a week old, so they arranged to meet in half an hour. Donnie hoped the booth he'd sat in for the last forty or more years would be free.

In his apartment, Will went inside to find clean clothes which, like his other possessions, were now in piles. As he went out the door, he looked back at the letter he'd torn to pieces and the pathetic little package that had come with it.

He sat down in front of Donnie a quarter of an hour late, apologised and they were soon sharing a beer. Will now on his sixth for that day unbeknownst to Donnie.

Donnie knew he shouldn't have asked but had to know. She was his friend too. 'Maybe you and Stacey and me could all go out to dinner this week. Somewhere nice.'

'Stacey's gone Donnie. She'd been seeing someone else for quite a while, she found it hard to...tell me.' Will said the last part of the sentence with a tone of self-disgust. That he was such a pathetic looser a girl found it hard to break up with him.

'Well there's always...'

Will cut Donnie off. 'Yeah. I know. I know. There are other women in the world. They're lining up to settle down with a full package cripple.'

'It hurts me to hear you describe yourself that way son. You're a good kid. A good man. That's rare. Think about all the people in those buildings, older people or single parents, they don't have much at all but they're living with dignity now. That was *your* idea. And you're making it happen.'

'Sorry I was rude before Donnie. 'You're the one guy who doesn't make me feel like I'm not trying.'

'I know you'll never stop trying. And you know if I could come with you to that place and help you fight you're way out I would, but I can't.'

Donnie looked into a pair of eyes that had now stopped trying.

He reached across the table and squeezed the man's shoulder and said. 'Don't leave me alone Will.' The words came in a rush, raw. And the family crier wasn't ashamed to be wiping the water from his eyes.

Donnie saw Will only sporadically after that and ended up only exchanging a minimalistic 'hello.'

About a month after sharing that beer he looked up to see Art's Urn was missing, replaced by his brother's hat, which had been how they decided to share Art.

Donnie knew he was finally alone.

A Visit to Broken Promise

This time it was hard to climb up. Very hard. He had brought a crutch he hadn't needed for a few weeks to help him get onto the railings. It was slippery as showers began to come and go, but on this occasion with hardly any breeze.

He had almost dropped the urn on a few occasions trying to juggle it and hold the pillar. Holding on for a pointless moment of reflection rather than slip and tumble over like an idiot.

He was finally standing still one hand onto the pillar. This time he was able to see the water far below. He hoped Donnie would understand why he'd taken the urn. Art had promised him they would meet there if what they tried didn't work. And Will believed for him nothing worked. Now Art needed to keep his word.

He heard a voice behind him. 'How you going kid?'

Will turned around to see Bernie standing a few yards away, in what was slowly becoming a downpour. While turning around, Will lost his balance and slipped on the wet railing, falling painfully on his shoulder on the pavement. The urn fell from his hands and cracked open near the curb, now swelling with water.

Will ignored the Urn and got up painfully and grab Bernie from collar of one of the pathetic, dated suits he wore.

'You want to know how I am Bernie. You want to know about my fucking day. Well most days I walk around feeling like I'm getting the shit kicked out of me. And when I'm not reliving the last time I had the shit kicked out of me Bernie, I imagine something new driving me insane with pain and confusion.'

'Is that the information you want Bernie. Do you want to know that the girl I loved Bernie, actually loved, left me for someone not as smart as me, not as good looking as me and someone who will never love her like I would have. But she left me for someone who functions Bernie.'

Will was now beginning to shake the old man. More and more violently

'And hey Burnie. I'm on the junk now. There are new guys in the neighbourhood who push the stuff. I can't handle the pain and the system can't give me morphine forever, so I have to go to the pushers and buy it with money I *steal* Bernie. That's right Burnie. I steal money from the person I respect most in the world, and who has only ever only shown me kindness and trusted me.'

All of Will's injured body was objecting to the pain of standing but he kept shaking the old man and was now yelling in his face.

'Still interested in how I'm going. Well I get a letter a little while back from some army cunt, who says that my brother got killed. He was a hero trying to take back the same shithole town, in the same shithole country, that the politicians had given back to the same shithead enemy a year ago. They send me this cheap silver-plated piece shit glass to remember the only person who was good to me among my fucking drug addled dysfunctional white trash family.'

'So that's how I'm doing. How the fuck are you doing Bernie?'

He threw the old man away like a doll so that he landed on his back in the gutter. The swelling water damming at his groin, trying to wash him away like a leaf. He swung his legs around and pushed himself up to sit on the curb. The rain was stinging now.

'I came here to, you know, maybe try to talk you out of it otherwise I was going to…join you if you'd let me.'

Will could barely hear him and sat beside him in spite of himself. The urn, with the earthly remains of Art, lay between them with ashes slowly being washed into the stormwater.

'I know I can't understand what's it's like for you and I always say things wrong. See I was hoping.' The old man shrugged. 'Maybe you'd like me. We could be friends. But I know it's…well, I don't have any friends. No one except Donnie has ever visited me in my apartment in more than twenty years and…ha…he's a good guy to everyone.'

'I was never going to amount to much. No good at school or sport. My wife said she'd divorce me if it weren't for the church.' He spoke quietly so Will could barely hear. 'She used to hit me. I let her. That's how weak I am.'

'I've sold most of my stuff, even my clothes, which I don't get much for. Would never make the rent except for the bit of work Donnie gives me. I don't want to live on the street or on someone's charity, so the river seemed like maybe a good idea.'

'Donnie and Art have been good to me when everyone else ignores me. When Art D'Amicio calls you by name and asks how you're doing. Well, that would make me feel ten feet tall. I guess when they more of less adopted you, I thought, working at the Laundromat sometimes and all, I might have a chance at shoehorning my way in as a cousin of something.'

The rain moderated to a steady downpour. About half of Arts remains had washed away. In the process a medal on a ribbon had been revealed. Will dug it out and tossed it over his shoulder into the river.

After a long time Bernie asked. 'What do we do now?'

'I have no idea.' Said Will.

Will suspected the door would be open and the lights still on at one in the morning. The two men, dripping with moisture sat at the table with Donnie. Who had several empty beer cans in front of him. They put the base section of the urn, broken in a jagged pattern, containing perhaps a third of its contents on the table.

Donnie got them beers and said. 'I see Art's lost some weight.'

The Doctoral Thesis.

Will came out of his apartment to find Bernie. He'd been relocated to Will's floor when he moved from his old apartment block up the road to become maintenance supervisor.

'You look like shit Will.' The old man said looking up while locking his door. Still tentative in this relationship.

'Yeah, and you're an old prick in a cheap suit.' This was their new approach and it seemed to be holding together. The proximity was testing Will though. 'I'd like to get together with you later and work out a maintenance plan for the next month.'

'Sure Will. Meet at Donnie's?'

'We don't need to bother Donnie with this shit Bernie. We can work this out ourselves. I'll come to your apartment around three. Have some beers in there maybe.'

'Sure Will.'

The younger man stalked off. Annoyed at himself that he was getting to like the old prick. Also that he was so petty to have ever disliked him in the first place.

He was still ruminating on something Donnie had said, no doubt after much consideration. *'You haven't tried everything Will.'* Will noticed he wasn't being called Kid. 'Your brother, Art, me. Think about us and try some different things to get well or even a bit better. I've been studying this stuff. Nothing will change at all between us Will if you don't want to. But I'll be standing right beside you if we can find anything worth trying.' Will wondered if he would go back to 'Kid' again if he wasn't interested in trying anything. He knew he hadn't tried hard enough. He owed it to his adopted uncle and now all the people who depended on him to improve their lives. And he much preferred Will.

The FBI agent he'd met at Art's funeral was catching up with Donnie that evening, and she'd said he'd be welcome to join them. It turned out Donnie had called her with some questions, and she said it would be better if they caught up face to face.

Emelia had reserved the booth Donnie wanted. Once the food had arrived, she said. 'Hard to know where to start. But first, I was wondering on the way in here, how many times Art walked up the road in a year.'

Donnie thought about it. 'Two or three, half a dozen some years maybe.'

Emelia smiled. 'Adds up over twenty five years. Not all were single. And that doesn't include the mob killings.' She was reflective. 'Art was by far the finest gentleman I ever met. When I was in an interview room with him, he made me feel like some sort of crazy cross between a princess and a genius. I know he was a great older brother. And surrogate father.' She looked at Will. 'To both of us. Yet he was a murderer. On a grand scale.'

'And you tracked most of them down. I mean, figured them out.' Donnie was curious, but also apprehensive as to what might be revealed.

'Most of the one hundred and twelve I knew about yeah. It became my hobby. I was finishing my degree for Quantico and looking around for a subject for a PhD. I wanted to get into the profiling area. Most serial killers, mass murderers, you name it, had been done to death, excuse the pun. I wondered if there were any old mobsters still alive who could provide enough continuity through their careers to make an interesting Thesis. I looked through the people in the pen who might fit the bill and I came across this guy Arthur D'Amicio. Meant nothing to me, I'm from Boston but a few enquiries suggested he might be an interesting subject. I looked into his records to find they were sealed. Probably why no one else took an interest. I ask my boss if I could look behind the curtain. He gets approval but says I might have to put up with a heavily redacted Thesis. His mob career alone would be enough for a PhD, but I can see there's something else about this guy. An unusual charge list with an even more unusual wall of tight alibis. And never a shred of evidence. It looked like the police weren't that interested. Often didn't follow any leads or collect evidence. Like they had far better things to do.

'The more I thought about it the more I came to realise that the main reason his records were under seal was not the crimes he'd confessed to, which were typical of Mob crime, but the long list of investigations in which he was a person of interest, but either rarely charged, or had the charged dropped though lack of evidence. The seal was in place to cover over what could be interpreted to be collusion between Art and local law enforcement in dozens of unsolved murders and cases of missing people.'

'He got caught in the big Mob and racket busting program the government finally set in motion to expose and break the Families stranglehold. Art was considered a senior member of the local hierarchy. He confessed to a list of mob activities, some he wasn't even involved with, but wasn't charged with nor confessed to any specific murder. He knew if there was a full investigation it would turn up some bodies. Quite a few. He said he was willing to rat on the big Boss if he could get immunity for quite a several of the small fry mobsters in the organisation and be allowed to make people think he'd left the country. The Bureau was reluctant, but they believed the process was reeling in some big fish.'

Donnie bridled. But before he could speak. 'I use the word rat Donnie, because those were Art's words. The Boss he gave away was dying of cancer. He died at home before the trial. They both thought it was funny. And sorry about the small fry I could have said...' She was searching for an alternative.

He helped with 'Small time would have worked as well.'

'Yeah. Sorry. Art and his Boss came up with a list mainly from other Families who they didn't particularly like and were happy to give up. The Boss dying and Art heading for prison in any event.'

'Anyhow I send a letter to Art asking him if there was any way he would let me come and meet him. I was upfront that I was wanting to do a Doctoral Thesis on his early life, but it would all stay under the same seal as the rest of his records. He wrote back, in that beautify flowing script of his, and more or less said, *name a time.*'

'I was expecting some sort of fading Marlon Brando. But I was brought into see this guy who was pleasant, erudite, keen to help and I was with someone eager to listen to someone who's fascinating; me. This was twenty years ago. He was in his mid-fifties.'

'He wanted to help so much, but there was a problem. He had no recollection of nearly all the crimes he'd committed. He could remember planning for some of them, preparing for some of them. But only a few actual murders. I think that's why he could continue to be such a nice guy. Until the next person needing to be killed came along.'

'But what about the stories. Like the dog story.' Said Will. 'Did he make those up.'

Amelia looked to Donnie as if for confirmation to continue. 'No. He believed the stories. When he heard about some murder he'd committed second hand, he'd believe the story that went with it. Half of them either never happened or were not like what happened in reality. As we found out with Jerry, if it suited him, meticulous as he was, he would find out the facts in detail. But generally, the past was abstract to Art.'

'Then how did you figure most of them out.' Donnie's curiosity growing.

She laughed. 'I went one day a month, for twenty years even when my PhD was done so I was a regular visitor. The Bureau has struggled with this initially but I told them it was unpaid work experience. Art had forgotten the details, but there were a lot of clues. Particularly once you started talking about a specific case and described who it was that went missing. What they'd done when they were alive or what else was going on at the time, there were these hints. Oblique references like a genie trying to get out of a bottle.'

She gave the impression she felt she'd been dominating the conversation. And looked around the table.

Donnie was thoughtful. 'Since Art died something's been niggling away at me. He was such a presence you know, but when he was a kid, till he was maybe, I don't know, fifteen, he was, quiet. And got pushed around a fair bit. There was nothing to him. Skinny as a rake, average height. A few years later he's with the Mob.'

Emelia revealed she could be a hard interviewer. 'Donnie you called me to try to understand Art better, and if what I knew might help. But you know as well as I do how all this started. At least two of the three reasons.'

'I don't want to talk about the Church stuff.' Donnie said quietly. Will realised he was not alone in having his demons.

'Sure. But what about how things were at home.'

Donnie shook his head. 'What was it about that era that made fathers; husbands, come home so drunk, so...mean? Pa was an ordinary guy, no saint. Worked hard when he kept a job. But when he drank.'

Donnie shook his head again. 'Usually it was just shouting, cursing at Ma. Breaking things. But sometimes we'd be upstairs and had to listen while she took a beating. We were scared. Angry. But we were only kids. One night, Pa's about to lay into Ma for some petty thing and Art comes down and says he'll take Ma's beating for her.'

'He was a man three times Art's weight. He went...insane. How Art didn't have any bones broken I don't know. And Art looked at him. Not angry, not afraid. It was like he was waiting for a bus ride to finish so he could get off.'

'Child Welfare took him away that day. Tried to take me too. Pa disappeared, which happened from time to time anyway. Art was gone for three months. Stayed in a foster home but he didn't say much about it. And yeah, it was a different kid came back from there now that I think about it.'

'Yes. He was different Donnie. I think it was the first time anyone had ever listened to the skinny kid. They told him that Priests that interfere with children were bad, terrible people. Fathers that beat their kids to a pulp should never be allowed to do it and never come near them again. And that bullies in the schoolyard that humiliate you, taunt you, steal from you, beat you up for years, have no place in a decent world. He was told that none of the things he was experiencing had any place in a normal community. His foster parents wanted Art to stay with them. They loved him.'

'I've built a complex timeline about Art, and it starts with a priest that was found in a sewer with the end of a baseball bat rammed deep into his throat until he suffocated.'

'That was Art? He was a kid.'

'It's one of the few incidents he has a vague memory of. I don't think the kindly woman I met fifteen years ago in her nineties who was Art's foster mother would believe the fuse she lit. She would never guess Art would take things quite so literally. She remembers this quiet, intense, yet somehow sweet boy with enormous potential caught in a net of violence and abuse. I let her know that her guidance at that pivotal time had contributed to the making of the finest gentlemen I had ever met.

Donnie scratched the top of his head at high speed and if scratching out a memory. 'A bully. Yeah. There was this kid who had picked on Art for years.' Said Donnie. 'I couldn't do anything I was four grades down. In those days you didn't tell your parents. Your father would say you were weak like a girl. Beat you some more. But I remember that kid went missing.'

'Second in the timeline. Went missing three months after Art came back.'

Donnie hadn't thought of it in nearly half a century 'It was a big deal in the neighbourhood. Police going door to door. Search parties. Never found a trace of him.' From Donnie's voice it was obvious he hadn't made the connection with Art.

'Art got a motorbike around that time.' Said Emelia.

'Yeah. Don't know where he got the money. Pretty soon he'd be gone most nights. No one told Pa. Pa was home on some bullshit deal where he promised to be good.'

Emelia continued 'When I talked about the boy who'd bullied him, Art remembered that 'like yesterday' he said. But only the bullying. When we talked about the boy, Art made an interesting comment about where his family lived.'

'He had them placed in what was then a rural area miles from here. I scanned the newspaper from the whole region, and I came across an interesting story about some remains found in a well five years back. They were covering it in to build over it. It was a dry well much of the year. But this wasn't a case of a body thrown in a well. This was a person lowered into a well because there were no broken bones. Possibly unconscious. Usually you'd die of hunger or thirst within a week in a well. But examination of the bones of this person suggested they starved to death over a period of months. Water and food had to have been lowered down. The connection with the lost child hasn't been made with DNA because from my investigations the family moved back to Ireland nearly thirty years ago. It may be the ideal approach as a law enforcement agent, but I thought I'd wait until Art...' She laughed. 'Went to heaven.' They all had a laugh at that. Emelia had decided that even after Art's demise she would let that sleeping dog lie.

But Donnie and Will sat digesting the latest revelation. 'The well thing. That's rough.' Was all Donnie could come up with. Donnie knew he was the person who had to provide details for number three in Emelia's timeline.

'It was inevitable that Pa would come home with a skinful and smash things up. It was only a matter of whether he'd beat on anybody, but he knew he couldn't lay a hand on Art now. Art was away anyhow on his bike. Art arrived home early in the morning one day as Ma was trying to finish putting on the heavy makeup she used when he'd belted her in the face rather than slapping her and yelling and stuff. She started early in the morning as a seamstress. She worked every day I can remember except Sunday's, until she lost her mind. Right up till then she was doing some sort of volunteering stuff.'

'She passed Art on the steps and just shook her head at him and disappeared down the street. Within half an hour of him arriving was getting ready for school and I hear Pa calling out. He'd been sleeping of the booze and Art had tied him to the bed. He either didn't notice me coming beside him or it didn't bother him.'

He was pouring whiskey down Pa's throat until it was bubbling up. Pa was coughing it out like a drowning man. Art smiled at him. 'You're never going to hit anyone ever again.'

Pa was shaking his head saying. 'No Art, never.'

Donnie had been staring into the middle distance and sighed. 'Then Art pulls out a baseball bat. He says to Pa 'Ankle, knee, elbow or wrist; because you need something to remember your promise by Pa.'

'Pa was shaking his head saying no. Art, had ne expression on his face and says. 'It's okay Pa, I'll choose for you.' Donnie took a deep swig of beer. 'I'd never seen anything like that. Art kept bringing that bat down till Pa's ankle must have been mush. And then...' Donnie was shaking his head. '...then he got out a can of gas and poured it all over Pa, drenching him. He sat there looking at him and pulled out a box of matches and lit one. He said 'Pa, you won't forget your promise will you.'

'Pa was now babbling all sorts of 'I'm sorry son and I promise.'

Art watched the flame of the match till it finally died out. He pulled out a blade so sharp it cut the rope like butter. Pa was paralysed by fear and a ruined ankle. It was then I realise that Art wasn't a skinny kid anymore. He turned his body into something tough and strong.'

'With one hand gripping Pa's hair and the other his collar he dragged him downstairs. He acknowledged I was there to the extent he nodded to me to open the front door. He dragged Pa halfway down the steps and threw him right onto the pavement. Then he turned away as if the whole thing had never happened. He says to me. 'Ready for school Donnie?' Donnie gave half a smile and half a shrug. 'He didn't seem to be trying to pretend to put that out of his mind. It was like it was already forgotten and he wanted to get on with a normal school day, after a normal morning.'

'But your father was a slow learner.' Emelia regretted how that came out.

'Pa never amounted to much when he was sober and was nasty as a drunk. But like a lot of men of that time and still now I guess, he wasn't much without his family. If he'd never taken a drink, he'd have been ordinary, and probably a loving father to the extent men were expected to be in those times. I like to think he kept coming back because he hoped he could be like that. We're all guilty of thinking something's fixed and it's actually still broken. Maybe unfixable. He should have lived nearby is what I think in hindsight. But we know what that's worth.'

'He'd been away a long time. It was not long before Art was recruited he turned up with flowers and what not. Had a brace on his leg and foot so he could walk without crutches. He got the family together and said that he had learned his lesson and he thanked Art for bringing him to his senses.'

Donnie shook his head. 'I won't bother going through it all again. This time the police were called when the neighbours heard the screams. By the time they arrived a neighbour was sitting with Ma and Pa was gone. She'd been knocked around, but nothing like in the past.'

'Pa never got the chance to. The screaming the neighbours had heard hadn't been from Ma.'

'A month or so later, we were washing the dishes. Even though she was a strict mother, she had a good sense of humour. We always did the dishes the same way. We'd say Ma washes them, Art dries them, Donnie puts them away and Pa smashes them.'

'This one-time Art was drying the plates. She knew he'll be leaving home soon. 'She said 'Art. Where's Pa?''

He thought for a while, looked at her and said. 'I don't remember Ma.' Donnie looked up at Emelia. Into her eyes. 'But you know where he is; don't you? You figured it out.' Donnie was conflicted.

'A hundred and twelve cases not associated with the Mob and a hundred and three closed out. Including your fathers.' She said nothing more.

'But you're not going to tell me.'

'Sure. I'll tell you Donnie. I don't want to. He was your father.'

Donnie thought for a long time. 'Yeah. I'll try to remember some good times with the old man. Sure, there's not a crowd of them. But I'll keep those.'

The Dog Story

Will shook his head and wished he had Donnie's 'Sunny Side of the Street' gene. There was a sense they'd like Will to contribute if he wanted to. 'Well I feel kind of privileged that I got to hear a story straight from Art. At the time he gave the impression that he told those stories all the time, but all I ever got was the dog story.'

Donnie was about to laugh and say that was a made-up story because he didn't remember any of the real ones. But a glance at Emelia let him know that there was indeed a dog story. It's just it wasn't the one Art told.

They both looked up at her with a look that said. 'Let's hear it.'

'The guy who killed Art on his last 'Walk' was the son of the main player in the dog story. I couldn't tell you while case was open. Jerry Macy's convicted now.'

'Art's Boss, and a neighbouring Boss had met and decided it would be good to avoid the need to constantly run security between themselves and so made a truce. But the Macy's Boss wanted to get rid of Art, who was always out doing his people. Macy's Boss believed with Art gone he could deliver a death blow to D'Amicio's Boss with his people. Jerry's father, like his son, wasn't very smart when it came to an assessment of Art. He came up with the idea of killing Art but also selling some tickets to people who also hated Art to watch it. Make money and get rid of someone who'd been humiliating him for years. He lines up four guys who are willing to pay to watch the show. He told Art he wanted to have a meeting to firm up the agreement on security for the two families.'

'As you'd expect this whole plan leaked like a sieve and Art had studied it from more angles than the people putting it together could imagine existed.'

'It was a case where Art had help because it was Mob business. He had some of his people arrive on time, one of similar build and dressed like Art. In Jerry's father's plan, the people with Art were supposed to go through the main door which would be locked behind them and Art's men taken out.'

'Macy also had men hidden in the garden and at various places in the house. Macy's men would then force Art into the 'meeting' room. With a dog.

'Macy was in the room and was none the wiser when his people were all dead, his family locked in their rooms and guards on the meeting room door. Art had seven men inside and four outside. All had been there for over twelve hours.' 'Inside the room there were now four paying customers and one guy holding onto a very large vicious dog. Art didn't arrive on time. Soon Macy was pounding and yelling at the door. No one was responding and it was locked.'

'Art steps out from the curtain in front of a lounge room window behind the men on the couches. He'd been there eighteen hours. Well in advance of the visitors arriving to study the room from every angle.'

'Macy is holding the dog by a choker chain with his right hand. He'd had no reason to think he'd need a gun. Art has his gun pointed at Macy's head. Part of Art's reputation is that he could choose which eye to shoot through and not touch the sides. He comes around and faces the couches. All the spectators each get shot through the middle of the hand Art decides is their favoured hand.'

'Art's gun is back on Macy in seconds. He motions the spectators to throw forward their guns and he kicks them against the wall. He pulls out a gun with his left hand and shoots each spectator in the knees and ankle to keep them there. Always leaving his gun trained on Macy.'

'Art went to a space on the wall near the door that was in full view when the door was closed, but hidden by an open door. A baseball bat had been sitting there, ready for Art to walk over and get it. He walked to the middle of the room and shot Macy in the wrist.'

'I got these details from two men in separate old people's homes, both in wheelchairs. Both say Art side steps the dog like a matador and swung the bat hard across its front legs. They could both hear the legbones break. The dogs landed on its chin and Art comes over at incredible speed and belted the big stumpy tail they have on some of those dogs five or six times.'

Emelia took a pause.

'Then Art picked the dog up by the collar and by that stumpy tail. It's completely insane with rage and agony. Macy is now being pushed towards a corner of the room by its snapping, foaming jaws. He squeezes in as hard as he can, but those jaws keep coming. Soon, there's blood, and bone, wallpaper and plasterboard flying around. Art keeps pushing that dogs face in until it's tearing through drywall and some splinters of the wooden supports.'

'One of the guys in the old people's home said that he found most disturbing, was Art's face. He said he'd never forget it. The look on his face was like someone waiting for a bus.'

'Once the dog was biting mainly wood, Art dropped it and shot it. He picked up the bat and went to one of the spectators. The others didn't know what for. But Art starts laying into him with the bat.'

Another pause.

'He kept going and going. And then he stands back. He wipes down his face and the bat with a towel he'd had behind the curtains. He knocks at the door and leaves with his men. Never having said a single word.'

The Tell All

'You can imagine how all of this would be material for an amazing book. Dozens of cold cases solved. A remarkable Jekyll and Hyde type killer with a fascinating history in the Mob.' She smiled sadly. 'And don't forget the idiosyncratic FBI detective who kept visiting the killer and following clues for twenty years.'

The mood had changed. Although Donnie could understand why she might want to write it, he wanted to see if some stories about his family matters could be dealt with sensitively or left out. Although he knew that once it came out, someone else writing a book would want to dig deeper.

'It's not something I could have done when he was still alive.' She said. 'After the funeral I was driving back to Boston, getting ready to be beaten up by the Bureau for sitting on this stuff for so long. Getting ready for them to redact the book so badly it'd make me cry. When I knew I never really intended to publish a book about Art.'

'The book had always been a justification to keep visiting him, and keep talking to him, and learning from him, about crime. But also because it became like visiting a friend, then an old friend and then, he advised me one day, he'd adopted me as a daughter.' She laughed. 'I've never mentioned this to my dad.'

'So I got all my papers to do with Art and burned them and threw every hard drive or anything with a trace of my investigations on it into the Mystic River. I don't want to remember Art by what was on those pages. And I don't want anyone else to. Art was a killer. A heinous, ruthless, vicious, murderer. And no one should operate above the law. And on a scale unheard of in this county.'

'But Art was someone who would never be violent if he didn't believe it was right. Even if a Mafia Boss told him he had to. Yet he wouldn't live in a community with rapists, thieves, bullies and pushers without doing something about it.'

'I'm pretty sure that's what the guy over there pulling beers believes. And that's the way I hope it'll stay. That's Art's reputation.'